RACCOON LOVE

RACCOON LOVE

A Memoir by

STEPHEN AKEY

BOOKS

Adelaide Books
New York / Lisbon
2021

RACCOON LOVE
By Stephen Akey

Published by Adelaide Books, New York / Lisbon
adelaidebooks.org

Editor-in-Chief
Stevan V. Nikolic

For any information, please address Adelaide Books
at info@adelaidebooks.org

or write to:

Adelaide Books
244 Fifth Ave. Suite D27
New York, NY, 10001

ISBN: 978-1-956635-37-9

For Erin Finnerty

But O that I were young again

And held her in my arms.

– William Butler Yeats

1

It all ends badly. Fulfillment turns into frustration, enchantment into aggravation, empathy into recrimination, love into – no, love never turns into hate, at least not in my case. In the twenty-three years we lived together, I could never bring myself to hate Lucy Kung, not in our last agonizing two or three years and not even in the more agonizing years immediately afterwards. This is a love story. That the love dies, that the infatuated boy and girl turn into harried middle-aged parents, mitigates nothing of the reality of that love.

I'm always mystified that people quote La Rochefoucauld's maxim, "True love is like a ghost, which everybody talks about but few have seen," as if it wittily encapsulated some worldly, unillusioned wisdom. It's the stupidest thing I've ever heard. Almost everybody falls in love. It doesn't have to last forever or be glamorous or lofty or transcendent to be "true." True love, the kind that for a greater or lesser period brings together two people and bestows on them the greatest happiness they will ever know, is as common as mud. From a love-sick schoolboy to the Goddess Aphrodite, romantic love rolls over most of humanity and even the occasional divinity like so many bowling pins. This greatest of all experiences, this biggest of all events, this only rival (and ultimate loser) to death, requires no money, no credentials, no status, no prerequisites, no previous experience. Some people, it's true, by reason of social injustice or quirks of fate or sheer bad luck, never really get to enter the fray, and no reasonable person would thereby claim that a life untouched by Eros lacks purpose or fulfillment. It may be that a life devoted primarily or exclusively to altruistic service or the pursuit of knowledge or the rearing of children provides comparable spiritual satisfactions without all the heartbreak and aggravation of romantic love. Most of us, however, will take the heartbreak and aggravation. It's the nearest we'll ever get to the Gods.

I met Lucy Ha Kung at the sundial in front of Low Library on the campus of Columbia University in the spring of 1980. I still can't pass that sundial without a pang. Such are the ravages of nostalgia. She was a child and I was a child, / In that kingdom by the sea – except that we were both in our mid-twenties (I twenty-four, she twenty-five) and really should have been far more experienced than we were. But part of the charm of our love story was its comparative innocence. We were late bloomers, so that many years later, when we were breaking up, Lucy could say with a simplicity that still breaks my heart, "Stephen, we grew up together."

I would like to say that we met as students, which is the fiction that we gave out to various acquaintances, but in fact our tenure at Columbia didn't overlap. I had collected my master's degree in librarianship the year before, and Lucy had begun her study towards a master's in urban planning two months after I graduated. In reality, we met through the auspices of what was the local precursor to today's online dating sites: a personal ad in the *Village Voice*. It's hard to imagine now just how ubiquitous the *Village Voice* was in the lives of several generations of left-leaning, intellectually inclined, vaguely bohemian New Yorkers. I read it mainly for the rock criticism and movie reviews, but

I couldn't help peeking at the personal ads. Some were witty, touching, romantic, and sincere; others, shall we say, put their cards on the table. If you wanted to know what it was like to watch your wife have sex with another man (or woman), the *Voice* personals was the place to go.

This wasn't my first go-around with the *Village Voice* classified section. A year earlier I had placed a personal ad there that got me what I had been pining for since the age of thirteen: a girlfriend. If it seems odd that a slender, gainfully employed, fairly good-looking, otherwise agreeable young man on the loose in New York City should resort to personal ads for female companionship, you don't know what shyness can do to a person – namely, harden into pathology, which is what was happening to me. I'm not going to tell that story here; I've told it elsewhere. But I am eternally grateful to the *Village Voice* and to my own uncharacteristic intrepidity for rescuing me from the male spinsterhood and gathering eccentricity that could easily have been my lot. For the many thousands of Eleanor Rigby types who walk its streets and huddle in rent-stabilized apartments much like the one I lived in, New York City is a cold and lonely place. I've known a number of Eleanor Rigbys in my life; I might have been one of them. The girlfriend I met through the auspices of the *Village Voice* and who bore with me for about four months before mutual incomprehension and rooted incompatibility broke us up, helped to forestall that fate. I wish I had treated her better. I wish she had read the *New York Review of Books* rather than *Cosmopolitan*. I'm not going to tell that story either. But at least we opened each other up a little bit, discovered some pathos and tenderness, had some laughs and some tears. When it ended, Katie went back to her mother's apartment in Co-Op City in the Bronx and I went back to my one-bedroom apartment in Park Slope to brood on the Meaning of Love and revert to the isolation that had already damaged me quite sufficiently. So the question isn't what the hell was I doing placing another personal ad in the *Village Voice* a year later. The question is what the hell was Lucy doing answering it.

I still have the ad, "yellowing with antiquity," as Blanche DuBois says, preserved in one of the nine volumes of diaries I kept in my nearly illegible handwriting during those years. It says:

> Shy handsome WN, 24, into lit and film, sks very attractive F, 20's w/similar interests. Must believe in love.

How typical. Here I was, a pathologically shy nobody making less than $14,000 a year in an entry-level job as a librarian yet insisting that my nonexistent girlfriend be "very attractive." Note also the bland assurance of my "handsomeness" – well, I was sort of handsome, if skinny, pale, poète maudit types are your dish. It turned out that my imagined dishiness did not at all correspond to the ideal held by the "very attractive" – indeed, rather beautiful – "F w/ similar interests" that I was soon to meet. But that's getting ahead of the story. Anyway, the bit about "must believe in love" was corny but true.

I was apprehensive enough to be inordinately disconcerted by the tiny typo that the *Voice* typesetters had let slip: "Shy handsome WN" instead of "Shy handsome WM." Would my "very attractive" potential girlfriends mistakenly write me off as a shy handsome white neurotic or shy handsome white nihilist or shy handsome white nut job? I had a lot riding on the accuracy of the transcription, and the fee – thirty-eight dollars for a two-week run – was a lot of money for me in those days. However, the matronly doyenne who oversaw the *Voice* personals operation from an office on University Place and who acted as something of a den mother to all the lonely singles and horny sadomasochists who anxiously queued up to deliver their hand-written love letters to the world, had gently reassured me when my turn had come a few weeks earlier.

"Sly, handsome white male, 24, into lit and film," she read much too loudly as I stood at the counter before her. "Is that right so far, dear?"

"No, no," I replied. "it's *shy*, not *sly*. Wait a minute. Do you think *sly* would work better?"

She gave me a grandmotherly laugh and said, "Nah, you don't look sly to me. Girls like shy guys."

Though I can't say the replies poured in, I eventually got a few intriguing responses: someone who called herself a "total woman" and hinted at a sexual willingness that sounded like the fulfillment of my most jejune fantasies; someone who was writing a musical adaptation of Sheridan's comedy of manners *The Rivals* and was looking for a "special" collaborator; someone, surprisingly, who had the courage to admit she was "lonely"; and an Asian (in those days "Oriental") graduate student who said almost nothing about herself but left a coy little message on a blue index card, something like, "Does one plus one equal downhill?"

I met a few of those women and it was the usual pile-up of unexpressed disappointments so familiar to anyone conversant with match.com and its congeners: she's chubbier than I expected, she talks too much, she doesn't talk enough, oh my God she likes *Billy Joel.* And the converse just as surely obtained: this guy is way too nervous, he looks like a wimp, oh my God he wears *sneakers.* So I was especially keen to meet the "Oriental" graduate student whose note had seemed so fetchingly understated and who had sounded, in the few brief times we spoke on the phone, poised and intelligent. I can't recall that first telephone conversation. How was I to know it would change my life forever?

But it wasn't all fetching understatement and poised intelligence. In that same note, the mysterious grad student had one apparently urgent question that she delivered with point blank directness: "Are you tall?" Well, I was five feet ten, a perfect averageness that, until then, I had never thought to be disqualifying. In her heart of hearts, I suspect that Lucy (five feet three) always regretted that I wasn't a few inches taller. Other than that they're great and that I love them, I have learned over the course of a long life and various romantic involvements never to make any generalizations about women. There are almost none that can't be contradicted and even the "positive" ones can be turned inside out by people (that is, men) of ill will. So here goes the only one I'm willing to venture: women like tall men.

Nor did I find it especially fetching when I asked her in our second or third telephone conversation why she had answered my personal ad and she replied that she had always wondered about the sort of people who wrote them. She had chosen me partly to satisfy her curiosity. I would have been more insulted if I really believed her. By then we had got to know each other a bit. (Talking on the phone was easy; it's when I met the person that I tended to screw things up.) She said that she had seen my personal ad while idly leafing through the *Voice* in the course of her part-time job in the sundries store or "bazaar" of International House in Morningside Heights. Although I worried about jumbling up her story with those of the other women I was meeting at the same time, I managed to get a few things straight: that she was studying in the Department of Urban Planning at Columbia; that she had grown up in the Philippines but was of Chinese ethnicity; that she had worked briefly as an architect in Manila after graduating from college there; that she had studied for a year in Toronto before coming to New York; and that she had a big family back home.

I would spend the next twenty-three years learning the details of this sketchy story. For now, I was intrigued enough to forgive her the minor insult to my pride that she had committed with the remark about her idle "curiosity." Hey, I was nervous too. If she wanted to pretend that I hadn't written "Must believe in love," I readily assented; it took the pressure off. Naïve as I was, I knew that she wouldn't have asked about my height if she were merely looking for a friend.

It pleased me that she turned out to be studying at Columbia, not because I had any love lost for that university but because it gave me a conversational opening. As I told her in our first or second phone call, "I hate that fucking place." I didn't, really. It's just that my studies in the School of Library Service had been so stupendously boring that I had to blame somebody, and I preferred to blame Columbia rather than my chosen profession – or myself. Also, raving about the intellectual shortcomings of Columbia University afforded me the opportunity of being impressively cynical. Such was my idea of courtship. But my exaggerated contempt, which Lucy seemed to find amusing, masked something deeper. For me, coming from an extremely modest social and intellectual background (the University of Connecticut by way of Glassboro State College), getting into Columbia had been a big deal. I had put my faith in an institution, as I saw it, and the institution had failed me. Actually, Columbia taught me something that would sustain me for the rest of my life: institutions don't matter; love does.

Although I still wasn't clear about the languages she spoke, or why she had left the Philippines in the first place, or even if "Lucy" was her given name (it wasn't), I knew that I had to reciprocate with a story of my own. The trouble was that, even over the telephone, her story seemed so much more interesting than mine. How could my banal suburban upbringing compare with her internationalism, her worldliness, her independence? More to the point, how could I hide the shameful, inescapable fact that I hadn't had a girlfriend in college? So I revealed just enough to convince her that I was real, without getting into the embarrassing details: that I had grown up the son of a school teacher and administrator in a divorced, middle-class family in Westport, Connecticut; that I had gone to a couple of state colleges where I had studied literature; that, not knowing what else to do with all my useless humanities classes, I had decided to become a librarian; that I had earned my MLS degree from Columbia the year before and was now working as a cataloging librarian at the Brooklyn Public Library and living in a one-bedroom apartment in Park Slope.

As it turned out, none of the things I worried about concerned Lucy in the least. She didn't give a damn where I went to college or how much money I made or whether my profession was sufficiently elevated. Was I interesting? Was I intelligent? Was I a kind and thoughtful person? Those were the only questions that mattered to her, in the beginning as at the end. When I look back on it, I'm amazed at how little either of us ever thought about money or clothes or real estate or the other accoutrements of success associated with the educated, urban middle class to which we belonged more or less by default. Years later, after we broke up, I was to discover to my cost that people do indeed care very much about such things.

I hadn't met her and I was already in awe. That turned out to be a life-long pattern. Almost everyone who knew her was at least a little in awe of Lucy, partly because her breathtaking creativity was conjoined to an unaffected modesty and simplicity of manner. But I didn't know that yet. All I knew was that the other women from the *Village Voice* hadn't met my expectations (nor I, it goes without saying, theirs), and that the "Oriental" graduate student, whom I was eager to meet, kept putting me off. That was understandable. She was busy with papers to write, faculty advisors to meet, presentations to prepare. I was lucky that she had agreed to a meeting at all, but she wasn't exactly shoring up my already shaky self-confidence.

It almost ended before it began. When she finally agreed to meet me at the sundial, ground zero of the Columbia campus and the traditional rendezvous of young people with a lot more confidence than I had (or maybe just better at faking it), she probably didn't anticipate that she would walk past me with barely a glance. Anyone with any experience of online dating will understand. You've been through all the motions, you've said and done all the right things, and at the final moment you think – Eh, do I really wanna go through with this? There will be others in the pipeline, and if he asks what happened, I can honestly say, I was there, where were you? So it was that on that sunny April Saturday at one PM in 1980, Lucy Ha Kung hurried by the sundial on the middle of the campus of Columbia University, slowed down just enough to steal a glance at me and the handful of others milling around, and prepared to move on. But I knew.

"Lucy?" I asked.

Yes, it was Lucy.

2

What we did as we climbed, and what we talked of
Matters not much, nor to what it led –
Something that life will not be balked of
Without rude reason till hope is dead
And feeling fled.

That is Thomas Hardy looking back forty-two years earlier to the courtship of his first wife, Emma Lavinia Gifford, and commemorating what feels to me like his moment at the sundial on the Columbia campus: half sublimity, half banality. And there are indeed, to my way of thinking, certain spooky parallels between Hardy and me: that we had loved so ardently in our youth; that in our marriages "Things were not lastly as firstly well"; and that each of us, to the frustration of our subsequent partners, might have spent a bit too much time brooding on the past. Hardy had the excuse of genius; I have none. Yet Hardy's great elegiac sequence to Emma in *Satires of Circumstance* accomplishes some of the psychic work that only memory can do: to meliorate the ravages of time; to honor our youthful idealism while acknowledging our profound foolishness; to face the future with a little more courage and a little less illusion. I don't know whether Hardy achieved all these goals; I know that I haven't. Yet it's more than nostalgia that pulls me back to Lucy and our love. It wasn't a dream. Will I ever again find that inwardness that once connected me so deeply to another? Probably not, but in remembering it, I remember what was best in me and preserve what remains – a few tatters, a thing of shreds and patches – for my loved ones.

There is this difference between Thomas Hardy and me: at his first meeting with the woman he was to marry, he and she *climbed* (up a slope in Cornwall beside a pony pulling a wagonette), whereas Lucy and I *descended;* that is, we walked past the main gates of the campus on 116th Street and Broadway and over to Riverside Park, which slopes down to the Hudson River, or would if the damned Henry Hudson Parkway didn't cut it off. It's true that "what we talked of / Matters not much" – the usual conversational filler of two people getting to know each other. What mattered was the feeling, which was one of increasing ease and naturalness as the minutes wore on. Golly, this "date" (if you could call it that) seemed to be going surprisingly well.

I do, however, remember one very specific topic we discussed once we reached the park and sat down on a grassy hill: the film *Lancelot of the Lake* by Robert Bresson. Was this grim exercise (not even one of Bresson's best) in stultifying social codes and numbing violence really what Lucy wanted to hear about on a lovely spring day with the maple trees starting to bud and an acrobatic roller skater (as I remember) doing pirouettes below us on the paved walkway? If I wearied Lucy with my mansplaining – a word not yet coined but all too fitting for the occasion – she was too polite to say so. Anyway, my guileless enthusiasm for a director of genius I had just discovered was genuine and must have charmed her at least slightly. That's what I was like in those days: burning for Art and Meaning. Lucy would gradually wean me from the pernicious habit of mansplaining. How could it be otherwise? She was smarter than me.

Since I was keen to demonstrate that I could listen as well as pontificate, it gratified me that Lucy had a few things to say as well. Mostly she talked about her vexed relationship with a classmate of hers from northern Italy named Paola, whose aggressive Roman Catholic orthodoxy was starting to rub Lucy the wrong way – altogether a more promising topic than *Lancelot du lac*. Rather than nattering on about Existentialism in French Cinema, Lucy chose to talk about something at once intimate (the decline of a formerly close friendship) and substantive (the place of faith in an individual's scale of values). I should have felt out of my depth, but somehow she made me feel smarter. Good God – could it be she might actually, you know, *like* me?

I certainly liked her. The ride back home to Brooklyn on the unairconditioned, graffiti-scarred 2 train, normally such an ordeal, passed in a flash. We spoke on the phone the next night and agreed to meet again on campus when I got off work on Thursday. Could I help it if my good looks were that irresistible? The incredible thing is that, initially, Lucy didn't strike me as especially attractive. Here some serious contextualizing is in order.

New York City in 1980 was far removed from the world in which I had come of age. That's why I liked it. Even as a child in white, upper class Westport in the 1960s, I used to look at the photos on the front page of the *New York Times* and occasionally wonder, Why is it always white men? Being highly unadventurous by nature, I stayed in my suburban comfort zone until bad grades and low S.A.T. scores brought me to the unassuming but racially mixed Glassboro State College in southwest New Jersey, where I learned this valuable lesson: black people exist. Also, being seventeen years old, this lesson: black women are beautiful. Well, that was progress of a sort.

Nevertheless, my roots in homogeneity went deep. I remember as a teenager my eldest brother telling stories of the single Japanese exchange student at his college in Pennsylvania. On one occasion the student had given my brother the gift of some exquisite rice paper. We thought that was hilarious. So yeah, I had come a long way and greatly appreciated it that here in New York, after all these years, I was finally mixing it up with people who didn't all look or talk or think like me, but I hadn't as yet met many Asians. All of which is to say, to my shame, that when I laid eyes on Lucy, she seemed a little *too* Asian. She didn't look much like the Aryan "playmates" and "pets" (yes, that's what they were called) I had spent way too much time ogling in the pages of *Playboy* and *Penthouse*. Far be it from me to objectify any woman sexually; but I was a little disappointed not to be able to objectify her sexually. The world, as Benedick says in *Much Ado About Nothing*, must be peopled.

It didn't take long for my concupiscence to rise, as it were, to the occasion. Our subsequent meeting on Thursday went swimmingly and I went home thinking, Jesus, I've hit the jackpot – she's a knockout! Everything that had seemed too "foreign" to me at our first meeting – her dainty, bridgeless nose, full lips, plump cheeks, and dark skin – now seemed, as indeed they were, ravishing. Also, at that first meeting she had pulled back her hair into a ponytail, which brought out the sculpted planes of her broad face but made her look slightly severe. Now, for our second meeting, she had let loose her glorious silky fall – so glorious that, a few years later, when she went to a hair salon in Park Slope to have most of it cut off, she came back home looking exactly the same. They had refused to cut her hair on the grounds that it was too beautiful to touch.

On that Thursday I took her to a Greek restaurant on 113th Street (the Symposium – still there, by the way), where she spoke some more about her exasperating friend Paola and I reasoned of God and Providence. Earth to Stephen: Get real – there's a beautiful woman sharing an intimate meal with you; this is not the moment to expound on David Hume's *Dialogues Concerning Natural Religion.* And yet, as absurd as it seems, my high-minded table talk did establish certain useful commonalities. For better or worse, I was the kind of guy who *did* talk about David Hume's *Dialogues Concerning Natural Religion;* if she could get past that, she could get past anything. More importantly, Lucy's talk about her friend's grating religious and political orthodoxy and my corresponding tirades against superstition and reaction were oddly compatible. We didn't know we were going to spend the next twenty-three years together. We did know that if we disagreed fundamentally on certain core beliefs in politics and religion and ethics, we wouldn't have got through the next twenty-three minutes. It's the greatest balancing act of them all – how to allow for differences of belief that foster rather than undermine a loving relationship. Occasionally you hear of church-going, free market conservatives happily married to secular, welfare state liberals. Congratulations. I don't know how they do it.

So there we were, a couple of classically left-liberal, New York atheists. Nice to get that known. Maybe now we could go up to Lucy's room for a cup of tea? It was she who extended the invitation. This will be hard to believe, but I had to fight the temptation to decline. The evening had gone so well; why give me a chance to ruin it? And it wasn't just a question of my shyness. I had grown so accustomed to negation in my Bartleby-like existence that my default response to almost any invitation was a mumbled and apologetic "I prefer not to." To give myself some credit, I was not unaware of this deplorable tendency. So I looked into Lucy's lovely brown eyes, strained to catch the outline of a nipple, and said, "Sure, I'd love a cup of tea."

We were to have a good laugh about that later on; I can't abide tea and hardly ever drank it again. Lucy drank all sorts of imported teas – the real stuff, from China and India. I can't say I loved her for the tea she drank, but even that was thrillingly romantic for me. In the white-bread suburbs where I grew up, tea meant Lipton's and you bought it at the supermarket. If falling in love was, as my readings in existentialism were then teaching me, an encounter with the Other, this was about as Other as it got: a woman from the other side of the globe, who grew up drinking real tea, worshipping ancestors at shrines, and speaking languages I couldn't get my tongue around. And yet even I, up there in Lucy's sixth floor dorm room in International House, had things on my mind other than existentialist concepts of the self. What, to be blunt, happened?

Nothing happened. We talked. We drank tea. We looked out her window onto leafy Claremont Avenue and the adjacent greensward. Yes, I might have let slip a golden opportunity; most men would probably think so. Why then did I feel so incredibly happy in that little dorm room with the marvelous girl perched inches away on her bed? There would be time, I fervently hoped, for the other stuff. For now, it was more than enough – it was downright intoxicating – to share an hour or two with the loveliest, the sweetest, the smartest, and by far the most interesting person I had ever met.

During the rest of the term I came up to Morningside Heights about twice a week. More tea, more walks in Riverside Park, more conversations about politics, friends, family, and the Meaning of It All. Lucy in the Sky wasn't much better at conversational superficialities than I was; within a few days we were talking about some of our most intimate hopes and fears. In fact, what we often talked about was the horror of life. It seems unfathomable that two young people, with so many advantages and so lucky to be where they were, could also be so grimly pessimistic. Partly, it was playacting. We were intellectuals – or thought we were – easily seduced by the glamor of alienation and tragedy. But a lot of it was a cover for anxiety and depression. God knows I had reason to be depressed; I was twenty-four-years old and this was the first time I had ever been taken seriously by an attractive, intellectual, and sensual woman. And Lucy had anxiety to spare: Would she stay? Would she return home? What would her parents think if she got involved with a non-Chinese man? When would she see her siblings again? Even into our mid-twenties, we're still learning how to be adults; it's a little scary out there. Hence all that mumbo jumbo Lucy and I talked about fear and trembling and the sickness unto death. Beneath it all, we were simply comforting and reassuring each other.

So serious! That's why I called Lucy's residence "International House of Pancakes." I needed to prove, however feebly, that I had a sense of humor. And I needed to prove it to myself as much as to her. She had it over me in so many ways that I clung to the one small area in which she didn't surpass me. In addition to speaking four languages (Fukienese, Mandarin, Tagalog, and English) to my one and a half (I knew a bit of Spanish), she was smarter, better educated, better looking, more sociable, more talented, worldlier. But I could make her laugh. We never competed with each other, then or later; she outclassed me so thoroughly that it wasn't an issue. Still, somebod*y* had to be funnier, and it was me.

Well, if a young man and woman start seeing a lot of each other over the course of a warm springtime and begin sharing certain intimacies, something pretty obvious is bound to happen: they will fall in love. And so we did, but there were obstacles to overcome, most having to do with my haplessness. I lived for those trips to Morningside Heights, for our strolls in Riverside Park, for our meals in funky diners on Broadway, for our conversations about architecture and scholarship and the presidential primaries. But I was starting to go nuts. So one evening when we were saying goodbye on Claremont Avenue, I decided to boldly risk it all.

"Lucy," I said as we stood under the street lights and the London plane trees in the enveloping warmth of May, "can I have a kiss?"

She smiled, gave me a peck on the lips, and returned to her dorm room, apparently thinking I was the most adorable little boy she'd ever met. Not quite what I had in mind.

Coupled with my ineptitude was my sincere desire not to seem like just another creepy guy pressuring a woman into a half coerced, half consensual sexual situation she might not really want. Later, Lucy would tell me a bleak story about being on the other end of exactly that sort of situation. I would have killed myself before exploiting a woman in that way. Very admirable, but gentlemanliness can be taken too far, and I practically drove mine off a cliff. So while I waited for an engraved invitation from Lucy reading, "Stephen: Please fuck me," I tried to interest her in my mind. It worked all too well. She thought I had a fine if somewhat unnuanced mind, but the body attached to it seemed not to arouse her in the least.

So I tried another tack. I would be her guide to New York. After all, I had lived here a whole year longer than she; my ignorance of my adopted city was surpassed only by my passion for it. I thought she might be making the same mistake I had made when I had first moved to Morningside Heights two years earlier, namely, confusing the side show (Columbia University) with the main event (New York City). Like a lot of Columbia people, she tended to stay fairly local. *What* – she hadn't been to Brooklyn Heights? Or Bleecker Street Cinema? Or the Bronx Botanic Garden? I would be her cicerone, more enthusiastic than knowledgeable, and together we would explore this crime-ridden paradise on its broken-down subway system. But first I had to ask her. I managed to screw that up too.

"Um, Lucy, you know, it's just, well, there's so much going on out there, and I thought maybe, you know, if you wanted I could show you some great places if you, I mean, if you . . . "

"If I wanted to see some more of the city with you? Sure, Stephen, I'd love to."

She told me afterwards that she thought the way I had posed the question was "cute." Yeah, that was me: cute, adorable, boyish, and wanting to get in her pants so badly I thought I would die. Fortunately, this comedy of miscommunication – entirely of my own making – would come to an end a few days later. The conversations in her dorm room had been getting, let's say, warmer – literally so, because it had been an unusually warm spring and Lucy had switched from her standard student wardrobe of jeans and buttoned up blouses to gauzy summer frocks. She was wearing just such a frock one May evening when, rather than perching on her bed, she lay back on it and spoke of her dreams: that she hoped to pursue a career, perhaps in academia, perhaps in architecture, as a free and independent woman with a partner or partners who would respect that independence and at the same time provide the sort of intellectual and sexual fulfillment that made for a rounded life. If this was the engraved invitation I had been waiting for, I declined the R.S.V.P. This time it really was shyness. I desperately hoped that Lucy might misinterpret my paralysis – my sweating palms, my tongue-tied monosyllables, my extremely uncomfortable erection that I was trying my best to conceal – as solidarity with her feminist self-determination. More likely, I had blown it all to hell. It felt like a very long ride home on the number 2 train that night.

So I was surprised when, the next night on the telephone, she immediately accepted my offer to show her around the

Bronx Botanic Garden the following Monday, Memorial Day. I half expected a terminal refusal, but no, she was her usual accommodating self. Jesus, if she still liked me after that miserable non-performance the night before, I was either incredibly lucky or maybe – *maybe* – not such a goddamn fool after all. It's hard to hate yourself when you're falling in love.

We met, as usual, on campus, took the 1 train down to Fifty-ninth Street and the D train up to Bedford Park Boulevard. Hard to believe, but in those days the Bronx Botanic Garden was free and never crowded. Also, the hemlocks in the Hemlock Forest hadn't yet succumbed to the blight of woolly adelgid. If they had, I probably would have mansplained about that too. Instead, we just walked through that lovely woodland and the native plant garden and the rock garden and the allée of tulip trees. We had reached the point where we didn't need to talk all the time, and I remember standing on a stone bridge with Lucy at my side, looking down at the Bronx River (there is such a thing and it's not as laughable as it sounds) and feeling a closeness and tenderness that needed no words.

We did, however, talk. A lot. That day Lucy told me that she sometimes had to struggle against despair and I said something about the necessity and dignity of the struggle. Yes, but she had to worry about things beyond my ken: Where was her homeland? What place, if any, could she find as an Asian woman in the West? How would her parents deal with the "betrayal," as they would surely see it, if she got seriously involved with a non-Chinese man?

"You know," I ventured, "we may get seriously involved ourselves."

Silence. She glared at me for an instant, then dropped her eyes. I had said either the most inappropriate thing in the world or the words she had been longing to hear. It turned out to be a bit of both. No more was said on that topic, but I felt hugely relieved to get it off my chest, and our serenity was unbroken as we gathered our few belongings and walked past the ornate greenhouse and through the gates on the way back to the subway and our return trip to Morningside Heights.

Soon enough, after a quick meal in one of our favorite diners, we found ourselves back in Lucy's room. The gauzy summer frock. The enveloping warmth. The bed, and Lucy stretched out on it.

"It's funny," I managed to say. "We've known each other a pretty long time and have talked about a lot of intimate things, but we've never really touched each other."

"I know," she said quietly. "I like to be touched."

I now draw a veil over the ensuing scene. Not that memory fails. I remember every kiss, every caress, every moan, every awkwardness with zippers and hooks. There was a great deal of the latter. We were not the skilled lovers we pretended to be. The only thing I said or did unequivocally right was to exclaim in all my innocence, "My God, your skin is like glass!"

Lucy found that very touching. The rest of the encounter, as she informed me in a long letter that arrived two days later, left a lot to be desired. She had called me soon after I arrived home that night. She needed to think things through, she said, and she wanted to hear my voice. The only thing clear to her was the truth of my parting words: "We have a lot to teach each other." A letter would be forthcoming.

Wingèd seraphs of the jury! I now enter into evidence the only letter that Lucy ever wrote me in all our years together. (We were almost never apart. I deeply regret, among much else, not having had the occasion to write her more than one or two love letters.) Well, she liked me. Exhibit A clearly demonstrated that much, if perhaps not so palpably as I would have preferred. And she partly blamed herself for what she called the somewhat "clinical" nature of our embrace: "You seem so peaceful and ascetic. I couldn't help but feel gross next to you in my carnality." Gross carnality? I don't see a problem here. In truth, Lucy was neither grossly carnal nor I especially peaceful and ascetic. But the walls were coming down – sex will do that – and we could begin to see each other for what we were: not the sophisticated intellectuals of our imaginings but ordinary, fumbling human beings with an ache in our hearts.

I had a letter for her too, which I hand delivered when we next met. It made her cry. I think it said something to the effect that my life felt more like death until she came into it. In her letter Lucy told me that she thought I was sweet and tender, which greatly pleased me. She also told me she that was seeing other men, which didn't. Slightly shocked but undeterred, I asked her to meet me after work on Friday for an artsy, romantic vampire movie, *Nosferatu* by Werner Herzog, at Carnegie Hall Cinema. She would be Isabelle Adjani, I Klaus Kinski. And then I would suck her throat.

After the movie (no throat sucking, just hand holding), she came to my apartment in Park Slope for the first time. From the appearance and relatively classy location of the building – a handsome limestone walk-up on Second Street and Eighth Avenue – I think she was surprised at what she found when crossing the threshold into my fourth-floor apartment: nothing. A bed, a card table, a few sticks of furniture. It wasn't so much a Zen-like simplicity as a depressing and oppressive absence. First of all, the rent ($365 per month, about 70 percent of my take-home salary) precluded the purchase of all but essentials. Even so, she wondered, couldn't I touch it up with a house plant or a picture or two? So I told her the truth: my life felt so empty that filling up my apartment with "things" would only make me feel emptier.

It felt a lot less empty after that night. Soon, Lucy was to fill the apartment with plants and paintings and quilts and her own home-made furniture. She was to bring to it what it had been so conspicuously missing: life.

3

Let me not to the marriage of true minds admit impediments. But what if getting over the impediments is the fun part? Lucy had some doubts. That's why she gave me that death glare in the botanic garden when I said we might get seriously involved. With my bumbling adoration, I threatened her notion of a free and independent creative life. Though it might have been something of a fantasy in the first place, she did, in a way, achieve it – just not the free and independent part. So during that turbulent and thrilling and sexy first weekend in my apartment, she laid down one rule: Just don't say the word "love," O.K., Stephen?

I don't know where I got the confidence to believe that she herself would soon be breaking that rule. No, maybe I do. I had to leave before Lucy on Monday morning, but when I got home after work there was a note for me on the kitchen table saying that after all that drama (my tearful ardor, her tearful hesitation), we needed a laugh. The note directed me to the bathroom, where I found, to my inexpressible delight, Lucy's panties hanging from the shower nozzle. I still have them. Just kidding! But I had a feeling I wouldn't be hearing about potential rivals anymore.

I myself didn't have much to come clean about – just Katie, the girlfriend from the Bronx and a lot of adolescent crushes. Lucy, I was strangely excited to learn, had a few more notches on her belt than I did. You did *what? Where?* Tell me more, tell me more. What she told me, far from being the titillating revelations that I feverishly anticipated, was that she thought she was cold, uncaring, unworthy of the love she hadn't yet given to anyone. Every word she spoke proved the contrary. O.K., maybe she shouldn't have laughed in the face of the puppyish college boyfriend when he confessed his adoration (my God, how did he pick himself up from the ground?), but all that gentleness and sensitivity sure sounded like love to me. Two weeks into our "relationship" and we were nearly speaking the forbidden word.

"Lucy," I said on one of those nights, a veritable Harlequin Romance of heaving breasts (mine) and scattered underthings (hers), "I won't ask you to say the same thing, but I just need to tell you that – "

"I know, Stephen, I know. It's beautiful, it's lovely, I appreciate it. But can't we just, you know, *relax?*"

That was good enough for now. Maybe I should have been a little more worried. In addition to her own self-doubts, Lucy had doubts of a more socio-political nature, namely, that men tended to be such miserable oppressive assholes that it might not be worthwhile getting involved with any of them. She didn't wholly believe it, but she didn't disbelieve it either. This was the era of the Angry Sisterhood. (In truth, it never went away – just underground for a little while in the nineties.) Lucy took her anger pretty far, and the object of her wrath, more often than not, was me. On the one hand, I loved it that she so passionately asserted her feminist principles and beliefs. On the other hand, it wasn't *my* fault that Ted Hughes had betrayed Sylvia Plath or that women on average earned less money than men or were commonly demeaned in pop culture or had to fight for control of their own bodies. Nor was I exactly bursting with the confidence that Lucy seemed to consider a male birthright. We would return again and again to the contentious subject of female anger and its place within domestic and social relationships. We never really worked it out. Has anyone?

Lucy never fully believed that I loved her because of, rather than in spite of, her feminism; we couldn't find the right way of talking about it. It was easier and a lot more fun to talk high romance, which I did to excess. If not for my staggering innocence, she might have thought I was having her on. As it was, she listened to me with amused indulgence as I droned on about her loveliness, her intelligence, her talent, her compassion, her independence; nobody this naïve could possibly be making it up. In the midst of my rhapsodies, she brought me up short with a question that hadn't occurred to me: Was I in love with her or in love with love?

I blame Plato. Young people should not be allowed to read *Phaedrus* or the *Symposium,* the two dialogues that most obsessed me, unless under the supervision of a weary and cynical philosophy professor; they might believe some of that nonsense. For mark you, Phaedrus, physical love may or may not conduce to the true beauty of the Eternal Forms, but if you're in love with a marvelous girl who leaves her panties lying around, how much more can you reasonably ask for? When she was in her early teens, Lucy had the formative experience of reading (surreptitiously) a Chinese translation of *Lady Chatterley's Lover*, but she hadn't let D. H. Lawrence's bizarre lessons in sex education turn her head. My head, at twenty-four, was more easily turned than hers, at fourteen. I might have had more realistic expectations about the give and take of actual intimacy if my preferred philosophical reading at the time had been, I don't know, Kant's *Prolegomena to Any Future Metaphysics* or Hegel's *Phenomenology of Spirit.* Fortunately, my Platonism, which Lucy sensibly disregarded, hadn't so blinded me that I couldn't see what was in front of my nose: "a real girl in a real place, // In every sense empirically true!" (Philip Larkin.)

All of which is to say that I loved Lucy for the reason that all lovers cherish their partners: it's the little things. The way she clumsily punched my arm when she pretended to be mad. The girlish way she found so many things "cute." Her mispronunciation of certain words and the music of her slight Chinese accent. Her charming inability to tap her foot in time to the simplest Beatles song. Her tears of compassion or sorrow, which she didn't shed so much as pour. All lovers have their own lists. Ours was growing day by day.

On that list I would include an old-fashioned blue dress with short sleeves and oversized white buttons. Some of Lucy's dresses, though she never meant to be provocative, inspired deliciously impure thoughts in me. Not this one. It made her look like a schoolgirl. It made me want to protect her. She was wearing that dress one Saturday in mid-June when we went to the Brooklyn Botanic Garden to sit back to back on the lawn underneath the Norway maples (since replaced by scarlet oaks – I've lived long enough to outlast seventy-foot trees). I couldn't stay long that morning. I had to meet a friend in Manhattan who was no fun and whom I especially didn't want to see that day. It didn't matter. I knew I would be coming back, not to an empty apartment, but to my girlfriend – finally, I could join the words "my" and "girlfriend" in a single sentence! – in the blue dress. I also knew I would be thinking of that moment in the garden with Lucy for the rest of my life. And so I have.

One afternoon away from Lucy, with a killjoy friend at the Museum of Modern Art, wasn't such a hard condition to bear. I could shut out most of Frederick's pedantry about the amalgamation of color and form in synthetic cubism and just try to enjoy the pictures. But Frederick, who lived with his parents in Queens, who itemized the bill for our coffee shop lunches down to the last penny, who never set foot in Central Park for fear of being mugged, who studied German opera and Yiddish with the same joyless diligence he applied to his job as a cataloging librarian, who had never kissed a girl or (what I suspect he would have preferred) a boy, Frederick the only child and perennial A-student whose smothering, overprotective parents had probably ruined him, was exactly the sort of friend that Lucy was saving me from. How had I entangled myself with a lost soul like this? Or was the lost soul me?

I once was lost but now I'm found. How sweet the sound. We were just letting ourselves fall lazily in love, walking around Park Slope, going to a few movies, meeting some of Lucy's friends at International House, Platonizing. One of the friends I met was her erstwhile antagonist from northern Italy, Paola. I was standing by the window with a couple of Lucy's other friends when she breezed into the dorm room wearing a half-open kimono, pretending not to see me as I conversed quietly. She affected great embarrassment upon "noticing" that Lucy's gentleman caller was present, and excused herself to dress properly, but not before flashing me her upper thighs. Typical Paola behavior, Lucy averred, tarting it up for me with a show of coquettish modesty. Another friend, not present in the room that day, posed a far greater challenge than Paola's failed Mata Hari routine. That friend would presently invite Lucy to spend two weeks at her mother's vacation house near Miami. This time I really should have worried. A vacation was fine. The friend, not so much.

I think Lucy would have loved me even if Anne-Sophie hadn't tried to poison her mind. Nothing like a little jealousy to keep things real. Anne-Sophie surely would have denied any such imputation; she really seemed to believe she was above all that. She certainly was above me – intellectually, at least. I had been hearing a lot about this brilliant Swiss phi betta kappa graduate from Columbia College, currently studying Chinese literature and culture in the Asian Studies Department. Lucy so wanted me to like her; she couldn't have known that Anne-Sophie had made up her mind to despise me before we ever met. To be fair, Anne-Sophie would have argued that I truly was an imbecile: shy, awkward, wholly unworthy of Lucy's intellectual gifts, a classic American provincial. For a few months Anne-Sophie and I shared a strange and secret bond, detesting each other without ever saying so. She had large eyes and a languid grace that I would have found attractive in anyone else. I'm prepared to admit I was pettier than she was. I merely aspired to arrogance; she had fully achieved it.

It was not Anne-Sophie's way to savage me openly; I scarcely merited the attention. But her best friend, who she insisted on believing was some sort of mystical Asian sage, suddenly had a boyfriend and she didn't. So when Anne-Sophie got Lucy into her clutches for two weeks of rest and recreation on the beach in Florida, she didn't need to mention my name. It was enough to discourse on the two groups of people she most despised, Americans and men. She had me dead to rights on both counts.

Lucy wasn't unreceptive. Apart from her reservations about my gender, she was in no danger of falling in love with love. Unbeknown to me, she had accepted the invitation partly to get some distance on emotions that were complicating her life more than she had anticipated. I was turning out to be a pretty nice guy, apparently, but did she really want to deal with all of this ardor right now? And could she fall in love with Mr. Average Nice Guy, if that's what was happening, without sacrificing the dream of pursuing her scholarly and artistic endeavors wherever they might lead her – far, perhaps, from a one-bedroom apartment in Park Slope?

Her vacation reading was a then-popular novel by Marilyn French called *The Bleeding Heart*. I haven't read it. If I'm not mistaken, it argues, as Lucy more or less admitted later on, that men are shit. So I was up against a lot: a feminist polemic of rage and despair, the poisonous insinuations of Anne-Sophie, and, most importantly, Lucy's own ambivalence. I'm under no illusion that it was solely my personal magnetism that won the day; after all, I could never be tall enough. I know that Lucy thought me sweet and tender; she said so. All my grand pronouncements endeared me to her less than the childlike way I tucked a Kleenex under my pillow at night. And my endless effusions about her kindness, her beauty, the wonder of her body, though a bit overwrought, surely touched her; I was nothing if not sincere. So there I was, a sweet and tender ordinary guy, not bad looking, fairly intelligent, who clearly adored her. Lucy too, in some ways, was an ordinary girl: she wanted to be loved. Marilyn French and Anne-Sophie didn't stand a chance.

I knew I had prevailed when she sent me a postcard that said, "Wishing I were in NYC. Wishing you were here? Missing you a lot. Love, Lucy." Deathless poetry, as far as I was concerned. She also said, in answer to a pressing question of mine regarding the (male) folk belief that women were always checking out guys' cocks on the beach: No, not really, but if I wanted to think so, go ahead. She was more excited about the prospect of seeing a production of *Mary Poppins* with Anne-Sophie's kid sister at a local theater. Nonetheless, we were brazenly abusing the United States Postal Service to make bawdy jokes on postcards. If that's not love, what is?

When she returned to New York, Lucy told me that the tropical heat and vegetation had got her brooding once again about the Philippines. Did she really want to go back? The more she thought about a meaningful and rewarding life as an independent woman there, the more unlikely it seemed. And although she wasn't too crazy about gross sexism in Western culture, she was even less crazy about grosser sexism in Eastern culture. (Her great grandmother, to Lucy's lasting horror and outrage, had had her feet bound.) I was in no position to judge, then or now. My job was to offer support, understanding, encouragement, and love – not hard, when Lucy was doing exactly the same for me.

Lucy's parents were in Manila. I didn't have to worry about meeting them in the foreseeable future. (In fact, I never did.) My mother, however, was coming up from Florida for a few weeks in July to see me and my two brothers in New Jersey. Did we really want to get involved with each other's families? It sort of killed the romance, didn't it? So Lucy gave me a few days in Brooklyn alone with my mother, who sussed it out anyway. As I was seeing her off at LaGuardia Airport, I said, "You know, Mom, I'm not so alone as you probably think I am."

"I know," she said. "I saw you stuff a shirt in your knapsack before we left. Mothers notice such things."

Well, love loves to love love, as James Joyce mockingly wrote. We spent the rest of the summer spooning over each other and sweating out the New York heat – which kinda turned me on. Lucy's skin, so soft, so luscious, got slightly clammy in the high humidity. She was self-conscious about it, whereas I thought this trace of earthiness – gross carnality! – made her even more desirable. I couldn't keep my hands off her. I couldn't even keep my nose off her. We used to hug in such a way that by lowering my head and locking my nose against the hollow between her eyes, all I could see was a huge, luminous field of brown – her eyes, which she raised to me, making her look, at that distance, like some unearthly star-child. Even better, almost, was kneading my thumb against her lower forehead to alleviate her headaches. Lucy, can you please have another headache so that I can have the bliss of rubbing your brow and watching your beautiful features relax? We were like a pair of raccoons in their den: creaturely, warm, furry, and clinging to each other for love and security.

It wasn't all raccoon love. In addition to our various fears and insecurities, there were practical matters that weighed heavily on Lucy's mind. That August she began receiving letters from one or two of her younger siblings. The news wasn't good. Lucy's parents were self-made entrepreneurs, and she had grown up with maids, chauffeurs, and private schools – all pretty standard in the Philippines, where there was a small upper class, a large lower class, and not much in between. But the thriving family textile business that had financed her life in New York and her education at Columbia wasn't thriving anymore; the creditors had come calling. The news would get worse, much worse, in the months ahead. There followed a great many tearful conversations at two AM in which I did my best to suggest practical solutions, which Lucy invariably countered with fresh obstacles. Finally, I figured it out. My role wasn't to offer advice. My role was to listen. I like to think I got pretty good at it. Lucy didn't have to say, "Stephen, I need to keep you up till two AM tonight, crying over the same things I've cried over a hundred times before, feeling guilty and helpless, rejecting any practical advice, accusing myself of selfishness and disloyalty. Got a moment?" She just needed to get withdrawn and quiet, and then her eyes would get a little puffy. I could take it from there.

One happy consequence followed from the disaster at home. For some time, Lucy had wondered about the desirability of continuing her studies in urban planning at Columbia; now it was a fait accompli. There would be no more money from home. She had been half lazing away the summer, with me in Park Slope and with her friends in Morningside Heights, but she couldn't afford to stay on at International House much longer. With her experience as a working architect for a major firm in Manila, she shouldn't have too much trouble finding an entry-level position in New York. Oh yeah, there was one other thing: we were in love. She moved in with me on Labor Day, September 1, 1980.

4

There are a few gaps in my diaries, so that I can't say exactly how we managed the move or even where I got the car to haul Lucy's belongings. To this day, driving in New York terrifies me, and I've never learned how to parallel park. Love must have inspired me to fight my way down the West Side Highway, across Canal Street, over the Manhattan Bridge, up Flatbush Avenue, and to a vacant parking spot near enough to my building.

It might be worth pointing out that what Lucy and I were doing was, technically, illegal. Although I would have loved to shock my elders by cohabitating in sin, "living together," after the tumultuous social changes of the sixties and seventies, barely raised anyone's eyebrow. Nonetheless, New York City housing law preserved certain remnants of the dark ages, among which was the proscription of cohabitation on leases not subject to negotiation. This barbarism was widely ignored, except by landlords, who enforced it selectively. There came a time when my landlord, at war with pretty much every tenant in his building, tried to enforce it against me. Too late. By then Lucy and I were married.

Once installed, Lucy set about transforming all that light-filled emptiness into what my apartment had never been: a home. Her tiny dorm room at International House had been teeming with African violets, spider plants, and philodendron.

Now she moved all of those plants into my top-floor apartment, adding from seed an avocado that eventually grew to nearly monstrous proportions. Then she got started on the furniture – not buying it but building it, principally a strong, spare, simple double bed where we were to live much of our lives. I knew she was talented. I didn't know she was Picasso. In the months and years ahead, I was to discover that there was virtually nothing she couldn't create with her hands: furniture, dresses, hats, gloves, quilts, paintings, prints, mobiles, architectural renderings, and, when our son was born, an unending menagerie of fanciful creatures made out of play-dough. For someone who could barely draw a straight line or hammer a nail without bending it, all this skill astounded me. She mended shirts and pants, she assembled appliances, she unclogged the toilet, she cut my hair with barber's tools (I never went to the barber's again), and when she knitted a sweater for me, it wasn't merely a comfortable and handsome pullover but a masterpiece of whorled patterning so intricate that I hesitated to wear it outside of the apartment – I ran the risk, unendurable for a shy person, of being incessantly complimented. And when at last she strapped on her tool belt and got to work with her power drill, I was so utterly out-manned that all I could do was laugh.

When I wasn't crying. We were still having plenty of two AM colloquies, and Lucy's tears were contagious. I cried for her sorrows and anxieties, but I also cried because I liked crying. So did she. Though our worries and fears were real, we laid it on a bit thick. The world was still a fairly threatening place to a pair of inexperienced young lovers, but in our bedroom we could give each other all the comfort and support that the world denied us. And what could be better, kissing away the tears, murmuring the loving words, quietly blowing our noses, and, almost invariably, having great sex afterwards?

All this storm and stress wasn't quite so silly as it sounds. Out there were falseness, compromise, bureaucracy. In here were nakedness, openness, innocence. In other words, all that high-minded stuff about "alienation" that I had been reading since I was eighteen wasn't entirely bullshit. We both had a sense of what the literary critic Dennis Donoghue (with whom Lucy was later to study at New York University) called "social and political formations largely indifferent to individual values." You have to live in the world, and we did, more or less successfully, but I never lost the sense, to quote Donoghue, that "my true self is my subjectivity, and my specious self is the fractured functionary who trades under my name." That's what Lucy and I were giving each other – our truest, deepest, most subjective selves. Maybe in the end a little less introspection and a little more worldliness wouldn't have hurt.

There were some tears, alas, that couldn't be shared. One day that fall, with Lucy out visiting Anne-Sophie, my eyes fell upon the diary that she happened to leave on the coffee table that she had recently installed. This was one of the rare times in my life that I had been guilty of snooping into other people's business, so I richly deserved what anyone can see coming. Idly and unthinkingly picking it up, I chanced to open to a passage that read:

Why do I find Stephen so unattractive? He's so gentle and so kind to me. And yet I don't feel the slightest physical –

That was as far as I got. It was almost enough to make me believe in God, or, more likely, a wicked demiurge arranging retribution with perfect foresight. I had been fittingly punished, but after the initial shock and the sting of tears, I recovered surprisingly quickly. First of all, I had enough presence of mind to note the date – sometime in April or May, before Lucy had left her panties on my shower nozzle. Since then, we had spent enraptured hours in gross carnality. Pretty clearly, she had grown to find me sufficiently attractive, so much so that I abandoned the running tally I kept for a few months until losing count; we were getting close to triple digits. It is with some reluctance that I refrain from detailing the what where when and how or even the special articles of clothing she sometimes wore for me on those occasions. But really, I think she came to find me attractive because I found her attractive. Like any woman or I suppose any human being, she wanted to be desired. That was never a problem. All she needed to do was accidentally brush against me or not wear a bra or casually apply a touch of lipstick and I needed to . . . well, let's just say I needed to love her in a special way.

Complications would arise. This story, as I've said, doesn't end well. But for now, our shared life was fairly idyllic and even our troubles knit us closer together. In a way, I was glad that Lucy really did have some quite serious problems; they gave me a chance to demonstrate my love, to be useful, for the first time in my life, to someone who needed me. On top of the bad news from Manila, there was bad news in New York. With her glittering résumé and usual diligence, she had gone out and found a job in a matter of weeks. But before she could start working as a junior architect for the New York Housing Resource Administration on Worth Street in lower Manhattan, she would have to upgrade her visa. Thus began a Kafkaesque nightmare of waiting, applications, appointments, documents, forms, reviews, authorizations, transcripts, signatures, and more waiting. This went on through the fall and into the winter. I could barely understand it then, let alone recapitulate it now. Dealing with the Immigration and Naturalization Service would be hard enough for anyone; for Lucy, whose sense of ethnic identity was always a delicate subject, it was agony. She resented

being treated, however subtly, as a "foreigner," and since fighting
the bureaucrats at INS was basically a full-time job, she was
subjected to that treatment nearly five days a week. Furthermore,
she knew that if she didn't get her visa troubles resolved soon,
she would lose her job. Her supervisors at the Housing Resource
Administration were patient and sympathetic, but they couldn't
wait forever. Well, I wanted to be useful. Here was my chance.
And all I had to do was listen.

Lucy listened too. God knows I had my own shit to deal
with. If I ever felt in need of some sympathy or a few tears shed
in my behalf, I could always tell a story from my wretched,
protracted adolescence lasting from junior high through
college. The bullying, the humiliation, the shame, the isolation,
the physical deprivation, and on and on. She grieved for me,
I grieved for her. Maybe there was something to my absurd
Platonism after all. It really did, at times, feel like a merging of
souls.

But I had had about enough of Anne-Sophie. She no
longer posed a threat, but even Socrates, when contemplating
the transcendent beauty of Agathon, probably didn't want
Eryximachus hanging around all the time, and Eryximachus
had to be easier to deal with than Anne-Sophie was. Not wanting
to tarnish a friendship that obviously meant a lot to Lucy, I held
my tongue for as long as I could, though I was sorely tempted
to tell Anne-Sophie to fuck off then and there when she ordered
Lucy one summer day at International House to go back to her
room and change: her panties were (just barely) visible through
her thin white frock. Jesus, Lucy finally wears something sexy
outside and Anne-Sophie has to spoil that too! Lucy might have
been the only person Anne-Sophie didn't completely dominate;
she certainly stomped all over me. I think it was after she snarled
at me for talking too loudly on the subway (as if you could have

a quiet conversation of the number 1 train!), then deliberately made me wait for an hour on the sidewalk rather than the promised five minutes she said she and Lucy needed to talk to her prospective landlord in Washington Heights – it was after these and a hundred other excruciations that I finally broke my silence.

"Um, Lucy," I said that night in bed with my usual magniloquence whenever speaking about a subject that made me nervous, "I don't want to upset you or anything, but I just have to say, well, you know, it's just that, um, the thing is, I'm having a really really hard time with Anne-Sophie and I . . . "

That was enough.

"Oh my God," she exclaimed. "How could I not see?"

She had wanted to believe that our shared affection for her would translate into shared affection for each other. If A loves B and C, and B and C love A, shouldn't B and C love each other? No, B and C wanted to push each other in front of a subway train. We agreed that henceforth I should keep my distance from Anne-Sophie as much as possible, which wasn't as possible as I would have liked. The whole situation weirdly resembled the plot of Henry James's *The Bostonians,* where Basil Ransom (the suitor) and Olive Chancellor (the best friend) battle over the soul of Verena Tarrant (the marvelous girl). Lucy's soul wasn't up for grabs; Anne-Sophie and I weren't *that* stupid, or possessive. Nevertheless, I have to say it: I'm glad I won. Anne-Sophie wanted Lucy to be the embodiment of some sort of Eastern wisdom and serenity, "the pearl of Manila," as her former friend Paola had once – cringingly – called her; I wanted Lucy to be Lucy.

Eventually Anne-Sophie and I worked out an unspoken détente, which lasted a couple of years, until Lucy too had finally had enough of her former best friend. In the meantime, we were still sometimes roped together, as on one weekend that October when the three of us, plus a Japanese friend of theirs studying film at Columbia named Setsuko, drove up to Massachusetts to see the fall foliage. Who conceived of that brilliant idea? It must have been Setsuko, whose sweetness and limited proficiency in English would have blinded her to the cloud of hostility and anxiety that enwrapped the three of us. Predictably, the trip was a disaster from the start. Anne-Sophie was two hours late to our agreed rendezvous at International House on Friday night, and everyone was already worn out when we arrived at our destination in Somerville, outside of Boston, at two AM. The next day it rained, and the four of us were stuck in the car on a slow, claustrophobic ride to Vermont. The whole weekend was like that, with Anne-Sophie alternately sulking and snarling, and Setsuko perhaps less oblivious to the tension than I had imagined. The only halfway amusing part of the debacle was Saturday night at a bar in Harvard Square, where Anne-Sophie, who called all the shots, insisted we squander more time. An extremely drunk Vietnam War vet (or so he claimed) hit on Lucy as soon as we walked in. Wow, I thought, this must happen to her all the time, or would if she ever hung around in bars, which she didn't. I got between her and the guy and distracted him with some ridiculous macho bluster about the war. Other times it wouldn't have been so amusing. Once, alone at night, she was walking by the newsstand at Grand Army Plaza in Park Slope when a guy felt her up and then laughed in her face. She came home wanting to take karate lessons. Hence one of the great lessons any straight man learns who marries or lives with a girlfriend: they have to put up with a lot more shit than we do.

Still, Lucy dealt with the shit better than Anne-Sophie, who saw feminism almost exclusively in terms of victimization and oppression. Lucy had a more complex view. Yes, victimization and oppression were a huge part of the story, but so were achievement, agency, and celebration. At any rate, I couldn't imagine Anne-Sophie saying what Lucy said to me one night, after I beheld with sacramental reverence her latest purchase of some frilly lingerie: "I like being a girl."

I've been hard on Anne-Sophie, but if she could speak for herself, she might say something like, "Yes, of course Stephen was a very great asshole, but I too had my struggles, I was young, conflicted, depressed. *Quelle horreur*! Why does this man think that I alone acted in bad faith?"

It's true. Sometimes the problem was me. A year later, in the summer of 1981, we went to an open-air Ramones concert on the pier at West Forty-sixth Street and were joined by a friend of theirs who was studying piano at the Manhattan School of Music. None of them knew the slightest thing about rock and roll and were most unlikely to appreciate a band as loud, unvarnished, and assaultive as the Ramones. Whatever mild curiosity they had was immediately dashed by the opening chords of "Blitzkrieg Bop," which sounded a lot like the opening chords of "Cretin Hop," which sounded a lot like the opening chords of "Gimme Gimme Shock Treatment" and every other song they played that night. In the momentary intervals between songs, Anne-Sophie witheringly asked me why "that man" sometimes held the microphone stand over his head and why that seemed to excite the audience so much. A little respect, please – this was Joey Ramone we were talking about! My reply was to leave my seat and join the mosh pit in front of the stage for the rest of the performance. In a coffee shop where we repaired after the show, Anne-Sophie continued asking mocking questions and I continued to sulk. Lucy laid into me when we got home. Of *course* Anne-Sophie was going to mock me – what else did I expect? But did I have to abandon her and her poor, mousy friend Nancy, who seemed genuinely shocked by the music and who could have used some of the warmth and humor I prided myself on sharing with people in uncomfortable situations? Really, Stephen, you can be such a . . . such a . . .

In succeeding years Lucy would have many occasions to fill in the blank. Initially, however, we never quarreled at all, so that the first time she spoke harshly to me – the subject was preparing meals, or rather my negligence thereof – I was so stunned that the tears immediately started from my eyes. Never mind that she was right and that in our first few years, to my lasting regret, she did more of the housework than I did. Until that moment after dinner she had never raised her voice in anger. What had happened to the marvelous girl? The marvelous girl was pissed. For God's sake, Stephen, toughen up! Lucy had no illusions about perfect domestic harmony. People who loved each other got angry too. Well, I learned. I also learned to fight back.

Occasionally we chafed over small things. I tended to be tidier than Lucy, but no one was going to erupt over a misplaced toothpaste cap. On the other hand, Lucy did erupt, and not infrequently, over a very large thing in which I was necessarily (in her view) implicated: the degradation and exploitation of women. Naïvely, I believed we could debate this subject in the same invigorating way we debated philosophy or modern art or literary criticism or architecture. I was a committed feminist, was I not? I had read Kate Millett's *Sexual Politics*, I believed all the progressive things about female empowerment that enlightened men were supposed to believe. And yet the problem was, as Lucy frankly admitted when she got angry enough, I was still a *man*. It was, in fact, someone of my gender who had recently used, abused, and jilted a close friend of hers from the Urban Planning Department at Columbia. When she got back home after hearing the whole sorry tale, she seemed to be angry less at the creepy guy who had dumped her friend or at men in general than at me. It made her only angrier when I suggested that women also lied, deceived, cheated, and broke hearts. O.K., O.K., let's calm down. I was sorry I said this, she was sorry she said that. But I stood convicted. Maybe I tried a little harder, maybe I was a little less insensitive than others of my sex, but I was still blinded, and always would be, by male privilege.

Me, blind? I was Mister Sensitive. I readily perceived the pervasive gender stereotypes taken for granted by less enlightened men, I daily congratulated myself on my elaborate respectfulness for all women, I never used the word "pussy" except as a licensed obscenity in certain moments of passion with Lucy. Hence, I was stunned when she remarked matter-of-factly that one of the diary entries I had made her listen to from my years as the world's most miserable and maladjusted college student was plain and simply a rape fantasy. *Rape fantasy?* I merely wanted her to understand how lonely I had been before she entered my life, how my futile longing for unobtainable girls had been transformed through her ministrations into a shared and loving sexuality. First of all, she never should have forgiven me for making her listen to such wretched prose, but that aside, she was entirely right that my diary musings as a horny eighteen-year-old had less to do with an honest reckoning regarding the nature of desire than with repressed sexual violence. And if I was capable of such barbarity, what man wasn't?

In later years, that same jilted friend of hers from the Urban Planning department used to ask me sometimes what, "as a man," I thought about this, that, or the other thing. As a man? How the hell should I know? Ask me what I think about the rhythm section of Talking Heads and I'll tell you. (The rhythm section of Talking Heads was really great; but any woman would have said the same.) I had opinions on everything under the sun and was only too glad to impart them. Yes, but the *way* I imparted them – that was what rankled, that was what Lucy heard as the hidden, despotic male voice that even her gentle, unassertive boyfriend couldn't quite suppress.

Lucy took it as an article of faith that women not only had the right to resent men but, as she told me on more than one occasion, the obligation to do so. Further, she believed that all men were guilty until proven innocent; she allowed herself to be pleasantly surprised when a man, like me, turned out to be not wholly beyond redemption. Fortunately, she applied these principles inconsistently, and for the most part was as gracious and courteous with men as with women, children, and dogs. If it seems hard to comprehend that she could have embraced such extreme opinions (substitute gays or Blacks or Muslims for men and see where that gets you), I, in part, embraced them too. We were young. We wanted to believe in a system that would explain the inexplicable and at last sort out all our confusions about the world. Maybe feminism would succeed where Marxism or Freudianism had failed. (Religion, "that vast moth-eaten musical brocade," to quote Philip Larkin, was never in the running.) I need hardly point out that this faith in a totalizing theory is at the root of some of the worst disasters of modern history. For burgeoning intellectuals like us, the surrender of this fantasy was the beginning of wisdom; ordinary people already knew it.

Over time our views grew to accommodate what I like to think of as reality. Lucy's anti-male bigotry evolved into a confident, thoughtful feminism with a residue of perhaps reasonable anger, whereas I grew increasingly defensive on the subject of male collective guilt, which she could never persuade me to accept. We hadn't had the last of these wrenching debates. Let others fight about the misplaced toothpaste cap! We fought about female self-determination and patriarchal assumptions that stood in the way of full emancipation. Eventually, of course, like everyone else, we ended up fighting about the misplaced toothpaste cap as well.

Park Slope was a heavily lesbian neighborhood in those days, and out of solidarity, Lucy always yearned for a lesbian friend or two. I, however, was the one who ended up with the gay friends – mostly men from my job at the library and the School of Library Service at Columbia. (They were not, as Lucy wanted to believe, exempt from the sexism that she attributed solely to male heterosexuals.) Early on, though, we didn't have many friends at all, either gay or straight. What we had was each other, and what we most enjoyed doing together was nothing in particular. Reading, listening to music, snuggling, walking to the newsstand on Saturday night to buy the Sunday *Times*. "Earth's the right place for love," said Robert Frost; he could have been talking about Park Slope on a Saturday night in the 1980s. Yes, already there were some complications, but we were discovering, as the great Irish novelist John McGahern wrote, "that the best of life is lived quietly, where nothing happens but our calm journey through the days." And living in Park Slope – beautiful, relatively quiet, rough around the edges, and still surprisingly diverse back then – accentuated our sense of blessed ordinariness. Those brownstones were full of average boring people just like us. We didn't smoke, drink, take drugs, go to chic restaurants and hip clubs or even know where they were. The occasional Ramones concert was about as wild as it got for us. I thought it would last forever. I was wrong.

Actually, it wasn't going to last longer than a few months if Lucy didn't get her visa problem straightened out. She wasn't making much progress, and the effort was bleeding her dry. Tears of rage, tears of grief, almost every night. Finally, late one evening in December, I offered, as the only possible solution to this hopeless problem, what might have been the least romantic marriage proposal ever delivered.

"Fuck it," I said. "Let's get married."

5

I called in sick to get married. We were in a hurry and the marriage bureau was closed on weekends. Neither Lucy nor I ever considered an actual wedding. For better or worse, the idea of dressing up in a suit and gown for people to gawk at us just about made me throw up. So on January 9, 1981, we met Anne-Sophie and Setsuko, who would serve as our "witnesses," at the Municipal Building in downtown Brooklyn. The bride wore an orange skirt and yellow sweater, the groom a flannel shirt and corduroy pants. It must have taken a heroic effort on her part, but for the first and only time in her life, Anne-Sophie treated me affectionately. She joked, smiled, teased us, even – *mirabile dictu*! – kissed me goodbye when we parted for the day. Everybody was in high spirits. Sitting on plastic chairs and benches in that enormous waiting room with all the other couples and their families from Africa and Asia and Latin America, we felt like invited guests at the funkiest, friendliest party in New York City.

Eventually, we were summoned to what was laughingly called a "chapel," where a bored clerk wearing Coke-bottle glasses recited the familiar litany with such haste that if I hadn't heard it a hundred times before in movies and on TV, I wouldn't have understood a word he was saying. When the bit came about placing the ring on Lucy's finger, I panicked. I never wore a ring; neither did she. (Elegant and understated earrings, yes.) For a moment I thought we'd have to go through the whole bureaucratic rigmarole, including the blood tests, all over again. But Giuseppe Nazzaro (his name is on the marriage certificate) came through like the heroic civil servant that he was.

"You don't have a ring for this beautiful girl?" he said. "Shame on you, Stephen. Here, use this one."

The ring he lent us for the occasion had been made from a coin. He was a numismatist and spent the next couple of minutes extolling the wonders of coins and coinage. We thanked him sincerely, and Lucy and I left the room "man and wife," to borrow the term he had used and that we sternly disapproved of. Afterwards we went to a diner in Brooklyn Heights, which I suppose was our version of a wedding reception. I ordered a cheese omelet and a milkshake. Setsuko took pictures of Lucy and me standing on Montague Street and smiling a bit sheepishly in our bulky winter coats and knapsacks. Would we ever be that happy again? As a matter of fact, we would. Until we weren't.

For our honeymoon we got back on the F train and went to see a double feature, the rarely screened Beatles' oddities *How I Won the War* and *Magical Mystery Tour,* at the Eighth Street Playhouse in Greenwich Village. Lucy still had to wait a few weeks before she could get her long delayed Green Card and begin her job, but I had to get back to work on Monday. I was still shy enough to be self-conscious about things like interactions with co-workers; office banter didn't come easy for me. So I was nervous about telling the news to my colleagues, mostly cataloging librarians from various parts of the world, in the technical services annex of the Brooklyn Public Library in Crown Heights – nice people, most of them, whom I barely knew. On the way to work that morning I stopped at a bakery on Seventh Avenue and bought a box of cookies, which I offered to all at our customary eleven o'clock coffee break in the staff lounge.

"This is to break the bad news," I announced. "I got married on Friday."

Ho ho ho, he he hah. Nobody paid much attention until a few minutes later when Farzanah, a piss-elegant woman from Iran, paused in the midst of a conversation, turned to look at me quizzically, and said:

"Stephen. You weren't joking, were you?"

"Well, no, actually, I wasn't," I replied.

Whew, glad I got that over. They were all very nice to me when the news sunk in, and they even threw a little surprise party for me the next day. It wasn't their fault the job was so fucking boring. Next I had to tell my family. That was easier. A couple of my siblings had already met Lucy and taken her to heart. Besides, getting married at city hall without a word of warning seemed like a typical Stephen move that didn't require much explanation. Lucy's case was different. When they had parted at the Manila airport two and a half years earlier, the last words her father had spoken to her were, "Now, don't go and get married to a white man." He was half joking. But only half.

The call came at 1:30 AM two weeks later. Lucy had written to her parents and siblings, explaining that she had met and married, well, *me*. She trusted they would understand and respect her decision. Unfortunately, the caller was not her mother or father but her sister Connie, who had a way of pushing Lucy's buttons. Connie explained that their parents were away on business, an unlikely story that I suspect Connie wanted Lucy to disbelieve. She did indeed disbelieve it. Clearly, her parents needed time to recover from the shock. Lucy had to know that was coming, but it didn't stop her from sobbing in my arms when she returned to bed. On the other hand, all of the seven younger siblings, some of them still in high school, were delighted. There soon arrived in the mail a package containing congratulatory missives from all or most of them, plus a few charmingly stern warnings from her brothers: "Steve, you take care of my big sister!" and "Hey Steve, we're gonna come over there and check up on you!"

Normally, I loved hearing Lucy speak Chinese on the phone, even though, when she spoke to her mother, it sounded as if they were yelling at each other. That's because they were. Nothing riled her up quite like one of her monthly conversations with Brave Orchid – the nickname I gave her, inspired by the all-consuming matriarch in Maxine Hong Kingston's memoir of Chinese-American family life, *The Woman Warrior*. I remember reading an interview in which Kingston said that, far from exaggerating her mother's ferocity, she had toned it down; no reader would have believed her otherwise. Lucy said the same thing. There was no way I could ever comprehend just how implacable her mother was. Still, I had a rough idea. Some years later, when our son's second set of teeth had come in crooked, Brave Orchid put the blame squarely where it belonged: on Lucy, for not pushing and pulling Jonathan's teeth properly with her own hands.

Both sets of parents had to be relieved that we weren't living in sin, but we were sufficiently products of our time not to believe in marriage as an institution. Although we celebrated our birthdays with special dinners and gooey chocolate cakes (my preference), our putative anniversary meant nothing. The only significant change in my life was that as of January 9, 1981, I had to stop calling Lucy my girlfriend and start calling her my wife. I never got used to it. "Girlfriend" was all romance and innocence, like the French *petite amie*. "Wife" had a creepy, possessive ring to it, like the German *Ehefrau.* Once a friend of mine referred to Lucy as "wifey." He wasn't a friend for much longer.

Anyway, she wasn't my "wife"; she was Lucy Ha Kung. As I wrote in my diary, "The thing is, we know we love each other forever & that our marriage is a purely superficial convention that has little or nothing to do with that love. If we keep that in mind & keep marriage out of mind, we'll be all right." I can almost weep for the innocence. Nevertheless, it's possible that being married boosted our confidence a bit. Exactly one day after our "wedding," we had a party to attend in a ground-floor apartment for all the tenants in our building. I couldn't have faced it alone. Walking into that room of total strangers (my neighbors, but that's New York for you), I cleaved onto my wife and we were one flesh, as the Book of Genesis says. We certainly bucked each other up; attending parties with the pot-smoking, left/liberal intelligentsia of Park Slope was a life skill we had not yet mastered. Nevertheless, we got through what was a very long evening of gossip and chatter and even made our first friends in the neighborhood: Maxwell, a hyper-articulate, Jewish, home-grown intellectual currently studying law, and his charming and low-key girlfriend Nina, who calmed him down, if anyone could. Welcome to Park Slope. If we could hold our own with these people, maybe this neighborhood could be to us what our places of birth had never felt like: a hometown.

A few months later Lucy and I threw our own party. This was, basically, a reunion of Lucy's girlfriends from International House. The Philippines, Switzerland, Japan, Nigeria, Nepal, Guyana: it felt like the United Nations in there, and I delighted, as at our marriage ceremony, in being the only indigenous white guy in the room. The women drank a little wine, got silly, laughed loudly, and took pictures with our Polaroid camera. (Lucy looks absolutely smashing in them.) My job was to entertain Dama, the hopelessly shy kid brother of the Nigerian woman Karen, whom she dragged around the city in a vain attempt to loosen him up or improve his English, whichever came first. I wasn't having much luck until I discovered, apropos of Bob Marley's recent death, that he loved reggae. Thereafter the conversation returned again and again to the few words of English he understood: "Bob Marley," "so sad," "tragedy," "political," and "Peter Tosh."

All of these women, to one degree or another, identified with the traditions and customs of their homelands. Not Lucy. She took a fair amount of heat for her indifference to Chinese history and culture, not to mention her still greater indifference to Philippine history and culture. Even the unfailingly polite Setsuko, a few years later (when her English had improved), once said, "You know, I look around this apartment and I don't see any sign that a Chinese person lives here." Lucy responded, later that night, by yelling at *me.* (I told you this was a sensitive topic.) But Setsuko was right. It wasn't Chinese scroll painters that spoke to Lucy and influenced her own art; it was Louise Bourgeois, Jasper Johns, Joan Mitchell, Robert Ryman, and other difficult and thoroughly Western postmodernists. Some people then and even more people now would have denied her that preference, seeing little but false consciousness or capitulation to coercive power structures in her allegiance to West over East. I was on her side. In spite of my unfortunate last name (rhymes with shaky), I happened to be Irish-American, but Irishness didn't mean much to me either. My resistance to identity politics may or may not stem from my sympathy for Lucy's difficulties, but I hope we may be allowed to decide these matters for ourselves or at least acknowledge the primacy of private consciousness over identarian categories. Existence, I willfully believe (along with Jean-Paul Sartre and a few others), precedes essence. If you want to observe Chinese New Year or practice Mandarin or study Confucianism (which Lucy particularly loathed), go ahead, and if you don't, don't. Undoubtedly there was an element of psychological conflict in Lucy's orientation towards Western culture, but there's an element of conflict in all the deepest areas of our psychology. Why not give her the benefit of the doubt? Why must her reasoned opposition to Confucianism (which she saw, rightly or wrongly, as a hierarchy of oppression) be reduced to a psychological case study? I know very well that these are enormously complex matters. To what degree should racial or ethnic identity be determinative? That wasn't the question. The question was, How do I comfort and support Lucy?

My only regret on this score is that my sweetest endearment – Pe Fung, her given name – never gained any traction. After a few attempts I went back to the silly pet names she clearly preferred: Crummy, Gloomy, Gloopy, and the like. Although I was no more sentimental about Ireland than Lucy was about China (neither of us had ever set foot in either country), I loved the idea of the lines of our ancestors, from so many worlds apart, converging after thousands of years at the sundial on the campus of Columbia University one day in the spring of 1980 – very sentimental, no doubt, but I still think the world would be a better place with a little more exogamy and a little less endogamy. Yes, while fornicating in the shower we were doing our bit for world peace!

We also did our bit for international communication. Chinatown was still the nucleus of the Chinese population in New York, and one night, at a subway stop in Penn Station, a lost and bewildered old woman threw herself on Lucy's mercy. Hopeless. She spoke only Cantonese. Lucy spoke Fukienese and

Mandarin. We knew she needed to get to Chinatown, and the only way to get her there was to take her ourselves. Dropping off a poor old woman at the Grand Street station hardly merited the Nobel Peace Prize, but I sometimes wonder if Lucy saw something of herself or perhaps her mother in that old woman's rooted Chineseness. Probably not. She was just being nice, as usual.

In the 1980s, Asian-Caucasian unions were rather less common than they are today. Occasionally I would pick up an innuendo about my great good luck in having a "submissive" Asian wife. Lucy was about as submissive as Genghis Khan, but never mind, I wasn't going to argue with racists. What did bother me was the never openly expressed idea that *I* was the racist – that I had chosen Lucy out of some kinky, imperialist sexual preference. And indeed, to some it might have looked that way. I never learned a word of Chinese, I didn't know the Han dynasty from the Ming, I couldn't even handle my chopsticks properly. I knew better than anyone, however, that the less I made an issue of Lucy's ethnic identity, the more loved, the more secure she felt. My role wasn't to solve every unsolvable existential dilemma in her life – I had enough of my own. My role was to make her feel loved and secure. If she had been an ordinary American girl from the suburbs, would I have loved her just as much? Yes. Except maybe for the silky hair.

One specific proposal did suggest itself: Let's go to the Philippines. She didn't say no, she didn't say yes. I didn't relish facing the terrifying Brave Orchid either, but Lucy would be with all her brothers and sisters again, and I would do my best to provide some amiable son-in-law cover between her and her parents. (Actually, I would have been the son-in-law "ghost"; that much I understood from Maxine Hong Kingston.) As a further incentive, I scoped out a national forest preserve not too far from Manila that we could visit on our own. Furthermore, with the acquisition of her Green Card facilitated by our society wedding, Lucy finally started working in February. With two incomes, we could start saving for the airfare. This conversation lasted for several years, long past the point when the revelation dawned on me: Lucy wasn't going anywhere near the Philippines, but she still needed to keep the door theoretically open. Fortunately, what I considered my clinching argument never came to an issue. Lucy, I used to say, you don't want to go back for a funeral.

If I was nervous bantering with my utterly unintimidating co-workers, Lucy, the only female architect in an office of fairly grizzled men, had reason to be more so. And in fact she spent part of her first lunch hour hiding out in the women's room. Yet within a few days she was riding between job sites in taxis and having lunch with suppliers in Italian restaurants – perks unimaginable to a grunt-level public librarian like me. Even so, the Housing Resource Administration was a step down for her. In Manila, she had designed hotel lobbies and houses for rich people. In New York, she was designing homeless shelters and food stamp offices in the outer boroughs. That wasn't an accident. We had decided, quite deliberately, to settle. With a little more effort, Lucy could have found a more prestigious position at a much higher salary in the private sector, and even I could have made some serious money as a corporate librarian in Manhattan, as a few of my acquaintances did. Those acquaintances of mine worked nights and weekends and wasted expensive theater tickets when deadlines ran late; that wasn't going to happen to us. Time, not money, determined our choice – time to read, time to think, time to create, time (never enough) to be lazy. Apart from believing (as I still do) in the mission of public service, we chose our humdrum 35-hour-a-week jobs because we preferred having some time to none at all. It was pretty simple, really. We were in love. We wanted time in which to love each other.

Living creative, engaged lives with even relatively civilized nine-to-five jobs proved more of a challenge than we had anticipated. I bitched about it more than Lucy did. We used to walk up and down the streets of Park Slope in the evening, peeking into the parlors of the beautiful first-floor apartments and speculating about alternatives to full-time employment. We never found any. Lucy would do quite well as an architect for the City of New York, rising several significant steps on the bureaucratic ladder and eventually earning more than twice as much as I did. I encountered a greater degree of frustration in my up and down career as a librarian, but I've written about that subject elsewhere. Say something once, as David Byrne immortally yelped, why say it again? Anyway, there were more important matters to consider than the mere question of making a living. There was also the acquisition of the French language. In the spring we enrolled in an introductory class in the continuing education department at New York University. Even if I hadn't met Lucy I probably would have taken the class, but I would have been miserable. Now, for the first time in my life, I could walk into a new classroom without the crippling self-consciousness that generally relegated me to a seat in the back and the avoidance of all social interaction. Was it a coincidence that the young woman who sat in front of us was continually hitching up her skirt to fiddle with her stockings? Lucy had no doubt that mademoiselle was making every effort to distract me. Probably she was. And probably, if Lucy hadn't been there, this low-rent femme fatale wouldn't have paid me the slightest mind. We had a good laugh about it. But I was indeed distracted.

We kept up with our classes for a few more years. French, I found, was stubbornly more resistant than Spanish, but a subsequent class at Alliance Française in midtown inspired greater confidence. Our young maîtresse was endlessly encouraging, and all the students but one were twenty-something couples just like Lucy and me. The exception was a divorced, middle-aged businessman named William who tried desperately to find common ground with us in class and even, on one or two occasions, in French restaurants where we shared a group meal. Many years of linguistic neglect later, I decided to brush off the cobwebs and register again at Alliance Française. You can see what's coming, can't you? I was William. Unlike my predecessor, I lacked the fortitude to stick it out. After two classes I fled, to study partitive constructions in the safety of my living room.

All this time, bad news kept arriving from Manila. I think Connie was playing on Lucy's sense of guilt, but the crisis was real and getting worse. For a while, her parents were housebound; outside of the big family compound, creditors and bill-collectors were waiting to pounce. Was this the best time (July, 1981) for Lucy to have to meet my mother, visiting from Florida? Sure, why not? We could all use a doting, gemütlich Irish-American mother-in-law who hangs on our every word. Although it took a day or two to sink in, my mother finally understood that this new daughter-in-law, who taught her how to crochet and laughed off all her house-guest anxieties with a breezy "Oh Peg, don't be silly," wasn't going to make the least fuss if she left a wet towel on the bathroom floor or opened a third can of Coke before finishing her first.

"She's such a beautiful girl," my mother kept whispering to me during the week of her visit.

"Hey Mom, remember me?" I replied a bit testily. "I'm pretty nice too."

My father, remarried and finally sober, rather liked the idea of having a Chinese daughter-in-law. He had been stationed in China during World War II and allowed himself to be sentimental about his time there. He did have a little trouble with Lucy's refusal to take the name "Akey" (never the remotest possibility). No, my brother Tony told him, it was worse than that; I had changed my last name to "Kung." Just kidding, Dad! Wish I could have been there.

At last she had met the parents-in-law, a rite of passage I never had to undergo. A more daunting meeting was coming up in November. Ten months after the "ceremony" in the Brooklyn Municipal Building, we were scheduled to meet with an officer from the Immigration and Naturalization Service, who would determine whether or not our marriage was a sham and thus whether or not Lucy qualified for permanent residency status. I knew there was nothing to worry about, but my insecurities lay elsewhere. For Lucy, the specter of this interview raised disturbing questions about identity, ethnicity, and belonging that she could never resolve. To put her at ease, I arranged for us to meet an acquaintance of mine who worked for a law firm specializing in immigration cases. Big mistake. My acquaintance supplied us with a raft of misinformation that only (and perhaps deliberately) exacerbated Lucy's anxiety. Lucy fretted particularly over the personal ad in the *Village Voice;* she thought that looked bad for us. Maybe we should make up a story about how we met? Oh, let's not, I said. In the event, none of her fears came to pass. We were in and out of there in ten minutes. The immigration officer instantly saw that we were for real and kept us just long enough to satisfy appearances. Another heroic civil servant! For that matter, *we* were heroic civil servants. Still, the whole experience had rattled her. I had an idea for unrattling her, or at least for making her feel a little more at home in the world. Why not become an American citizen? Let me think about it, she said. So she thought about it. And said yes.

6

I wasn't there when Lucy took her oath of citizenship in lower Manhattan with assorted other hopefuls from around the world. Guests weren't invited, but she said it was a welcoming and touching ceremony. Now she could rail with a clear conscience against the Reagan administration, vote for Democrats, and raise her voice as an enfranchised citizen – which makes both of us sound more political than we really were. John Adams could have been thinking of useless aesthetes like us when he wrote, "I must study Politicks and War that my sons may have liberty to study Painting and Poetry, Mathematicks and Philosophy." Politics for Lucy and me was like broccoli: necessary, not very appetizing. After a year and a half together, we still lived for art and culture. But if we were late bloomers in romance, we were also late bloomers in the arts. My problem was not enough talent; Lucy's problem was too much. She had more creativity than she knew what to do with. Should she set up as a freelancer and design interiors and studios? Should she paint? Should she make prints? Sculpture? Clothes? Quilts? On our evening walks up and down the majestic brownstone streets of Park Slope, we hashed out the possibilities. And the impossibilities. The many artist friends in subsequent years who came to know her as an inspiring role model serenely turning out one splendid semi-abstraction after another would have been surprised to witness these early struggles, which entailed much self-doubt and many tears shed at two in the morning. In the vale of soul-making that was our bed in the small hours, a box of Kleenex at the bedside, I found, was indispensable.

The struggles continued for another year or so. Where to begin, how to channel all that creative energy? I would have killed for such a problem. The most I could aspire to in those days was a handful of half-assed book reviews published in *Library Journal*. In another French class, after the students and teacher had learned about Lucy's creative endeavors, some wanted to know what the hell I did. "Je suis sa muse," I replied.

I loved it that our interests and inclinations dovetailed so perfectly: Lucy an aspiring artist with a feeling for literature, I an aspiring writer with a feeling for art. Nevertheless, I had no illusions about which partner was the authentic creator. Lucy's talent so abashed me that it took me years to believe in my own – a knock, needless to say, on me, not her. In the meantime (fall 1981), I enrolled in an art class in the Brooklyn Museum Art School with the goal, not of discovering the hidden artist within me (there was none), but of simply learning to see better. And to be a better muse.

I learned two things on the first day of that course: that without Lucy by my side, as in our French classes, entering a new classroom was the same agony of self-consciousness and head-down, eyes-averted diffidence that it had been for me in college. I got through the ten Saturday morning sessions without managing to speak to a single person other than the instructor. Clearly, this confidence thing was going to be a long-term project. Of course, if I had had any skill (or if the other students had had less of it), I would have felt less insecure, which brings up the second lesson I learned on the first day of class:

unless you were born to it, like Lucy, making art was hard. The morning we spent creating our own abstractions, far from being the fun, finger-painting exercise I had remembered from the first grade, turned out to be so grueling that it made the rigor of life studies seem comparatively relaxed. Nor did I understand until then how draining the effort of looking – really looking – can be. But that's what I signed up for. And I learned how to look.

Ever the diligent student, I filled sketchbooks at home with drawings of house plants, tea kettles, radiators, and the toilet bowl. All of those sketchbooks were lost (or tossed) when we split up, including the one containing the most prized possession of my life: a pen-and-ink portrait of Lucy reading in bed, with her knees propped up under the covers and a little still-life on the table beside her. Striving to apply everything I had learned about modeling and perspective from my art class, I ended up achieving a folkloric simplicity that made Grandma Moses look like Michelangelo. No matter. Lucy was for me in that portrait what the Duchess of Alba had been for Francisco Goya, or Susanna Lunden for Peter Paul Rubens, or "La Velata" for Raphael, except that they could draught and I couldn't. If I had had any talent, it would have been just another boring life study. Instead, I somehow managed to produce a genuine *ritratto con amore*. It even resembled her a bit.

That wasn't the only picture that was lost. In her pre-abstraction phase, Lucy painted an acrylic portrait of me seated in a director's chair reading, not Joyce's *Ulysses,* but (ever the pedant) a book *about* Joyce's *Ulysses*. It hung in the living room for many years and called to mind not Grandma Moses but Matisse. I sat for it in my standard uniform of flannel shirt and tattered sweater. As Lucy once said, "It's loose and kind of offhand, but if I do say so, I think I really got you." She used to claim that one day she would make a bonfire of all the paintings that she hadn't sold or given away. For all I know, my portrait might have gone up in flames.

Lucy did in time find her way to a medium that fully engaged her creative energies: quiltmaking. The quilts she made over the next five or six years, while having the unfortunate effect of turning the apartment into a tapestry factory and thus causing some domestic friction, dazzled everyone lucky enough to see them. She started out fairly simply, designing and executing elegant and minimalist geometric abstractions in the manner of classic Amish and Shaker prototypes, but she soon turned to bigger, bolder, more experimental designs. Basically, she ended up producing huge abstract paintings in fabric. No scrap of textile went to waste, and I delighted in seeing pieces of my old shirts and pants turned into the materials of art. That was my life up there in the upper left corner, or at least the life I lived when I was wearing that particular pair of blue jeans. Also, certain primal acts took place on or under those quilts, which is to say, we had fun breaking them in. Where life ended and art began was, thrillingly, impossible to discern.

When not in use, the quilts hung on our walls (at my insistence) on sturdy frames that Lucy constructed herself. She recycled them continually. She was forever boxing them up and mailing them off to quilting contests and exhibitions, where she occasionally had a sale or won a prize. To this day friends and family members are in possession of gigantic, intricate, and sumptuous quilts worth thousands of dollars that she dispensed as casually as candy. I have one of her early ones, quite tattered by now. Lucy, I think, has none. Once she finished a work of art in any medium, she could think only about the next one.

For Lucy the process was everything, the product comparatively little, which is why she eventually gave up quiltmaking for painting; the quilts were just too damn time-consuming. This was a sobering lesson for me. Lucy didn't waste any time glorying in her past achievements, as I, who archived my college term papers as if they were holy writ, would have done; she just got on with the job at hand. What really turned her on about quiltmaking was sketching out possible designs on graph paper in notebooks that she carried about with her. The actual quilting, which she did on a sewing machine or sometimes farmed out to local seamstresses, was mostly a matter of mechanics. She was like a great movie director (Luis Buñuel or Alfred Hitchcock, for example), who, after working out the principal ideas in the screenplay or storyboard, regarded the filming itself as somewhat mechanical. Anyway, seeing a real artist at work day in and day out taught me something I needed to know about myself: I wasn't one.

In the absence of any artistic breakthrough on my part, I had to settle for the revelation of a new world opening to my eyes and ears: birds! This was not, in my opinion, the worst of all possible trade-offs. Maybe our discovery of birdwatching (or birding, to use the proper nomenclature) wasn't quite so momentous as it seemed – it just felt that way when we saw our first black and white warbler flapping around the limb of an oak tree like a zebra-striped windup toy. Was it possible? Had the world around me always exploded in springtime with this riot of form and color and movement and music? Had the sky and the trees and the bushes and the meadows and the marshes always teemed with this secret life? Why hadn't somebody *told* me? I will try to restrain myself from excessive zealotry, but I'll need to say a few words about birding for two reasons: one, it comprised a fairly significant part of the life Lucy and I shared; and, two, you should try it sometime.

The idea, as Lucy and I sat one day in the Brooklyn Botanic Garden listening to an invisible bird pour out an incredibly voluble aria of discontinuous phrases (a catbird, as it turned out, not even one of the more skilled members of the family Mimidae), was simply to learn about and identify the common garden birds that we often heard and sometimes saw. So we signed up for a five-week birding class in the spring of 1982 sponsored by the Garden and led by John "I'm Not Crazy, I Just Love Birds" Yrizarry, a naturalist and illustrator of some repute and inexhaustible enthusiasm. Even without John's endearing eccentricities (including full-bodied imitations of the stop-and-start movements of certain waterfowl), we would have fallen hard for birds. I felt like Adam in Paradise, putting names to all the species that presented themselves to eye and ear. At the beginning of our learning curve, everything was new to us. A common yellowthroat was just as exciting as a cerulean warbler, and a lot easier to spot. We bought field guides and studied up over dinner and in bed. For once in my life, I was better at something than Lucy, who didn't have much of an ear for the songs. She might have been a more evolved, intelligent, generous, and creative human being than I was; but I knew a white-eyed vireo when I heard it.

I now supply a list of the 295 species we saw in our twenty-three years together. Just kidding. We did rack 'em up, however, in and around New York City (one of the key nodes on the migratory flight path known as the Atlantic Flyway) as well as on vacations to the Adirondacks, Vermont, and Florida. Nothing lasts forever, including the lives of birds. Or our marriage. Not the least of my heartbreaks in the last few years of our life together was Lucy's loss of interest in birds or even any interest in my interest. Another bond had been broken, not to mention a special, intimate connection much like the one we shared on and under her quilts. It wasn't just loggerhead shrikes or ruffed grouse that drove us deep into the palmetto scrub of Florida or the spruce forests of the Green Mountains. Sometimes when we got out there far enough away from the world, we took our lessons from the animals. Gross carnality in the woods! I never felt more tender and loving to Lucy than after we had rutted like beasts.

It was a blessing getting out of the city to watch birds and hike and paddle a canoe and do, well, other things in remote parks and wilderness areas. We didn't get away often enough, but our resources were limited and even the matter of renting a car, like so much else in Gotham, was absurdly difficult. (If you were twenty-five or younger, you had to have the rental contract co-signed by the devil, or something like that.) Nor was New York City in the 1980s exactly shining with promise. We still loved it, we still frequented the galleries and museums and theaters, but the notion, to take one small example, that the rusting, dried-up cistern of Bethesda Terrace, the architectural centerpiece of Central Park, would ever be anything but the locus of a dangerous and depressing drug bazaar, was inconceivable. Would the *New York Times* ever cease publishing long articles about the horrible deterioration of the subway system or the horrible deterioration of the parks system or the horrible deterioration of the school system or the horrible deterioration of the criminal justice system? So like many others, we started thinking about getting out. The first step was to start reading the classified ads for librarians in *American Libraries* and *The New York Times,* which I did fairly diligently, Maybe in a more affordable town one of us could support the other or we could get by on part-time jobs. While we endlessly and tediously debated the pros and cons over the next five or six years, two unforeseen developments shifted the ground beneath our feet. The first was that, for a variety of complex factors still debated by sociologists and urbanists, New York City began pulling itself out of its slump. One day in the fall of 1981 I was cutting across Bethesda

Terrace when, lo, a miracle. The Angel of the Waters fountain was working! A policeman told me the water had been turned on a few weeks earlier. Having given up all hope, I was caught completely unaware. There was still quite a bit of graffiti, and the Minton tiles underneath the terrace were years away from restoration. Even so, if Bethesda Terrace could be saved, maybe the day would come when I wouldn't have to keep a spare twenty or forty dollars in my pocket for potential muggers. And it did.

The other development was of a more internal nature. By the time Lucy and I finally realized that we really didn't want to leave the city and probably never had, it was too late anyway. Little by little, New York had unfit us for life anywhere else. Even now I ask myself if I'm ready for a quieter and simpler life in Vermont. It's a lovely prospect. Why does it unnerve me?

Fortunately, we had the option of an occasional respite in Florida, where my mother had relocated a few years earlier, and suburban Connecticut, where I had grown up and where my father lived with his second wife. He and I had never been close, so trips to genteel, bucolic Wilton were infrequent. On our first visit he rigged up a blanket as a screen between two trees to demonstrate his golf swing for Lucy. Fascinating! But after years of absent and alcoholic parenting, he was trying, in his own way, to make amends. Lucy was touched – she hadn't seen what I had seen. But I too was trying to make amends. We all got along more or less happily, which meant, for the most part, listening to him tell stories, something he did with virtuosic proficiency. He also obtained passes for us to use in the woods surrounding the pristine Saugatuck Reservoir. However fraught our relationship, I owe to him the sighting, in that reservoir, of my first scarlet tanager – not a minor event in the life of a birdwatcher.

Our annual trips to Florida, to visit my mother and younger sister, lasted longer and were altogether more relaxed. Lucy didn't come that first winter, but she might as well have; I couldn't shut up about her. You ought to hear the way Lucy deals with building contractors, you ought to see all the sketchbooks she keeps, you ought to taste the Chinese noodles she cooks, you ought to hear her stories about her crazy Buddhist grandmother. I must have been unbearable. I was like that with everyone I knew in those days. Lucy this, Lucy that. No one ever complained, though. She lived up to the hype.

I still would have liked to go to the Philippines. Imagine the birds we would have seen! Yet if Lucy refused to go to her native country, there was no stopping her native country from coming to her. In July of 1982 an old school friend of hers, vacationing in the U.S., invited herself and her mother to stay with us for a few days. It's not that Lucy was rude to them, but she wasn't exactly warm and fuzzy. If she had any lingering attachment to the life she had left behind in the Philippines, this visit effectively quashed it. Although it pained me to see the way sweet, pretty, guileless, and affectionate Becky looked up to Lucy almost as if to an older sister, I understood why Lucy would not or could not reciprocate. Becky had recently married a rising young business executive. The future looked bright: conjugal love, material comfort, vacations to Disneyland, babies. True, the servants were getting uppity, always demanding more pesos and finding inventive ways of shirking their responsibilities, but life in the stratified precincts of the upper class in Manila was good. Even the ruling Marcos dynasty furnished choice diversion. Becky and her mother talked about "Ferdinand" and "Imelda" and their spoiled princelings as if they were colorful characters in a prime-time soap opera rather than corrupt autocrats who might (and in fact did) assassinate inconvenient opponents. By the end of the four- or five-day visit, the strained smile on Lucy's face had vanished. Becky never caught on, partly because I worked doubly hard to be hospitable. But it was easy for me. I wasn't confronted, as Lucy was, with an inverse version of the self I wanted to be. And when I was so confronted, I reacted much the way she did. Only worse.

For my first year or so in New York I kept up with my only remaining friend from the University of Connecticut, Gene Sullivan, a bearish ex-serviceman whom I had met as a fellow worker in the dish room of a campus dining hall during one of his sporadic attempts at higher education. On his two or three visits to me from his dying mill-town in central Connecticut, he complained about his life there, while expressing no great enthusiasm for New York – it was crowded, it was noisy, it was expensive, it was dirty. Well, yes, it was all those things, but I got tired of hearing it. Although I might have engaged him in a conversation about urbanism or sociology or culture or even just taken him to an off-Broadway play to stop him from grumbling for a few hours, I had a better idea. I would ditch him in a subway station. And I did. After watching with feigned distress the doors of a southbound express train close behind him, I never saw him again. Gene was the mumbling, fatalistic, blue-collar version of the person I might have become, just as Becky was the cheerfully incurious upper-class housewife of Lucy's nightmares – except that Lucy didn't dump her former schoolfriend on the platform of a New York City subway line without a word of warning or farewell.

Maybe Lucy could have treated Becky and her mother with a little more deference; I certainly should have been a better friend to Gene Sullivan, or at least brought our friendship to a close more honorably. But if Lucy didn't want to return to the Philippines or express solidarity with her "people," that was her damn business. In subsequent years I've come to know a few women from other Asian countries who, at least in one respect, share her perspective. None of these women have any illusions about the West; hypocrisy and injustice are universal. Yet they choose to live here, or so they have told me, because of the obstacles blocking them from living as unencumbered professional women in their native countries. They could be right, they could be wrong. All of them have ventured far more than I ever have to attain freedoms that I take for granted. The least I can do is shut my mouth and listen.

We had a few other visitors from time to time, but mostly it was just the two of us. We did everything together. Art films at Carnegie Hall and Bleecker Street Cinemas, Talking Heads and B-52s concerts in Central Park, original productions of Sam Shepherd plays, major and minor exhibitions at the Met, the Modern, and the Whitney, weekend trips to Washington and Boston, regular dinners at a red sauce restaurant in Greenwich Village, where the Old-World waiters called the young Chinese woman "*signorina*," as if she were some *bella ragazza* in a Rossini opera. (No doubt my love for mediocre Italian food dates from these intimate meals on Thompson Street, usually before a movie or an Off-Broadway play.) Does Lucy remember the sweltering Saturday night in July when we went to see Brian De Palma's *Dressed To Kill* at a once grand and now decrepit movie palace in downtown Brooklyn and the entirely African American audience made knows its pleasure, fear, dread, and relief by standing up and shouting at the screen? It was like an avant-garde theater experiment in breaking the fourth wall, except that, unlike most avant-garde experiments, it was fun. (I'm still grateful to that audience for cueing us when to look away from the horrific violence.) Or would she remember our one and only trip to Bear Mountain on the no longer extant ferry service up the Hudson, where we learned, having absolutely no alternative, to boogie to the salsa music emanating from the boom boxes of a thousand festive Spanish speakers? Their destination was the Olympic-sized swimming pool and barbecue pits. Ours was the hiking trail to the top of the mountain. It was ninety degrees that day. We should have gone swimming.

Apart from the time we spent at work, we were rarely out of each other's sight. Maybe a little time apart every now and then wouldn't hurt us? I worried that I might start to feel slightly depleted; my inner resources weren't inexhaustible. And then I came across this passage in Montaigne's *Essays:*

> We must reserve a back shop all our own, entirely free, in which to establish our real liberty and our principal retreat and solitude. Here our ordinary conversation must be between us and ourselves, and so private that no outside association or communication can find a place.

Lucy was slightly hurt when I broached the subject, but she already had a back shop of her own: her quilts and the creative ferment inside her head. All I had was my piddling book reviews and some articles for a couple of literary reference works. For some time I had been contemplating returning to Columbia for a masters in English; this seemed to be a good time to do it. As usual, I had no practical objective; I just thought it would be fun. Literary studies would be the back shop of my soul. This time around, the university hadn't given me a scholarship, so there was no question of quitting my job. If I had known how difficult Columbia was going to make things for a part-time grad student, I might not have bothered. It was most unlikely, to be blunt about it, that faculty superstars were going to make themselves available to students who had to work for a living.

When it was good, it was very good; when it was bad, it was unspeakable – better that, I suppose, than mediocrity, which I rarely encountered in my two years in the English Department at Columbia. By the time I quit in 1984, a victim of Columbia's extortionist fees for part-time students (who paid double the tuition of full-timers), I felt I had sufficiently replenished my soul and gained a little confidence. I too could talk the talk. Lucy found enough inspiration in my example to enroll a year later in the Masters of Liberal Studies program at NYU. (We never saved a dime. Pissing away our money on diversions like utterly unnecessary masters degrees was why we worked for a living.) Always a bit self-conscious about her somewhat technical (and, from my point of view, awe-inspiring) educational background in mathematics and engineering, she doubled down on the humanities, with classes on nineteenth century romanticism, twentieth century American poetry, and stuff like that. She let me sit in on a few of her lecture classes, one with the aforementioned Dennis Donoghue, another with Paul Zweig. Zweig, then in his mid-forties, wound up one lecture on Kierkegaard before beginning another on Whitman, the subject of a forthcoming biography of his (*Walt Whitman: The Making of a Poet*). What we didn't know at the time was that he was dying of cancer. Two or three years later we read about the process of his death in his posthumously published memoir, *Departures*. He died as he taught, with grace and honesty. We were still young enough for death to seem slightly abstract. Suddenly, it had become a little more concrete.

And then Lucy got sick.

7

Lucy had already had a bout or two of cystitis, the probable cause of which, her gynecologist had tactfully informed her, was a common one: too much fucking. If that was true, it provided little or no consolation. Nor could I be of much help; you urinate, as you die, alone. There are worse things than cystitis, however, and a gynecological test in October 1982, revealed one of them: an ovarian cyst, possibly but probably not cancerous. That "probably not" hardly reassured us, but I knew I had to be strong and supportive as never before. Naturally, the first thing I did was to blurt out my worries about the medical fees (only partly covered by insurance). After that inexcusable blunder (which made her cry, and made me cry for making her cry), I managed to sound convincingly and sincerely optimistic. I was stupid enough to believe that Lucy was simply too young, vibrant, and beautiful to have cancer – a delusion we were lucky enough not to be disabused of. How many millions, similarly ingenuous, have found out otherwise?

Although we would have liked to get the thing over with immediately, two months of further testing, consultation, and bureaucratic haggling ensued before Lucy could check into St. Luke's Hospital in Morningside Heights for the surgery. A friend of hers, visiting her parents for the Christmas holidays, let me stay in her apartment on 111th Street, two blocks from the hospital. I hope this doesn't sound morbid, but spending all that time with Lucy in her hospital room was sort of, well, *fun*. It was just the two of us, alone with ourselves and everything that mattered. Her illness recalled us to the primal realities of love, life, and tenderness. The one primal reality we did not want to think about was death. Anne-Sophie, inescapably present during all visiting hours, made sure we did.

During her week at St. Luke's, Lucy had many visitors, including her Nepalese friend Hasri, who happened to be a nurse in that very hospital and who frequently dropped by to ensure that all was well. Anne-Sophie, on the other hand, moped around tragically, as if Lucy's demise were a foregone conclusion.

"Don't you find hospitals depressing?" she challenged me after the doctors had exiled us to a waiting room for a few minutes.

"Well, yes," I replied, "they are, in a way. But people come to them for a reason."

"Fine, yes, I understand, it's all very simple, isn't it? Some people will always be *rational*. I must learn to be more *sensible*, yes?"

So who loved Lucy more – the cold, rational husband or the supersensitive friend? It was a hell of a time to pick a fight, but I refused to be baited. Anne-Sophie really did love Lucy, if she wasn't (and this might explain a lot) at least half in love with her. Hence the air of constant martyrdom. Lucy could never love her in the same way, and then there was that *connard* Lucy was married to. How could she not despise me?

Fortunately, Lucy was too drugged most of the time to notice Anne-Sophie's melodramatics, which continued well after the operation had proved successful. The nurses were stern with me at first; the left ovary had been removed and Lucy needed a lot of rest. But they soon conceded me extra time alone with her, so that I could brush back her hair or kiss her sleeping face. I thought she looked a little like John Keats in that deathbed sketch by Joseph Severn – which was a terrible comparison, since Keats was dying and Lucy was vibrantly alive, but there was something about the unprotected beauty in Keats's face that I saw in hers. When she woke up for a few minutes, I'd read to her from the *New York Times* or gossip about the nurses. I felt like King Lear with Cordelia: "We two alone will sing like birds i' th' cage." Would Lear and Cordelia have lasted another twenty years like that? Mercifully, Shakespeare kills them off before we can find out.

The doctors sent Lucy home in a week, still fragile and in some pain. Three days later it was New Year's Eve and she insisted on riding the subway to the Upper West Side for a party thrown by Setsuko that she would not allow herself to miss. Lucy was the most devoted friend a person could possibly have. There was no sacrifice she wouldn't make for them, no criticism that ever escaped her lips. She certainly didn't mind criticizing me. I deserved it – sometimes. That night, I think, I deserved nothing but forbearance for shepherding Lucy through an extremely ill-advised outing and putting up with Anne-Sophie's scorn for most of the evening. I was a clueless American, an untraveled naïf. I was a literal-minded materialist with no sense of the numinous or the spiritual. I was to blame for the C.I.A. I was oblivious to the gross sexism of the movie *Kramer vs. Kramer*. (I saw it again a few years ago. She was right.) Anne-Sophie passed off this character assassination as playful banter designed to amuse the six or seven friends present. Since she had no sense of humor, I'd say I bantered rather more amusingly than she did, but it didn't matter. All I cared about was seeing Lucy, after her medical ordeal, mixing cheerfully with her friends, a bunch of lovely and interesting people except for you-know-who. The strain of the long evening, though, showed when we tried to get a taxi home. Lucy's pain had increased as the evening wore on, but as usual in those days, it was nearly impossible to get a driver to take us to Brooklyn. "Thanks for nothing, shitface! Why don't you drive into a fucking wall?" I screamed at the third cabbie who had ordered us out of his car. Very unlike me. I must have been thinking of Anne-Sophie.

That was the best Christmas I ever had – watching Lucy sleep peacefully in her hospital room the day after her operation. But then it was back to the work-a-day grind and the effort to carry the sweetness and tenderness of the hospital room into the rest of our lives. I didn't always succeed. Earlier that year I had taken a new job in the Cataloging Department of the New York Public Library at Forty-second Street. Swift disillusion followed. Hadn't I already learned this lesson? Didn't I know that affiliation with any institution, no matter how lofty – and the Forty-second Street Library was very lofty indeed – signified, in the larger scheme of things, precisely nothing? I had let myself be seduced by those marble lions guarding the entrance and the august reputation of what was, after all, a very great library, into believing that my admittance carried some sort of redemption or validation. If I needed redemption or validation, I wasn't going to find them in the gleaming lobby of that glorious building or any building in the world. Though I hold no grudge against the New York Public Library, I knew I was going to hate that place within my first twenty minutes on the job. It was like working in a morgue. The silence. The stiffness. The tedium. The endless rules. Nevertheless, in the two years I remained there I carried out to the best of my ability my exacting duties (cataloging serials – a very tricky business) and made my small contribution to one of the major research libraries of the world. (You can still find my catalog entry for the microform edition of *Screw* magazine: "Sex – Periodicals / Editor: Al Goldstein.") It's just that when I got home most days at 5:30 I wasn't in the best of moods. So I laid down one condition that Lucy accepted with a good grace: anything I said within the first thirty minutes of stepping through the door couldn't be held against me.

Lucy patiently bore my pissing and moaning. During my first month on the job, in July of 1982, she came up from downtown a few times to meet me on my lunch hour. We strolled through the Fifth Avenue department stores, which allowed me to cool off (my office wasn't air-conditioned) and feel human again. Unlike me, she more or less liked her job. Designing offices and health clinics was more interesting than checking microfiche indexes to make cross references for government bodies or typing in search keys on primitive databases ("FIN PA & MUL 8") for obscure books and journals that I wouldn't have read on pain of death.

Given the reality of my working life, I probably invested too much in my literary studies at Columbia, which I began that September. There, at last, I could drop the pretense of being the concerned young professional that I kept up at work and show something of my true self. And I remember sitting at my first seminar table, discussing with eight or nine fellow literary obsessives the relationship between ideology and esthetics, and thinking, Yes, this is where I belong, this is what my life has been pointing me to, this is what I genuinely love. As it happened, one of the "texts" assigned by our exemplary professor, John Romano, was *Theory of the Novel* by Georg Lukács, where I read the following:

> The melancholy of the adult state arises from our
> dual, conflicting experience that, on the one hand, our
> absolute, youthful confidence in an inner voice has
> diminished or died, and, on the other hand, that the

outside world to which we now devote ourselves in our desire to learn its ways and dominate it will never speak to us in a voice that will clearly tell us our way and determine our goal.

Sound familiar? Neither the English Department at Columbia University nor the New York Public Library at Forty-second Street nor any other meritorious institution to which I might conceivably aspire could do the work that I needed to do for myself. Any melioration of the "melancholy of the adult state," if such a melioration were even possible, was to be found not in the necessary and important mission of a great library or university but in the confines (in my case) of a one-bedroom apartment in Park Slope and the necessary and important mission of loving my partner. Lucy already knew that. I had to keep learning it over and over.

Not all of my seminars were as invigorating as the one conducted by John Romano (who dropped out, by the way, to write screenplays in Hollywood – there's an unconventional scholar for you). And I soon found out, of course, that a graduate seminar room is not merely susceptible to institutional jealousies and intrigues but virtually a laboratory of those things. Not being a Ph.D. candidate, I could let most of that stuff roll off my back. The unasked question in virtually every seminar was always the same: Who's the smartest person in this room? Definitely not me.

After a day of cataloging *Quarterly Bulletin of Coal Statistics*, I relished an evening of hashing out Northrop Frye's theories of recurrence or disentangling what Helen Vendler thought about what Lionel Trilling thought about what Matthew Arnold thought about Wordsworth's "Intimations Ode." Certainly the papers I wrote – "Ontological Sickness in *Notes from Underground,*" "Stylistic Discontinuities in the *Quijote*" – had the requisite grad school earnestness. But when I turned in my "masters essay" on W. H. Auden's *Bucolics* for two faculty readers, I found myself siding with Jeffrey Perl, who had been rather less impressed than Edward Mendelson (Auden's literary executor). Yeah, it was pretty good, Professor Perl said, but what exactly was the point of just another pretty good New Critical essay? He might have phrased it more simply: Mr. Akey, your heart isn't in it. I had enjoyed most of my readings and my seminar discussions, but I had also begun to weary of meeting students who read five critical texts for every creative one and who couldn't get it through their heads (in a few cases) that I had gone to a state college. (Unbeknown to me, my classmate Adam Gussow was living a second life as a blues musician in East Harlem, the subject of his memoir *Mister Satan's Apprentice*. So much for my own class assumptions.) I had signed up for this program to replenish my soul. To put it crassly, was my soul getting its money's worth at whatever exorbitant price I was paying for each credit? Columbia made up my mind for me when, in January of 1984, an administrator told me that, as a part-timer, if I wanted my degree I'd have to buy it at double the tuition. It was all a matter of some byzantine proviso about something called "residence units." I told her that was insane. She got very huffy, especially when I said that Columbia University could go fuck itself.

Lucy worried that my graduate studies were pulling me away from her. Not true, though deciphering the opaque "discourse" of Roland Barthes required a lot more time glued to my armchair than I would have liked. She also worried that I was becoming excessively friendly with two female classmates, which wasn't true either, except that I did have a weakness for beautiful intellectuals, Lucy being the foremost example. Fortunately, Jane, who might have had a crush on me, merely had a beautiful soul, and Penelope, an English rose who had studied poetry with Seamus Heaney, was married. I just liked hanging around with smart women. What's the problem? Well, as subsequent events would reveal, *I* was the problem, or at least a big part of it.

Lucy never met Jane or Penelope. Whatever distress those passing friendships of mine caused her was fleeting. Lucy had her "issues," but I had more, and worse. I had just spent two years in the English Department at Columbia University learning that the self had become so "problematized" by the ubiquity of media-saturated discourse that it had internalized its own alienation. Lucy never heard the news. Though struggling like anyone with the usual anxieties and insecurities (some deeply rooted, some circumstantial), she lived her life without agonizing over her putatively riven consciousness or worrying overmuch about what others might think of her values and beliefs. An article of faith among art-world intellectuals was that advanced art must henceforward be "ironized" by the inescapable pull of pop culture. She didn't get that message either. While she appreciated the wit and inventiveness of Roy Lichtenstein or Claus Oldenburg, Andy Warhol's deadpan portraits of Marilyn and Elvis had nothing to say to her. In her art, as in her life, she didn't give a damn about mass consumption or celebrity culture. No one could have been less snobbish or more unselfconsciously egalitarian in her dealings with people. She simply looked around, saw what was out there in the world of network television and *People* magazine, and had the confidence to dismiss most of it, without a trace of superiority, as not germane to her art or life. All the intellectuals at *Artforum* said that couldn't be done. She did it.

I lacked that confidence. Hence, I tended to overreact to annoyances that Lucy brushed off. I thought superficial, cocktail party chitchat was the end of the world; Lucy thought it was just cocktail party chitchat. In November of the following year we were invited to a Thanksgiving dinner with friends of friends – three or four young businesswomen – in an apartment on the Upper East Side. Was I grateful? Was I gracious? Maybe you can guess. I spent the evening inwardly seething and grinding my teeth as I listened to them talk about summer in the Hamptons and real estate prices in Manhattan and what it took to get a reservation at Le Cirque. Lucy was on me as soon as we reached the elevator.

"What's the big deal, Stephen? You think you're gonna die because you met some people you consider boring and superficial? Well, they're out there. You didn't see me sulking, did you? That was Irene's sister and her best friends. They were trying to be *nice* to you. Sometimes you just . . . Oh, never mind."

Right again, as usual. Not only were there legions of boring and superficial people out there; sometimes they seemed heavily concentrated in New York. One day around that time I saw an advertisement in the *New York Times* that said the following:

> They've seen Sam Shepard's *True West:* Jacqueline
> Onassis, Louis Malle, Kevin Kline, Rex Smith, Baron
> and Baroness Rothschild, David Bowie, John Kennedy,
> Jr., Cher . . . Have you?

What nauseated me was not merely the narcissism, the vulgarity, the assumption that all of us were or should be in thrall to celebrities. What nauseated me was that, aside from "Baron and Baroness Rothschild" and one or two others, I recognized every name on that list – and it went on for twenty more names. I didn't even know what to call this stuff. Inauthenticity? Bad faith? The culture of narcissism? Whatever it was, it seemed to have infected me in a way that it did not Lucy; maybe growing up in Manila, in a culture less blighted by consumption, conferred certain benefits not given to citizens of the prosperous West. Nor did my classes at Columbia afford much of a refuge. Academia has its own star system, so that while studying the leaching-out of personhood in modernist literature, I was simultaneously experiencing the same phenomenon. At any rate, when the microphone of the eminent scholar Frank Kermode malfunctioned in the course of a lecture, I witnessed three graduate assistants spring into action as if he were Madonna demanding Evian water for her lapdog. The care and feeding of my soul, it appeared, were being threatened by the very things that should have nourished it: graduate study at a prestigious university, life among "sophisticated" New Yorkers. Time to take stock. All I knew for certain was that Lucy was still my lodestar, the person who brought out what was best in me. I had better be at my best. We were going to have a baby.

8

We had been thinking about parenthood for quite a while. Although I liked to ruminate about grand abstractions like Self and Other and Personhood, our decision owed nothing to metaphysics and everything to instinct; we just wanted to have a kid. With our cramped one-bedroom apartment and our savings and investments at exactly zero, we knew this wasn't an ideal time, but we also knew that there would never be an ideal time. Why not do this now, when we were young enough to have the resilience but mature enough to be reasonably capable parents? A night hardly ever passed anyway without some "gross carnality." Nothing changed; it's just that the carnality no longer required intrauterine contraceptive devices. A few months later we were parents-to-be.

I remember the first time the baby kicked – not me, admittedly, but its mother. We were sitting in the airport lounge in Sarasota, Florida, in March 1984, waiting for our flight home after a week's visit with my mother and younger sister. They were vigorous kicks, Lucy said. As she did with most things, Lucy took her pregnancy pretty much in stride. Being pregnant was neither a joy nor a punishment. She would take all the necessary pre-natal care but suffered no illusion that, to quote from one of the childcare and pregnancy books we were then reading, "taking pleasure in your expanding form is good preparation for working with and expressing yourself through your body in labor." On the contrary; she looked forward to getting her body back. Yet genetics had been kind to her; it had bestowed on her certain corporeal features, shall we say, that enraptured me to dizziness and granted her, as the months progressed, a relatively mild pregnancy.

Although Lucy required no fussing, it didn't hurt that my mother, during that week in her Sarasota condominium, had fussed over her anyway. The reaction of Lucy's parents to the news of her pregnancy had been somewhat underwhelming; Brave Orchid, as Lucy expected, was not one to gush over mere matters of life and death. So it pleased her to get a little mothering from Peg, chiefly in the form of superfluities of comfort food and touchingly naïve questions about her "people" back in Manila. Furthermore, she could see that Peg's need to fuss exceeded her need to be fussed over. With her accustomed graciousness and tact, Lucy let her fuss away.

It was during that visit that we saw our first swallow-tailed kite. The birding at Myakka State Park and Corkscrew Swamp was sensational. I figured we should pack in as much birding as possible. We knew that with a baby on the way, it might be a long time before we saw our next swallow-tailed kite. Yet I fiercely resisted the notion, insisted upon by friends, relatives, and almost everyone except my mother, that parenthood entailed the cessation of virtually all recreational, cultural, and intellectual activities. Basically, people kept telling us, your life is over for the foreseeable future. I didn't believe it. Allowing for inevitable compromises, sacrifices, and frustrations, I considered it quite possible to live an active, intellectually engaged life amid all the diapers and baby food. I was about half right.

Although we boned up on T. Berry Brazelton's books about childrearing, I wasn't too worried about our prospects as parents.

Lucy, I had no doubt, would be an exemplary mother, as indeed she was. Being the eldest of eight children, she had already had considerable experience caring for babies. Realistically, the best anyone can do is to be a "good enough" parent, in the terminology of W. D. Winnicott, but I thought her emotional intelligence and prodigious creativity boded well for our child. As for me, I couldn't wait to hold a baby, cherish it, comfort it, watch it grow, make it listen to the Clash. The practical and financial difficulties were, of course, overwhelming. Would there be room enough in the apartment? How long could Lucy afford to remain on maternity leave? What the hell happens when she goes back to work? We would deal with these matters as they arose. Expecting a baby was already teaching me something I needed to learn: how to let go.

I also needed to learn how, or when, to stop thinking so damn much. On that score, a baby had more to teach me than I it. My tendency to analyze everything to death sometimes grated on Lucy. We once got into a ridiculous tussle over the novels of Agatha Christie. It wasn't enough for me merely to disdain them; I wanted to proscribe them. Had I read any of them? Of course not! I had read Edmund Wilson's brilliant hatchet job, "Who Cares Who Killed Roger Ackroyd?" which told me, in my view, everything I needed to know about the vapidity and moral vacuity of the English detective novel. Lucy said I sounded like Jerry Falwell thundering about godless liberals. Abashed, I offered a suitably contrite apology – but only after I had thought about it for a while. In fact, I *was* a godless liberal, which should have taught me (if liberalism teaches anything) to refrain from making such absolutist pronouncements. The only pronouncement that really fit the case was Lucy's: Stephen, she said, you need to listen to your heart a little more.

Shortly before out trip to Florida, Lucy's former roommate at York University in Toronto came to visit for a few days. I tried not to get in the way; they needed time to catch up, and Lucy had warned me that Mary, a dancer and aspiring writer now studying for a masters in librarianship, was a delicate orchid. Still, I tried to be a good host.

"So who are some of your favorite poets, Mary?" I asked.

"Oh, I like William Blake a lot."

"Why Blake?"

"I don't know. I just do."

The more I tried to draw her out, the more I alienated her. I think she thought I was evil because I aspired to write literary criticism. If Mary's sub-Blakean mysticism represented an alternative to my analytical propensities, my analytical propensities didn't look so bad, and in truth Lucy found that she didn't have all that much to say to her sweet, shy, and almost pathologically "sensitive" Canadian friend. They did have one powerful bond that I envied. One afternoon a few years earlier they had looked up from their studies to see, perched on the window sill of their dorm room in quasi-suburban Toronto, a screech owl peering at them curiously. It stayed for quite a while. In forty years of birding, I've never seen a screech owl. Doesn't seem fair, does it? I don't begrudge Lucy her sighting. I just wish I could have been there with her.

Lucy had looked forward to her reunion with Mary in part because of the progressive deterioration of her friendship with Anne-Sophie. I absolve myself from any string pulling on that score. Over time, Lucy had come, quite independently, to share some of my aversion to her former best friend. More could be said about that extremely intelligent and complex woman; but she wasn't much fun. One day, while I was still working at the Forty-second Street Library, she arranged (through Lucy) to meet me to return the Nikon camera she had borrowed from us. I wasn't expecting profuse gratitude, but this time she outdid herself. I was pleasantly surprised that she didn't keep me waiting in the lobby of the library on my lunch hour longer than she did. She arrived, approximately on time, fixed me with a look of weary contempt, held out the camera from a distance of about three feet, dropped it into my hand, and, without a word, turned on her heel and walked away. I almost laughed. In fact, I did laugh when I told Lucy the story later that night. Lucy wasn't amused. I think she would have been less angry if Anne-Sophie had subjected her rather than me to that particular insult; she would have taken the hit for my sake. Of all the things I could say about the dissolution of our marriage and that I have no intention of revealing, I submit one wrenching detail: the day would come when Lucy would look at me the way Anne-Sophie had.

"In headaches and in worry / Vaguely life leaks away," admonished W. H. Auden. Take heed, Stephen. I fretted over my job, I worried about the future, I brooded over past mistakes. Worse than any of this anxiety was the nagging doubt that I hadn't lived enough – that I hadn't taken enough drugs or fucked enough women or learned to ride a motorcycle. Even I could see the puerility of these fantasies, promulgated by ubiquitous cultural images of masculine self-assurance and internalized by my fractured self. That didn't make them any easier to overcome. Lucy and I weren't having a baby as a means of self-improvement, but if incipient fatherhood was forcing a reckoning with my less admirable tendencies, so much the better. Which is to say, the Red Cross helped make a man of me.

A few months before her due date, Lucy and I had registered for an infant care course on Tuesday nights at the Red Cross Center on Amsterdam Avenue near Lincoln Center. We were tired when we got up there after work, but we knew that more was riding on this class than on any other, far grander ones we had recently taken at Columbia and New York University. We started with dolls – holding them, bathing them, changing their diapers. A few months earlier I had been debating Claude Lévi-Strauss's theories of structuralism; now I was nervously cradling a doll's head under the supervision of a Red Cross instructor a thousand times more knowledgeable and confident than I. If I had deliberately sought a corrective to human vanity and presumption, I couldn't have found a better one. No one cares how cultured you think you are, Stephen; can you change this diaper without poking the doll's bottom? Having surrendered my pride and made a few more or less successful passes with wrappings and bobby pins, I found these practice sessions to be surprisingly fun. It helped that I had Lucy at my side to guide and assist me, and that our instructor – younger than any of us and not herself a mother – never condescended or criticized.

Not all of the students had someone at their side. A middle-aged African American woman stood out from the dozen or so younger, mostly white couples. Otherwise reticent, she told us that she had had a baby many years ago but feared that she had forgotten most of her child-rearing skills. Whether or not this pregnancy was an accident, she was clearly determined to get it right the second time around. If she felt self-conscious or out of place, she didn't let it show. She just put down her head and got to work. I think it safe to say that I derived more from this life lesson in courage and determination than I did from my rarefied readings of Claude Lévi-Strauss.

In contrast to the Red Cross Infant Care course on Tuesday nights, our Lamaze Childbirth Preparation course on Monday nights taught us very little of real use. Although Park Slope was more heterogeneous in those days than people might imagine, this class, held in the ground-floor brownstone apartment of our instructor, managed to hit all of the stereotypes. The six or seven young professional couples sat in a circle on the floor, listening to the instructor lay down the law: the readings, the exercises, the meditations, the hospital tours, the consultations, the whole holistic megillah. Over the mantlepiece was a blown-up color photograph of our instructor giving birth; be sure to bring extra film for the delivery, she advised us, unable to conceive that some of us might not want to take pictures of that particular event. She was so devoted to the cause that the two-hour classes sometimes ran closer to three, a real hardship, I thought, for women in advanced stages of pregnancy. I lived in fear that she would catch me out on the voluminous readings I hadn't done. Anyway, I knew my role was limited. It was Lucy who had to do the breathing exercises and bring a child into the world. If I could get her to laugh about our instructor's demented literal-mindedness, well, that was a start.

If only to relieve ourselves of the anxiety caused by Mme. Lamaze, we went up to Boston for a few days in mid-July for a change of pace. I still have a picture of Lucy in a sleeveless maternity dress sitting on a bench in the courtyard of the Public Library on Copley Square in the soft morning light – certainly the most beautiful pregnant woman I've ever seen. In fact, I expected my desire to wane as her body waxed, but that never happened; our gross carnality continued unabated until almost the seventh month. Boston without Anne-Sophie (as on our previous excursion) was a much more agreeable place. By day we relaxed in the Public Garden and toured the museums, by night we channel surfed in our crummy hotel room and followed the news of Walter Mondale's groundbreaking selection of Geraldine Ferraro as his vice-presidential running mate. It's a good thing we went when we did; Vermeer's "The Music Lesson," which had taken our breath away in the Gardner Museum, would soon be stolen and (as it appears) lost to the world forever. Anyway, I loved holing up with Lucy in our hotel room, just the two of us on rumpled sheets and an ice-bucket holding our chilled Mountain Dews. We would never again be alone in a hotel room.

We returned to a hotter, noisier, more congested city, but Lucy, uncomplaining even under these circumstances, worked until a few weeks before her due date. Why stay home and worry about something she couldn't control? And indeed, two days before giving birth she went to see *Boudu Saved from Drowning* at Bleecker Street Cinema. Advice to anxious women in advanced stages of pregnancy: go see a splendid Jean Renoir movie. It did wonders for Lucy.

I would have to wait a few years for my chance to see *Boudu Saved from Drowning*. I was still cataloging those wretched serials in the Forty-second Street Library and, in the evenings, preparing to embark on a new career. Working in one of the most beautiful buildings in America was a nice perk, but I was fed up with serials cataloging. I wanted to work as a reference librarian in the main reading room, where I might proffer bibliographic assistance to Norman Mailer or Toni Morrison or any of the other thousands of regular users who aspired to write important books and sometimes did. Unfortunately, I happened to be an experienced and nominally proficient catalog librarian; no supervisor, I discovered, in the New York Public Library or out of it, was willing to consider me in any other capacity. Not that I made things any easier for myself. When I finally got an interview for an in-house reference position in the main reading room, I proudly, deliberately, ostentatiously shot myself in the foot.

"So, Stephen," the lovely and gracious head of reference asked me, apropos of my professional development and career plans, "where do you see yourself in five years?"

"I don't see myself anywhere," I said.

"I'm not sure I understand. Do you think you could explain?"

"Yeah. It's very important for me not to think like that. Maybe I'll be here, maybe I'll be somewhere else. Whatever I'm doing, I want to make sure I'm living in the present and not putting off my life for the sake of some 'plan' that may or may not have any meaning."

"Oh." She glanced at her assistant. He glanced at her. "How . . . admirable."

I wouldn't have got the job anyway, but I'm consoled by this thought: I really didn't have a plan. I still don't. It seems to work for me.

I did, however, have a wife, and a child on the way. Some reasonable, short-term planning seemed appropriate. Having failed in every attempt to break out of my cataloging straitjacket, I read with great interest that summer an article in the *New York Times* about the Board of Education's desperate shortage of teachers and its desperate plan to fill the gap. For the time being, the Board of Ed was going to suspend its requirements for certification and attempt to recruit a few thousand rookies, who would take a crash course before being thrown to the wolves that September. I signed up.

The timing couldn't have been worse. We had finished our Red Cross and Lamaze classes, but Lucy still needed me to be there in the few weeks remaining till the due date. Instead, after work in early August, I found myself in a classroom in Norman Thomas High School on Thirty-third Street and Park Avenue, with fifteen other assorted wannabes listening to a young assistant principal trying to cram as much educational methodology into our heads as ten nights of three hours sessions would allow. Mr. Han was focused, organized, firm but flexible, in short, everything we were supposed to be. Did he have any idea how abysmally some of us – those who managed to get through this grueling class, negotiate the Board of Education's

Kafkaesque bureaucracy, and then scare up a job – would crash? Surely, he did. But what could he say? When someone asked him to confirm or deny wild stories she had heard about novice teachers fleeing from their classrooms in tears within their first hour on the job, he just smiled. He must have looked at me and thought, This guy is cannon fodder.

I would like to say, before anyone else can, that my brief and catastrophic career as a public-school teacher in Brooklyn was a mess entirely of my own making. Whatever it took to control, let alone teach, five classes of underprivileged minority students in an over-crowded, underfunded, dysfunctional New York City High School, I didn't have in me. Others succeeded. I failed. The stories were all true. Legions of novice teachers in New York public schools fled their classroom on their first day of their jobs. If I had had any sense, I would have been one of them. I lasted for four weeks, bringing nothing but misery to myself, Lucy, and our new-born child and contributing to the miseducation of my already marginalized students. I wish I could say I left when I realized I was part of the problem rather than the solution. I realized that from the start. The primary cause of my resignation was more immediate: I was breaking down in tears every time I tried to describe to Lucy a day on the job.

Tears of a different sort were shed two and a half weeks before I entered my first classroom. The occasion was the birth of our son on August 22, 1984, and the tears weren't necessarily of joy. The labor wasn't going so well. We had already taken the long cab ride the day before from our apartment to New York Hospital on York Avenue and Sixty-eighth Street. False alarm. Naturally, the contractions started again almost as soon as we returned home. So, three hours later, at five in the morning, we found ourselves in another cab sailing over the Brooklyn Bridge and up the FDR Drive. I told myself I would always remember looking down that night at the great black river spreading out beneath the lights of the three bridges. And I have.

Within a few hours of her admittance, it was discovered that the baby's head had lodged itself painfully against Lucy's spine; hence the unusual amount of difficulty she was experiencing in the early stages of labor; hence the total fucking nightmare that the labor became as the early morning turned to late morning to early afternoon to evening. The first thing to go was the Lamaze breathing techniques. Some of the nurses reproached Lucy for not following the script, but I, who had never experienced anything like this degree of pain, was hardly in a position to criticize. My job was to ease the pain on her spine by massaging her back, which I did till I thought my arms would fall off. The horror was only beginning. Could she please please please have a little ice to slake her agonizing thirst? No, she couldn't; it only made her vomit, which she kept doing anyway. By late afternoon she was pleading, "Steve, *help* me, make them stop!" Little by little, as I watched the person I most loved in the world being, as it plainly seemed, tortured to death, I lost my self-composure. Normally self-conscious about showing my feelings in public, I ceased caring what the doctors or nurses thought as my choked sobs turned into clamorous, calamitous, snot-dripping hysteria. Clearly, my presence wasn't abetting the health-care professionals, let alone the patient. Doctor Hanson called me out into the hallway for a little talk.

"Steve," he said, "I know this isn't a normal delivery, it's really rough, but she's getting there, you have to hold on. You weren't expecting anything like this, I know. It's O.K., the baby's there, we can see it, it's just a matter of getting it out."

I made a great effort to hold back my tears. "Yeah, but even if it's just a matter of time, I don't see how she can last another five minutes, let alone two hours."

Doctor Hanson, bless his heart, reassured me some more, and I went back into the delivery room a little stronger and slightly more determined. The baby was born a half hour later. I held Lucy and cried. This was supposed to be, as all the world had told us, the greatest moment of our lives. It wasn't.

9

Jonathan was a fretful, colicky baby who grew to be an adorable little boy who grew to be a handsome, talented, and exemplary young man. I'm going to leave his story pretty much untold; that book has yet to be written. At first, however, he was just another raccoon like us, clingy, creaturely, and clangorous – only more so. He and his mother certainly had a nice hospital room. Lucy needed a couple of days to recover, as well as time to accustom the baby to nursing – not, as it turned out, such an easy matter. But at least we had a little time to catch our breath and look out on the East River and Roosevelt Island, which had been, before this drastic change, a pleasant excursion for us on a few occasions. Maybe it still could be.

The shrieking began three days later, almost as soon as we got him home. Wow, this was going to be a lot harder than we had expected. Not only was it possible to spend an entire day locked in an apartment doing nothing but tending to a crying baby, it was possible to spend weeks, *months,* that way. So we made an effort to give each other little breaks, which mostly meant doing some furtive reading in the other room till the next explosion required the intervention of both parents. Not that I had the magic touch. Whatever we may want to believe to the contrary, hungry, uncomfortable newborns are wailing for their mothers, not their fathers. And though my infant-care skills were improving day by day, my primary role was to help Lucy to help Jonathan, who still seemed more raccoon than human. Despite our frustrations, we loved our baby and were not as yet tempted to "strangle him in his crib," the oft-repeated regret that Lucy's mother had used as a rhetorical ploy to keep her eight misbehaving children in line. How charming!

We weren't the only ones disconcerted by Jonathan's shrieking. Our neighbors, as they soon made clear, didn't like it either. "Shut up that fucking baby!" one of them screamed through the open windows from what sounded like several floors below on a hot Saturday afternoon. Well yes, that was exactly what I was attempting to do; would the concerned neighbor care to give it a try? Even worse were the neighbors in contiguous apartments. Tenant X complained that the crib was too near his apartment; when we moved it, tenant Y complained that it was too near to hers. Tenant Z, who lived below us, thumped his ceiling (our floor) with a broom handle whenever he had reached his limit, which was almost daily. This went on for several years and wasn't much improved when Jonathan stopped shrieking and started crawling. One night, tenant Z went up on the roof and spent the next several minutes stomping over our ceiling. Message received: we had the neighbors from hell.

How did we end up with such a crew – uncivil, ill-tempered, and unreasonable even by New York standards? Chiefly bad luck, exacerbated by the ill effects of a prolonged rent strike. Getting this apartment in late 1979 had been a near-miracle. There were easily a hundred people waiting on the street to see it when the landlord opened it up for a viewing one Sunday afternoon in November. (We had all seen the listing in the *New York Times* real estate section the night before – that's how you got an apartment in those days.) Why me rather than the ninety-nine others? I've always thought it was due to my profession. The landlord liked it that I was a librarian; he figured I'd be a docile and undemanding tenant. But when, by the next winter, he ceased to provide heat and hot water during some of the coldest stretches of the year, I voted with the other tenants to go on strike. Whatever esprit de corps had sustained us in the early days had long since dissipated as the strike dragged on. The more agreeable tenants, including our friends Maxwell and Nina, had moved out, while less agreeable ones, including a couple of squatters, had moved in. Hence the stomping over our ceiling and the icy stares in the hallway. Still, it was an airy one-bedroom apartment in the middle of Park Slope. Where else were we gonna go?

The sheer awfulness of our neighbors had one very concrete effect – it made it harder to raise our child. All the childrearing books said the same thing: after a few months you simply have to let the baby cry sometimes. We tried, but then the thumping from the floor and the pounding on the walls would start, and we'd have to lift Jonathan from his crib. Thus, our neighbors prolonged, to their distress no less than ours, the period of middle-of-the-night wailing long past what would have been its normal expiration date. There were compensations. Life affords few joys more blissful than that of retrieving a crying baby from its crib and nestling it contentedly between the pillows shared by its doting parents. The shrieking turns into soft gurgling, and the warm milky babyish smell lulls all three raccoons into peaceful slumber. Until the next explosion. One night, unaccountably, Jonathan had been sleeping for hours without a peep. Something seemed missing. "Let's go get him!" I said to Lucy. She laughed, but we were tempted.

So how did Lucy fare, staying home alone most days with an obstreperous newborn? The crying wore her down too, but being the primary life giver, she was much better than I at soothing the baby. He didn't cry and fret all of the time, only most of the time; in the intervals she worked on her quilts, which were becoming ever more elaborate and intricate. And she still had her classes at NYU. On Wednesday nights she studied modernist poetry with Dennis Donoghue while I paced the apartment with Jonathan on my shoulder. He had me wired like a machine; the minute I stopped, he screamed. We both could have wept with joy whenever we heard the key turn in the lock. Our Goddess of Hearth and Home was back.

The Goddess of Hearth and Home, in her human incarnation, was only a hard-pressed young mother who could have used more help than she got from me in subsequent weeks. But I had just begun my job as an English teacher at John Jay High School in Park Slope. My chief familial responsibility was to forestall a nervous breakdown, in which I succeeded but only at the cost of infecting the apartment with my noxious despair when I returned home five days a week at 3:15. Never before had my self-pity reached such empyrean heights (or depths), but even I knew I had nothing to complain about compared to those kids. I had had my chance; they never did.

It's hard to comprehend educational and socio-economic failure on the scale I witnessed at John Jay High School, which was, ironically, situated in the heart of Park Slope's commercial strip, though virtually no Park Slope parents sent their children there. (Basically, the school was populated by poor minority kids from around the borough.) I have nothing to say about educational failure and reform that hasn't been said before, though I note with relief that the huge, monolithic building on Seventh Avenue now houses four smaller, specialized schools and that the crowds of teenagers milling about after school lets out seem distinctly less volatile than they once did. John Jay High School was an authentic American tragedy, and I helped to make it so.

I thought it was a cliché from the movies, but my students really did call me "teach." Blackboard Jungle was *real*. They set a desk on fire (or tried to). They talked over every word I said. They painted their nails. They got up to look out the windows. They slept. They ate. They fought. They did not, as Ed Boland recounts in *The Battle for Room 314,* a memoir of his year in the trenches at a public school on the Lower East Side, stand on a desk and scream, "SUCK MY FUCKIN' DICK, MISTER," but they might as well have. I had zero control over my students, who were, as I was frequently reminded, the best in the school, juniors and seniors who had been selected for a specially designed "college bound" program. A handful were truly disturbed. A handful were genuinely threatening. But most were just ordinary kids, exactly what I would have been in their circumstances. They deserved a better school. They deserved a better teacher.

There was another handful, so overwhelmed by all the others that I barely noticed them at first. These were the four or five kids who really wanted an education, who could write coherent sentences or liked to read or shyly asked me to critique their poetry. They broke my heart because I broke theirs. My classes were utter chaos, but they could talk to me before or after and get a little encouragement from their hapless but well-meaning preceptor. And then I was gone. On my very last class on my very last day – I knew I wouldn't be coming back the following Monday, having finally made up my mind after another sleepless night and four weeks of hopeless vacillation – at the end of that class at the end of that day, Munir Zarabi, a lovely, quiet boy who dreamed of going to Hunter College, approached me with a smile, stuck out his hand, and said, "Have a great weekend, Mr. Akey."

That handshake still haunts me. Munir Zarabi clearly wasn't getting into Hunter College, not with the seventh-grade academic "skills" (a rung or two higher than that of most of his classmates) he had acquired from John Jay High School. And what had I done except to turn my back on him? In an effort to assuage my guilt or at least prevent myself from crying whenever I thought of him, I told myself three things: 1) I couldn't have helped Munir or any of my students anyway; I was the world's worst teacher and my classes were getting only more out of control; 2) I was heading for a nervous breakdown; and 3) I had responsibilities above all to Jonathan and Lucy, who had the right not to be enveloped by the seeping cloud of misery that shadowed my presence. A week earlier, looking for emotional support or a shoulder to cry on, I had called up a fellow novice who had taken the two-week educational training seminar with me and who had got a job at Seward Park High School in lower Manhattan. Sam had given by far the best sample lesson in our seminar, but he was more than a potentially superb teacher; with his modesty, humor, groundedness, and soft-spoken competence, he seemed to me almost a saint of everyday life. On his worst days, Sam told me, he had to fight the temptation to flee from his bus stop in the morning and run back to his bedroom, telling himself, "They can't arrest me, they can't arrest me, they can't arrest me." But that was just to buck me up. He believed he was making a dent in the New York City public school system and he believed that I could too. He said the schools needed intelligent and caring people like me. And then, just before hanging up, he said something else:

"Be strong, Steve."

I hadn't been strong. I had let down Munir Zarabi and Keisha Washington and Ida Martinez. But I hadn't let down Lucy and Jonathan. Or they hadn't let me down. Throughout the whole ordeal Lucy had patiently borne my shell-shocked silences, and Jonathan, when not fretting, had attained to a degree of cuteness unsurpassed by any other known baby, human or raccoon. Fortunately, they didn't have to endure my agony for much longer. Within a week I had applied for and got a job at the Brooklyn Public Library, where I was a known quantity and where just about any warm body would do. They put me in the Telephone Reference Division of the Central Library – part-time at first, full-time a few months later. It had been a roundabout journey but I had finally broken into the desired ranks of reference librarianship, even if I had to start from scratch and at a lower salary to do so. It turned out to be, for a few years, just the job I was looking for, but I've told that story as well. Say something twice, why say it again?

With a new baby, a new job, and less money that we had ever had before, I figured it would be a good time to buy an electric guitar. So I did. I never did learn to play an A barre properly, but it amused Jonathan to hear me flail away at it for the next few years. Now that things were slightly more settled, Lucy and I could, we hoped, rediscover some of the intimacy that had inevitably dissipated with the overwhelming cares of parenthood. Easier said than done, as any new parent will tell you. Apart from sheer fatigue, we had cause to worry about our diminished sources of income, our precarious rental situation, our hideous neighbors, and a thousand other mundane things. On the one hand, the world; on the other, our souls. We would spend the rest of our lives together seeking, and never finding, our ideal yin and yang, but we spent endless hours talking about it. That in itself, I think, tipped the balance in favor of our souls.

Our souls were almost all that we did have. We certainly couldn't claim an abundance of money or possessions or friends. The first two didn't matter; the third did. Our relative isolation might have established a bad precedent. We depended so much on each other that perhaps we created expectations that couldn't be met. I, at any rate – and in spite of my high-minded reading – never claimed to be other than the stumbling, average guy I was. In the end, no doubt, I stumbled a bit too much.

The International House crowd had broken up by then, and Anne-Sophie and Lucy were, to my lasting relief, pretty much estranged. That left, on Lucy's side, Irene, the Columbia classmate who had let me borrow her apartment in Morningside Heights when Lucy had been hospitalized at St. Luke's two years earlier. They would remain, as I assume they are to this day, very close friends, so I'm proud of my role in fostering that friendship in its early days, when Lucy worried that they didn't have much in common. Irene was everything Anne-Sophie was not: warm, funny, down-to-earth, middle-brow. What they shared was admiration, bordering on awe, for Lucy's quiet self-possession and staggering talent. Also, Irene didn't despise me.

I had a few friends too, mostly gay men from the library, more comfortable, like me, discussing Edith Wharton than the National Football League. What little I knew about the density of social relations I inferred from such sources as Wharton's fiction or the gossip of my friend Al Avant, who was chummy with Pauline Kael, Arlene Croce, and other leading figures in the New York literary world. I had no hope of breaking into that world. I just thought it would be nice for Lucy and me to have a little circle of close friends with whom to share companionable evenings or celebrate the occasional birthday. We did, eventually, form part of just such a circle, and it was exactly as engaging and stimulating as we had hoped. And then Lucy and I split up. I should have read my Edith Wharton more carefully. From one day to the next, the people I had thought my closest friends vanished. I had become Lily Bart.

So for the next few years it was mostly the three of us, holing up together in our raccoon den. Lucy had to return to work after six months, so we staggered our hours as much as possible and dropped Jonathan off with a babysitter in the neighborhood – a far-from-ideal arrangement familiar to most middle-class families in America. Evenings had a magic way of disappearing in a haze of formula preparation, bottle sterilization, laundry folding, and dishwashing. Lucy never complained. I did. A lot. That first year was pretty grueling, but as babyish giggling gradually supplanted babyish shrieking and as Lucy and I grew more efficient and confident in household management, I found less and less to complain about. I found, in fact, that lying around on that big homemade bed, cuddling the baby and each other, dreaming, dozing, telling stories, listening to music, and using all our silliest pet names – I found in all of that a bliss so oceanic that it sometimes frightened me. I knew the day would come when Lucy and Jonathan would be taken from me, or I from them, and I derived scant consolation from the lies I later told Jonathan about the naturalness and rightness of death and dying. What kind of world was it that would damage and destroy life and love like this, that would annihilate such tenderness and innocence? Why couldn't God exist so that I might have the satisfaction of hating Him? A more thoughtful atheist (or believer) might have replied that a world that bestowed such tenderness and innocence in the first place was a world very much worth cherishing. At the time, however, that seemed like a maddeningly unsatisfactory answer, so I appealed to one of my friends at the library, a witty and erudite Francophile who I sensed would understand my undirected rage at the cosmos. He did, and proposed a novel solution: read *Les chants de Maldoror* by the Comte de Lautréamont. I never tested his proposal, but it's possible that some transgressive French proto-surrealism would have provided a touch of perspective that I, in my transports of *l'amour fou*, otherwise lacked.

One effect, easily foreseen, of Jonathan's enforced time with the babysitter, who ran a little family operation with her mother and teenage daughters, was that he picked up illnesses from the other kids, and we picked up illnesses from him. I don't advocate runny noses and sore throats for anyone, least of all helpless babies, but the frequency of our mild illnesses and passing fevers incubated a contagion of tenderness and vulnerability. How voluptuous it was to lie there, tending to whoever happened to be stricken at the moment, wiping away the snot, nuzzling flushed cheeks, reading aloud children's books that Our Little Friend (as we called him) couldn't understand. Perhaps I should speak for myself. Lucy and baby Jonathan needed no invasion of bacilli to break down their emotional defenses. Not so the sneezing, wheezing, sniffling paterfamilias sharing the bed with them. Illness made me the man I wanted to be: loving, undefended, egoless, and so sensitive that when Lucy read Jonathan the story of the Velveteen Rabbit, *I* cried, not he. Furthermore, my hyper-vulnerability left me as susceptible to laughter as to tears. "I am dying, Egypt, dying!" I would exclaim, or, "Love me forever! I am lonely, lonely!" That bed felt like our life raft. We could be silly and extravagant and no one was there to censure or disapprove.

It might have been appalling that I could express my deepest love for Lucy only after throwing up on the floor (as once happened), but there was another domain, apart from illness, that brought out the best in me. The curious thing about sex after childbirth was that it got better. There had, until then, been certain inhibitions to overcome and even an occasional failure with the machinery. No more. Even now I can't quite decide which were more deliciously whorish, the white stockings or the red. (The white, the white!) No one but the two principals will ever know the secrets that made our nightly rituals so exciting.

I will say, however, that after childbirth and the experience of caring for a newborn, nothing physical repelled me anymore. On the contrary, I came to have a Whitmanesque appreciation for the sanctity and rightness of every bodily part, especially Lucy's. Although our Kama Sutra nights were thrilling, for me the real climax was post-coital. Yes, yes, that had been a very nice orgasm, but now I could luxuriate in the best part of all: squeezing Lucy tight as we drifted asleep, caressing her beautiful face, and murmuring the loving words over and over again. I regret that I couldn't be so tender and caring every waking moment, but I also know that if I had tried to be, the world would have flayed me alive by the time I got to my lunch hour.

With all that love and sweetness and vulnerability, not to mention loads of hot sex and even a fairly interesting job for a change, was I happy? Sometimes. I'm reminded of the anguished question Emily Webb asks in Thornton Wilder's *Our Town* – "Do any human beings ever realize life while they live it?" – and of the Stage Manager's laconic reply: "No." [Pause.] "The saints and poets, maybe – they do some." I was no saint or poet. I fussed, I fretted, I sulked, I brooded over missed opportunities and fantasized about nonexistent ones. After the trauma of my adolescence and the desolation of my college years, my capacity for happiness had withered but not died. In spite of all the shit out there and in my head, there was a world elsewhere – the one inside my apartment with my "ripe and pearly spouse" and Our Little Friend. I knew very well that Lucy had saved my life, and I told her so, frequently – sometimes even without the helpful pre-condition of an orgasm or a bad head cold. I was, I liked to think, getting better at this happiness thing. And now – now that I'm an old guy with a lifetime of loss and disappointments behind me? Now I look at the world and I can almost weep for the beauty and wonder I see everywhere. But Lucy never forgave me. I had been guilty of what Jorge Luis Borges, in a wrenching autobiographical poem titled "*Remordimiento*," called the worst of all sins: not being happy when he should have been.

I'm not sure that happiness, as opposed to purpose, meaning, engagement, and self-knowledge, was ever the goal. Lucy herself, given to occasional bouts of melancholy brooding and unappeasable insecurity, didn't exactly brim with *joie de vivre* either. But on the way to the tragic sunderings and utter annihilation that await us all, there was no reason not to have as much fun as we could. Furthermore, we had the obligation to raise our child in an atmosphere of playfulness, laughter, and even (something I think I was especially good at) downright silliness. If altering the lyric of the old torch song "What's New" and bellowing it out in my best baritone as "What's old? / On the bread there is mold," doesn't strike you as hilarious, well, you're not a giggly little boy.

All this good stuff got only better with the arrival of my younger sister from Florida around the time of Jonathan's first birthday. She had had some hard knocks lately, but her new job – taking care of Jonathan during working hours – offered her a needed change of pace while offering all of us what there could never be enough of: more playfulness, more laughter, more silliness, more love. There followed many days and nights of group hugs, piggyback rides, and finger painting. Having rescued Jonathan from the sick house of our local babysitter, she returned to Florida a year and a half later, ready to begin a new chapter in her life. I still owe her.

All very nice, this love fest, but how the hell do you fit four people into a one-bedroom New York City apartment? Sometimes there's simply no substitute for being married to an architect. By the time my sister moved in, the landlord, rumored to be wandering the streets muttering to himself in a state of increasing dereliction, had essentially abandoned the building as well as his two or three other properties in Park Slope and Brooklyn Heights. The remaining tenants had organized sufficiently to manage the building ourselves and pay a monthly maintenance fee, which meant, among other things, that another tenant and I ended up putting out the garbage twice a week, not that we got anything in return but grumbling and complaints. Anyhow, a number of apartments had sat vacant for quite a while, including the one immediately adjacent to ours. That was all Lucy needed. Even if she hadn't got grudging permission from the head of the tenants' association and its lawyer, she probably would have knocked down the wall and connected the two apartments. She had fun drawing up the plans and still more fun, with an able-bodied colleague of hers, smashing the wall down with a sledgehammer. (I looked on enviously – my job was to keep Jonathan out of harm's way.) In a stroke, we had doubled our living space. Even though we paid double the monthly maintenance (still well below market value), our nearest neighbors hated us for it. Lucy didn't quite reckon on that, nor did she have to deal with those neighbors, a high-powered professional couple who called me over one night for a quiet conversation. Within seconds the husband (six feet four) was looming over me and spitting in my face in a frenzy of uncontrollable rage. Who did you think you are you goddamn what gives you the right you miserable and on and on and on. For the first and only time in my life I had the perfect exit line. After impassively allowing this insane tirade to wash over me, I turned toward the door, reached for the handle, and as I stepped into the hallway calmly remarked, "It's been a lovely evening, you're a charming couple, and we'll have to do this again sometime." It never got any friendlier.

We would remain in that building for the next nine or ten years, making the best of it, as did, come to think of it, our unneighborly neighbors, who couldn't have enjoyed this infighting any more than we did. Lucy immediately set about transforming our cramped one-bedroom apartment into a cramped three-bedroom apartment. She didn't get much help from me. I hemmed, I hawed, I carped, I complained. Why not put this here and that there? Couldn't we get rid of some of this . . . *stuff?* Pretty typical: the librarian telling the architect how to design her own apartment. In the end, I agreed to every one of Lucy's choices, which were, of course, the right ones, but only after making myself a thorough pain in the ass. And I humbly and sincerely apologized; it just took me a while. So what's my excuse? I had yet to learn the wisdom of the pop adage of the day, "Don't sweat the small stuff." I hadn't had much experience screwing up relationships; give me some time, please. I think, eventually, I got to be pretty good at intimacy, at the give and take, at the shrugging off of abrasions, at the acceptance of imperfections, foibles, and blind spots. Given the three-to-one ratio of imperfections, foibles, and blind spots on my side, I had better be good at it, but that was hardly an overnight process. Lucy got tired of waiting. What I didn't know was that every mistake I was making – every thoughtless comment or stupid joke or erring glance, every sin of omission or commission – was being inscribed in her Book of Doom. Years later, when we were arguing over larger matters than the disposition of appliances in our expanded apartment, it all came out: Lucy never forgot (or forgave) a thing.

She continued to push and pull at the apartment for the duration, and I learned to become a somewhat more congenial collaborator. To begin with, there was more wall space to be covered with her sumptuous quilts, which I urged her to hang everywhere in spite of her reluctance. (She was afraid of seeming ostentatious.) On the blank narrow space of our new hallway we created a picture gallery of reproductions cut out and framed from art books: Paul Klee, René Magritte, Hendrik Goltzius, Albrecht Durer, Jasper Johns, Winslow Homer, and other mostly dead white masters whose gender and ethnicity, in that benighted epoch, we failed to consider problematic. We also had what I called the "rec room," where I played my guitar, Lucy knitted, stitched, sketched, and quilted, and Jonathan played, sang, danced, and tumbled. My sister had introduced a small television set into the household, which found a place in the rec room and where we allowed Jonathan to watch a few nature programs and *Mister Rogers*. It was a wonderful day in our neighborhood. Would you be mine? Could you be mine? Won't you please please be my savior?

10

If the aspiration to completeness is expressed anywhere at all, it may be in our own muddled daily lives – as, in a way unprecedented in history, many women and men are now trying to express, in their sometimes bewildered confrontation with particular choices: a commitment to work, to citizenship and social justice, to personal love, to the care and raising of children, to the household, to friendship and hospitality, to other values as well. All this, many hope, without the compromises and failures of recognition that have characterized so many centuries in which the lives of men and women were separated. As they do this they sometimes encounter painful conflicts (conflicts, for example, between obligations to care for children and the demands of a career for uninterrupted time and thought; between either of these and the intensity of attention that personal love requires).

Those words appeared in the January 30, 1986 issue of *The New York Review of Books* in an essay/review by Martha C. Nussbaum titled "Women's Lot." Though likely intended for readers more like herself, a professor of philosophy at Brown

University, than me, a grunt-level staffer at the Brooklyn Public Library, Nussbaum's essay described with uncanny precision the life Lucy and I were living. The key words jumped off the page: "muddled," "bewildered," "painful." There was more: "This life can feel overcrowded . . . It is frequently hectic, breathless, lacking in grace and ease." Yes, that was our life all right, a maelstrom of scattered toys, dirty laundry, unread newspapers, and nasty neighbors. Yet all of this mess, as Nussbaum went on to say, was in the service of something larger: the construction of "a new and fuller meaning for that venerable philosophical expression, 'the complete human life.'"

Assuredly, Lucy and I came nowhere near constructing or expressing "the complete human life." And yet, in a half-conscious way, we aspired to. If nothing else, we set the bar very high. Maybe this is a myth I need to tell myself, but it wasn't just the usual accumulation of tensions, abrasions, and resentments that did us in; it was, at least in part, our idealism. Many couples worry that they may not be connecting as deeply or lovingly or instinctively as they once did; Lucy and I made a religion out of our worries. We shed buckets of tears over nothing, over unreal fears and imagined slights. Lucy, in particular, was apt to pick a fight for the comforting reassurance of making up – anything to keep us talking, touching, loving, feeling. We might have taken slightly too literally Rainer Maria Rilke's beautiful but not easily applicable apothegm, "For one human being to love another: that is the most difficult of all our tasks, the ultimate, the last test and proof, the work for which all other work is but preparation." If you really believe those words, as we did, it's hard to settle for less than everything.

In some ways we fit the bill – being the kind of middle-to-upper-middle class "professionals" that Martha Nussbaum had in mind – in other ways we didn't. Our stake in personal love and the care and raising of a child far surpassed our rather dutiful "commitment" to citizenship and social justice, which consisted, essentially, of voting once every two years. As for work, we differed from many of our cohorts in having fairly decent jobs rather than highly demanding (and fittingly remunerative) careers. Perceptive and powerful as it was, Nussbaum's analysis took for granted class assumptions alien to our respective backgrounds. As she half admitted, Lucy's parents were just up from the peasantry, and although I grew up in a posh Fairfield County suburb, my family lived in what passed for the other side of the tracks, where I felt a lot more comfortable. In particular, I could never entirely buy into the idea of "fulfillment," so central to what members of the educated classes conceived of as "the complete human life." The counter view – that life is a bitch and then you die – I tended to find more congenial. To love and be loved was fulfillment enough for me, yet I wanted to love and be loved in exactly the sort of nonhierarchical, nontraditional, value-laden way that Nussbaum described. She was right. This life was full of messiness and frustration and difficulty. We couldn't conceive of, and wouldn't have wanted, any other.

Nor did I have any doubts about who had created the conditions to make such a life possible – it was women, not men, women whose bellicose feminism sometimes offended and annoyed me but who insisted on nothing less than a wholesale and liberating realignment of the way both sexes lived and loved. Women like Lucy. How insignificant the reigns of particular presidents and prime ministers seemed compared to the radical transformations of social and domestic life wrought by millions of unsung women. You didn't have to live half a life anymore; you could fail, as you inevitably would, on terms not dictated by your gender.

Unlike her less talented, less creative, less ambitious husband, Lucy did believe in the idea of personal fulfillment, which derived less from her peasant/mercantile family background than from her ardent feminism. In the end, I believe, she came to see me, at least partly, as an obstacle to her fulfillment. I was just *there:* obdurate, unenlightened Stephen who had made too many mistakes and clogged the way forward – "the magazine husband who one day just had to go," to quote Bob Dylan. Do I delude myself in thinking that the deepest fulfillment Lucy was ever to know occurred not after her life with me but during it, when we were young raccoons so madly attuned to each other that we could overcome with a touch or a tear drop – or even a labyrinthine argument about the state of our souls lasting till three AM – all the crap that got in the way? Just asking.

I envied Lucy the sort of creative fulfillment she seemed regularly to achieve with her quilts and later with her painting. Now that I've experienced at least a taste of that fulfillment with a few books and publications here and there, I can honestly say: It's O.K. But I could write *Moby-Dick* and it wouldn't bring me anything like the fulfillment I shared with Lucy on some of the most ordinary of occasions. Parenthood kept us at home most nights, but now and then I slipped out to attend a club show featuring a band slightly too intransigent for Lucy's taste – X or Public Image Ltd or Graham Parker and the Rumor. Although I picked my bands carefully and the shows were generally first-rate, coming home was always the best part. As I slid under the covers long after midnight, Lucy would wake just enough to murmur, "Oh, you're back. Was it a good show?"

"Great," I would reply. "You shoulda seen Billy Zoom."

Then I would hold her tight, breathing in the scent of her hair and the warmth of her body as she dropped back asleep. Usually I was too wired after a concert to sleep well or at all, and dragging myself into work a few hours later would be hell, but I didn't mind. I had seen Billy Zoom throwing out triplets on his spangled Les Paul, and here I was, squeezing my Sleeping Beauty, who would pretend to be interested the next night at dinner so that I might recount in tedious detail the highlights of the show. Some nights I just lay there, Lucy cradled in my arms, replaying the banal love songs that I had just heard and couldn't get out of my head: "My soul cries your name / Over and over again" or "I feel the heartbeat of the world / In the hands of this girl" or "I've been dreamin' too long / I guess something's always wrong / Unless I wake up next to you."

Something else happened in bed that was equally exciting, ritualistic, and intimate: reading. Ovid, Wordsworth, Dickinson, Yeats, Wallace Stevens, the Book of Job, and a few contemporaries I had discovered in my articles for reference books – oral literature, or at any rate literature (mostly poetry) for the ear as much as the mind. I did the reading, Lucy the listening. Uh-oh – was this yet another instance of male hegemonic coercion and lethal mansplaining? I don't think so. Lucy liked listening, I liked reading aloud, and we both let the poems speak for themselves, with only a passing comment here or there. There may be other and better ways of reading poetry, among which would be the various critical methods we had studied and practiced in graduate school, but it's hard to think of one more conducive to intimacy. Rather than reaching for any particular interpretation, we attended to the music, the mystery, the power. I'm sure we missed more than a few nuances. Still, there are worse ways of spending your time than sharing William Carlos Williams' "Asphodel, That Greeny Flower" ("It is ridiculous / what airs we put on / while our hearts / gasp dying / for want of love") with your life partner.

Lucy kindly indulged me in some other bedtime reading, namely, the articles I was then writing for a series of literary reference works. Not much music, mystery, or power there, but I needed to hear the sentences out loud, and she was my ideal audience, mostly because she liked everything I wrote, or professed to. That "professed to" made all the difference. If my editors didn't like something, they said so. Lucy just said yes. She knew I could work out the rough patches later on. Lacking anything like her confidence and talent, I needed all the affirmation she could give me. Her reward, some years later, was that she finally got to hear some pretty decent writing; my literary apprenticeship lasted into my mid-thirties. Anyway, she listened to every sentence of my first book, which even the least sympathetic reader would concede was more interesting than my reference articles on "Trader" Horn, Max Brand, and other forgotten travel writers and cowboy novelists undertaken for the "Wilson Authors Series." Another heartbreak. I stopped reading to her in the end. She had stopped listening.

Even less imperishable than my articles on Trader Horn and Max Brand were the humor pieces, inspired by Ian Frazier, Veronica Geng, and other *New Yorker* writers, I was then composing with a view to publication in that very magazine. Lucy thought they were pretty funny. I thought they were magnificent. Heeding my friend Al Avant's advice, I submitted them directly to Veronica Geng, whom he knew slightly and who, he assured me, would actually read them. Indeed she did.

Her reply arrived a few days before Christmas in 1987. I didn't save it. In fact, I would have burned it if we had had a fireplace; disposing of it with the kitchen slop would have to do. The gist of her criticism was that I was a contemptible hack. To do her justice, my pieces really weren't much good, although I still have a soft spot for the parody of Shakespearean criticism turning obsessively on the Bard's gynecological imagery. Even so, it amazed me that an established writer would take the trouble to savage a complete nobody who had been careful not to presume too much. I felt like I was in a Balzac novel – the provincial aspirant learning in the harshest possible way the mores of the Capital. Lucy rallied to my defense with her accustomed tactfulness, and I reflected that the provinces – our little apartment in Park Slope, filled with love and laughter and badly needed consolation – afforded more of the world to me than could ever be obtained in the literary capital on West Forty-third Street.

Did I offer the same sort of support for Lucy's creative endeavors? I did; it's just that artmaking, unlike writing, was so damn expensive. I needed notebooks, paper, pens and a typewriter; Lucy required a studio and seemingly half the stock of Pearl Paint on Canal Street, where she shopped with the avidity of a kid in a candy store. (By contrast, I always felt abashed shopping for guitar gear in the music stores on Forty-seventh Street; invariably, some sixteen-year-old phenom, trying out the latest wah-wah pedal, would put me to shame.) For now, she could produce her quilts at home, but artmaking would become an increasingly costly operation. I never asked how much of our income went into her studio and art supplies and I learned not to worry about it. Someone had to spend the money; it might as well be Lucy. Although I regret sometimes quibbling about the expense, I knew that art didn't come cheap. Later, she would befriend many other artists, some of whom achieved respectable commercial success, but even they scarcely broke even.

Among the changes wrought by parenthood was that we now did certain things apart that we had previously done together. Necessarily so. If we ever wanted to go to a movie or a museum or a gallery again, we'd have to go alone. As trial and error had proved, babysitters were a luxury and a worry we couldn't afford. (Our first one had left Jonathan with a mysterious bruise on his head.) So the Holy Family would split up sometimes, Saint Joseph off for some birdwatching, the Blessed Mother out for an evening with her friend Irene. While I missed having Lucy to confer with and sometimes felt self-conscious about being alone in a crowd, these solo outings oddly enhanced our intimacy. Revival house movie theaters turned out to be, for me, something like the back shop of the soul that Montaigne had described. Not only was I able to escape to a favorite Cary Grant movie, but I could tell Lucy all about it when I returned home. And after messing around with a two-year-old all day, I got to hear her reports from the outside world; she had seen a terrific exhibition of Jasper Johns' prints, or Irene had been on another disastrous date. These customary separations brought something new into our life: narrative. The telling was almost better than the doing. I sometimes went out of my way to do or see something just to have the pleasure of telling Lucy about it. For years I had had no one with whom to share my stories, opinions, perceptions, or even jokes. I used to worry that my best thoughts would all die on the vine. Now I had the most sympathetic audience in the world. Eddie Bracken had shown up to deliver a few words at the Film Forum screening of *Miracle at Morgan's Creek.* He was an old man now but still Eddie Bracken. So poignant! The crowd went nuts! He couldn't stand Preston Sturges! Remember how hard we had laughed at the hotel registration scene when we had seen it a couple of years earlier?

Even without the stories we saved up for each other, I would have relished seeing Lucy after one of our brief separations. I could never understand the hostility that passed as folk wisdom among long-established couples. "Ugh, I have to get back to 'the wife'" – that sort of thing. I couldn't wait to get back to "the wife," who had a name and was still, in spite of ample opportunity for disillusionment provided by six years of cohabitation, the person whose company I most relished. Admittedly, I sometimes kvetched when I got home from work and my yearning for occasional periods of solitude was neither alienating nor unhealthy. Nonetheless, thinking of Lucy as "the wife" in a domestic arrangement determined by convention and practical realities was unimaginable. No matter what I did, no matter where I went, that maximally interesting and intelligent person was waiting for me on the other side of the door.

That Cary Grant movie, by the way, might have been *The Awful Truth,* which in my more delirious moments I regarded as the greatest movie ever made. But all the best romantic comedies of the thirties and forties, which I had discovered with Lucy a few years earlier and now saw mostly on my own, made me delirious. *The Awful Truth, Bringing Up Baby, The Shop Around the Corner, The Lady Eve, His Girl Friday, Ninotcka, Twentieth Century, The Thin Man, Palm Beach Story:* I loved them so much that I half feared turning into one of the Mole People who lived underground in the theaters of the Museum of Modern Art, never venturing upstairs to see any of the art and suspicious of any film made after 1960. Nevertheless, I found in those movies an idealized view of worldly eros that Lucy and I couldn't always live up to but that did us no shame. Lucy had other ideas. After listening to me rhapsodize about the playfulness, wit, and wised-up sexiness of those screen idols, she sharply reminded me that I wasn't Cary Grant (Eddie Bracken might have been more like it), nor she Katherine Hepburn and that if I had a notion that our life in any way resembled an airy screwball comedy, I had better get it out of my head right now. She was right, of course. And yet.

I still love those movies and I still think they rival Shakespearean comedy as idealized projections (and criticisms) of romantic love. So did Stanley Cavell, a Harvard philosophy professor whose study of the genre in *Pursuits of Happiness: The Hollywood Comedy of Remarriage* I was then reading with perhaps insufficient skepticism. In spite of Cavell's wooly, self-infatuated prose, the book teemed with brilliant insights: that those movies "harbor a vision which they know cannot fully be domesticated, inhabited, in the world we know"; that the central pair are expected "to find happiness alone, unsponsored, in one another, out of their capacities for improvising a world, beyond ceremony"; that the lovers "simply *appreciate* one another more than they appreciate anyone else, and they would rather be appreciated by one another more than by anyone else"; and that, somewhat disconcertingly, most of those movies "end in undermining and in madcap and in headaches because there is, as yet, no envisioned settlement" for the issues they raise.

Lucy was right to tell me to sober up, that art wasn't life, and that not only was I not Cary Grant but that Cary Grant wasn't Cary Grant. (He was Archibald Leach, a cockney ex-acrobat who cycled through five marriages and at the end of his life resorted to LSD as a drastic form of therapy.) Still, we did appreciate each other in a way that at least resembled the mutual appreciation of our cinematic avatars. Like them, we each had a partner who was a worthy antagonist, who shared the other's private references, who enjoyed being with each other more than with anybody else, who knew, to put it more simply, how to have fun. If, for instance, we got separated at one of the rare parties we attended, we knew that when we traded notes afterwards, our impressions would line up almost exactly. Wasn't so and so hilarious, and don't you think we should give Madame X a wide berth if we ever run into her again?

The thing that impressed me most about the classic romantic comedies and that I considered applicable to our own case was that the principal conflict encountered by the central pair was internal rather than external. Those movies, to borrow the grad school terminology still rattling around in my head, lacked the "senex" or blocking figure that divided lovers in comedies from Shakespeare to Oscar Wilde. Whatever misunderstandings came between Henry Fonda and Barbara Stanwyck, or Jimmy Stewart and Margaret Sullavan, or Joel McCrea and Claudette Colbert were of their own making, not imposed upon them by disapproving parents or snobbish in-laws. Part of the fun of those movies was watching the lovers discover the resources within themselves to arrive at the solution that had been there all along. Which is what Lucy and I did – until we didn't.

No human beings could possibly jabber as fast as the characters in those thirties talkies, but if, as John Milton said, "a meet and happy conversation is the chiefest and noblest end of marriage," Lucy and I conversed as volubly, if not so wondrously, as any screwball couple. Out in the world, we both tended to reticence and self-consciousness or, more charitably, we thought before we spoke. Back in our den, what popped into our heads popped out of our mouths. Or out of my mouth. I had been waiting to speak my peace through too many years of mute loneliness; inevitably, I spoke it too heedlessly. Did Lucy really need to know what I thought of the luxurious red hair of my grad school friend Penelope? Sometimes my conversation wasn't as "meet" as it might have been.

One archetype of romantic comedy that unquestionably fit our case was that of the woman always being a step ahead of the man. I was Orlando to her Rosalind, Benedick to her Beatrice, Ralph Kramden to her Alice. Her G.R.E. scores were nearly perfect; if literature students had had to know anything about math, I would have been doomed. But of course, Lucy was smarter than I was in the way that really counted – emotionally. She neither fussed nor complained nor judged people, habits that I was slowly weaning myself from, largely through her example. We're all damaged goods, but she seemed less mangled by her childhood than I by mine. And although utterly unathletic and even a bit clumsy, she carried herself with a graciousness that wasn't meant to impress but did. All of which compelled the question that I sought strenuously to avoid: Were women better than men? That question went to the heart of our debates – fights, actually – about feminism. Lucy espoused a "difference feminism" that I considered prejudicial and in the long run damaging to the interests of women. If you could say that women were emotionally superior to men, you could also say that men were intellectually superior to women, or at any rate allow bigots to make that claim. Why then did I prefer the company of women, with their softer voices and less combative style and that marvelous way they had of touching and kissing each other? On the whole, I thought it best to attempt no resolution of these intractable matters. I still don't know whether women are better than men, but I'm pretty sure that Lucy was better than me.

"You're a lucky guy, Steve. You don't know how lucky."

Thus spoke a colleague of mine, one of the few other male heterosexual librarians on the staff at the main branch of the Brooklyn Public Library. Being too cheap to buy the *New York Times* himself, he had stopped by my office – I was then running the unspeakably boring Central Reserves Department, a promotion of sorts – to borrow my copy for a few hours. I had asked that he return it before the end of the day so that I could bring it home to "my wife." That was all it took. Poor Janek, whom I scarcely knew, just stood there, looking at the floor, wanting to talk but not knowing how. He managed to say that he was having "trouble" at home, and to cover for his embarrassment I offered a few bromides about the difficulty of marriage, which I myself didn't believe. Lucy and I later saw him dining, alone and forlorn, a few tables away from us at a Chinese restaurant in the neighborhood. I probably should have invited him to join us, but I worried that that would make him only more self-conscious and miserable. He would have seen just what a "lucky guy" I really was. And that I knew it.

Presumably, Janek and his unhappily married spouse were fighting over more nitty-gritty matters than the feminist debates of the 1980s that so much preoccupied Lucy and me. We argued over Judy Chicago's must-see "Dinner Party" exhibition at the Brooklyn Museum, over the tactics of the art insurgents known as the Guerrilla Girls (necessarily blunt, in Lucy's opinion, absurdly reductive in mine), over the assumption of the incommensurability of male and female experience in feminist literary criticism, over the unrelenting dogmatism of feminist discourse. It wasn't that Lucy always disagreed with me; she too thought that the reduction of individual women's identity to their genitals in "The Dinner Party" was a bit dodgy. But she considered me insufficiently supportive of the Cause, and she didn't like my tone. One time we returned from a family gathering in which my brother had told a few innocently off-color jokes at the expense of women. Lucy had laughed. My God, I told her, you would have had my head on a platter if I had said half so much.

"That's right," she replied. "I expect more from you."

In recent years the figure of the shambling manchild pulled kicking and screaming into adulthood through the ministrations of a patient, indulgent, and, needless to say, incredibly "hot" girlfriend, has gained currency in pop culture. Aren't these guys adorable? Lucy wouldn't think so, and I got no credit, understandably, for not being an overgrown schlub incapable of cooking dinner or seriously discussing the state of our relationship. I didn't mind being held to a high standard; I just wish, in Lucy's mind, I could have reached it every now and then. There were indeed occasions that call to mind the situation described by Robert Graves in his memoir of World War I, *Goodbye to All That*. His unconventional marriage (at the time) to the feminist and artist Nancy Nicholson provided the great benefit, as in our case as well, of shared convictions and philosophical alignment. And yet living with an extremely committed feminist, for Graves and for me, also provided certain challenges; as Graves wrote, "male stupidity and callousness became such an obsession with her that she began to include me in her universal condemnation of men." Lucy put it more simply one day when she was especially disgusted with men or me or both. "I wish I was a lesbian," she said.

One or two of Lucy's friends, from other parts of the world, couldn't understand her feminism at all. Selda, a pop artist who dressed in the bold primary colors of her paintings, considered it an amusing aberration, an endearing eccentricity on the part of her otherwise sensible friend. Why, men were wonderful (as Katherine Hepburn exclaimed in *Philadelphia Story)!* Why shouldn't women want to please them? Faced with such obscurantism, Lucy reacted as could have been foreseen, which is to say, she treated Selda with the same warmth and affection that she bestowed on everyone else. Lucy was no ideologue. We sometimes saw the radical feminist activist Andrea Dworkin, who really was an ideologue, lumbering around the neighborhood in her overalls. Some people thought she had a brilliant mind. Maybe she did, but if that kind of militant shabbiness was one model of feminist engagement, Lucy wanted no part of it. And when we met an older hippie woman at a picnic in Prospect Park one summer, Lucy said afterwards what I wouldn't have dared: My goodness, couldn't she have at least shaved her legs? I appreciated Selda's relaxed Mediterranean savoir-vivre about the general wonderfulness of men, but I knew it wasn't going to win me any arguments. Why must we argue anyway? I think I can answer that question with another, posed by Derek and the Dominos and quite beyond the reach of even the most ardent, searching, and broad-minded feminism: Why Does Love Got To Be So Sad?

Eric Clapton's guitar could do most of the explaining for him. Lucy and I were stuck with words. I was a little better at them than she, naturally enough – I being a writer, she an artist. I like to think I had a knack for finding the right words to say when she needed to hear them. We can never hear enough of those three little words, but we also want to hear variations on the theme. Yes, yes, you love me, but why? Be specific, please. And so I told her.

Lucy, I would say when she seemed a little down or in need of comfort, everybody's in awe of you. You have no idea. You ought to see the way your friends look at you. You're twenty times more talented, pretty, and intelligent than any of them, and you act as if each one of them is the most special person in the world. And Max Michaels at that party last year – he just couldn't get his eyes off your tits, I'm sorry, it's true. You're a total dish! So give yourself a break, O.K.? You're lucky to be you. Can we go to sleep now?

Admittedly, my knack for finding the wrong words to say when she didn't need to hear them was rather impressive too – but let us speak of abiding love, for the present. I was always pretty good at reading the signs. Like anyone I've ever known, starting with myself, Lucy had her share of "issues," many, in her case, having to do with the impossible dilemma of body image. This was especially frustrating for her in that her worries about her appearance contradicted what she knew to be true – that women wasted far too much time, energy, and money getting themselves up to look pretty for the delectation of men. Everyone wants to look good, everyone wants to feel sexy, and to see Lucy casually apply a touch of lipstick (the only makeup she ever wore) or bend over to adjust a (low) heel was delectation enough for me. But who's kidding who (or whom)? Men endure nothing like the pressure exerted on women to conform to idealized standards of beauty. No one knew that better than Lucy. And yet even she – beautiful, intellectual, feminist Lucy – felt "fat."

We were looking at some old photographs. Corny as it sounds, compiling and revising photo albums was a treasured activity. (I still have all of them. After we broke up, she never wanted to see them – or me – again.) Do you remember what you were thinking when Paola snapped that picture of you on the bus? Isn't that a nice one of my mother and you? But something was bothering her about three or four pictures taken a few years earlier of her and two girlfriends sharing a festive evening in our apartment. Silence. And then:

"I'm fat. I'm ugly."

It's true that the two girlfriends had more slender body types, and one of them, an Afro-Caribbean beauty oblivious to the effect she had on men (or at least on me), might have been the one friend better looking than Lucy. It wasn't a question of jealousy. She was beating herself up for internalizing norms that she consciously rejected. I tried to find a better way of saying that.

"Lucy," I protested, "how could you say such a thing? All I see in those pictures is how happy you look, how much fun you're all having. Why would you want to change anything? You look so sweet, so girlish, I just wasn't to bend you like a pretzel and fuck you every which way to Sunday. Would I lie about that?"

Although I never doubted the three little words that Lucy spoke often and feelingly to me, she was less profuse than I at verbal elaboration. Which is to say, I kept waiting for her to tell me how wonderful I was. She never did. This led to the absurd expedient of *asking* her to tell me. Though my character flaws were all too apparent, we could at least agree, I thought, on my better-than-average sense of humor. Once after a night out with friends when I had been at what I considered my sparkling best, I steered the conversation to my desired goal:

"I really got Cindy laughing tonight."

"Hmmm."

"I always get Cindy laughing. She thinks I'm really funny."

"Hmmm."

"I am, you know."

"What?"

"Funny."

"Of course you're funny."

"I mean, I'm *very* funny. I'm *unusually* funny."

"Stephen, what the hell are you talking about?"

It went on like that for a while, but I did eventually extract the avowal I had been longing to hear: that she loved my sense of humor and loved me *for* my sense of humor. Had to work for it, though.

One avowal needed no prompting. I might have been childish, I might have been selfish, I might have been irresponsible, I might have thought with my dick, I might have been, to use the phrase she repeated many, many times in our last few years, a *fucking asshole*. Yet from first to last she granted me one huge concession that didn't, alas, quite make up for everything else. Stephen, she would say in admiration or exasperation (depending on the case), you don't have a malicious bone in your body. You go out of your way to be nice to people. You would never do anything deliberately to hurt anyone.

Ah, but what I might do and did do undeliberately – that's another story.

11

There were other women in the world. I noticed them. Unfortunately, I did more than notice them, but let's start with the noticing. I've always thought that one of the nicest things about being alive is the sexual frisson that sometimes arises between men and women. It's not as if you're going to do anything about it. You've got your life, she has hers, and neither party is looking for any complications in an already complicated life. Yet for just a moment there's an unspoken current of complicity that passes between you. My goodness, doesn't she look elegant in that satin blouse, and maybe she thinks you're *unusually* funny. So you linger over your hallway conversation and notice the way she smiles at you. Then you go back to work, feeling a little more human, a little more alive but otherwise unchanged. What you do not do is go home and tell your wife about it. Unless you're me.

Of course, it's likely that Lucy would have experienced the same sort of frisson with some of the men who crossed her path. If so, she never told me. Would I have objected? Far from it. I saw the way men sometimes looked at her. They could only look; I could do a lot more than that. For better or worse, I wasn't prone to that kind of jealousy. Because she didn't object to my effusions about attractive women, I thought she wasn't jealous either. I thought wrong.

Common sense, you might suppose, would suffice to restrain me from some of those effusions, but I disdained common sense in favor of the higher value of complete truthfulness. Yes, I know – anyone that stupid probably deserves anything he gets, but Lucy believed in the same thing. I once asked if, in principle, there was anything I could do without informing her. No, she replied, because, in principle, everything I did affected her. What if – unlikely, but you never know – I impulsively said yes to a drug dealer in Washington Square Park and got high for a few hours? That was her business too, she said; if I was going to be an incoherent jackass, she needed to know. I conceded the point. We wouldn't lie or prevaricate, we would confide in and trust each other absolutely. That's what love meant, didn't it? No, it didn't. It meant sacrificing a high-minded idealism to the simple human needs of the other person. One of Lucy's needs was not to hear me gush about some of the women that I "noticed." Yes, Gong Li was a very beautiful actress. Couldn't I even go to the movies without bringing home my obsession with female pulchritude? I genuinely believed that talking about this stuff was a healthy expression of a shared sexuality that we could channel into our feelings for each other. Why then did Lucy, unlike some of her female friends, never seem to gush about her favorite male actors or register any other men as desirable at all? I recall exactly one exception, having to do with Lou Reed, of all people. After a terrific concert at the Bottom Line in 1983, she confessed to finding him seductive in his deadpan way. It's possible that, out of deference to my fragile ego, she hid from me her raging desire for Lou Reed, his bass player, the drummer, the bouncer, the guy who took the tickets, and half the other men she knew, but somehow I doubt it. Once, in a conversation initiated by one of her girlfriends, she pretended to find the actor John Cusack sexy, but I could tell she was bluffing. I was her guy, not John Cusack or Lou Reed's bass player or anyone else.

In my otherwise blighted adolescence, I had the fleeting consolation of a reciprocal crush with a pretty girl. What could be more innocent? Suddenly that girl, now a blooming young woman, emerged from the shadows to write a friendly letter and pay a brief visit on her way through New York. Consistent with our policy of full disclosure, I shared with Lucy not just my delight at the prospect but the warm and loving sentiments Maria had expressed for me in her letter – altogether too warm and loving, in Lucy's opinion. Whether or not Maria had crossed a line, Lucy had no doubt that I had. She claimed that I was handling this situation abominably, slighting her feelings and overindulging Maria's for the sake of my appalling male vanity – all pretty much true, as I failed to see at the time. What was not true was that I wanted to fuck her. Well, O.K., I did, but only in the sense that most men have involuntary visions of sexual thrills that bubble to the surface only to be beaten back to the murky substratum from which they arose. When Maria finally arrived at our apartment for her visit, we spent a couple of hours conversing awkwardly and, as Lucy bitterly said afterwards, making "goo-goo eyes" at each other.

Relative innocence availed nothing. Lucy would not be persuaded that I had no designs on Maria, that Maria had no designs on me, that we wouldn't have even if we could have, that tonight's argument merely rehearsed last night's argument, that I loved Lucy and only Lucy, and that it might behoove us to get a few hours' sleep before the morning overtook us.

Lucy never obtained from me the confession that she wanted – that I was still crazy about Maria and that if she hadn't lived halfway across the country I would have found a louche hotel room somewhere for our squalid trysts. On the contrary, these drawn-out battles provided a good occasion to confess something else: that however "susceptible" (Lucy's word) I might be to the charms of Maria or my grad school classmate Penelope or Gong Li or Susan Sontag, I had no illusion that I would ever meet anyone who embodied all those qualities of intelligence, talent, kindness, and beauty that attracted me to Lucy in the first place. That did no good either.

I was tempted to give Lucy her desired confession. Although I would have had to lie, it might have bought some peace. But no, any such confession, in the long run, would have had quite the opposite effect. To quote Wallace Stevens, "Her words accuse you of adulteries / That sack the Sun, though metaphysical." (Later, they wouldn't be quite so metaphysical.) The least I could do for now was to assent to Lucy's demand that I write a tactful note to Maria suggesting that we might want to tone down our rhetoric just a notch. You can imagine how well that went over. Now, instead of having one beautiful woman furious at me, I had two. Simmering, seething Lucy. Bristling, bewildered Maria. Poor, put-upon Stephen. For many people, that first adolescent crush stays with them forever. Lucy never had that formative experience. She couldn't understand that Maria and I might have a special affection for each other. Which excuses nothing. I could have kept that affection close to my heart. Instead, I got all spoony and made goo-goo eyes.

Lucy ended up hating Maria, and Maria ended up hating me. A fine mess. Assuredly, I would have preferred our hushed, bedtime readings of poetry to these enervating quarrels, and yet there was something strangely addictive about them. We weren't haggling over the phone bill. Although the chief topic – my gross insensitivity – hit rather too close to home, we never doubted the necessity of hashing it out, even at the cost of a reasonable night's sleep. Attraction, repulsion, excitement, frustration, yearning – sounds a lot like sex, actually, which is how these nightly dramas generally ended. Unwittingly, we might have been establishing a dynamic that would come to constrain us, namely, that of conflict generated principally for the sake of resolution. The sex is great but there are easier ways to get there. Nevertheless, when I think of Lucy in a skimpy tee shirt raging at me in the middle of the night or of my half defensive, half admissive reactions, I think also of truthfulness, trust, openness, authenticity, selfhood. Those two half-naked people sharing a bed and exchanging words of anger or contrition, shedding tears of rage or pity, and moments away from making love – those people weren't faking it or dialing it in or going through the motions.

Going into work the morning after one of our intimate, erotic *agons* always felt slightly unreal. I had no idea where authentic selfhood was to be found, but I was pretty sure it wasn't at the weekly departmental meeting on Wednesdays at 9:15. I had been to my share of those meetings and conscientiously took notes or asked suitably pertinent questions. I was a librarian; my job was to help people find information and to make myself useful to the reading public. How could I not buy into that program? But I worked for two enormous institutions with complex bureaucratic hierarchies and a commitment to the dubious "expertise" of expensive management consultants. Inevitably, I felt somewhat alienated from the fruit of my labor, or to put it in less Marxist terms, those compulsory training programs with the management consultants took the piss out of me. The day-to-day stuff was fine, even gratifying at times, but the meetings made me want to cry. I used to tell Lucy about the jargon, the groupthink, the sheer bullshit I was periodically subjected to at work. She could hardly believe it; at her office, they trusted her to draught and design without too much interference. All of which is to say, I guess, that I had a fairly typical American job. And that meant that my home life – my real life, the one that counted – more than ever seemed a sanctuary from the false, the inauthentic, the meretricious, the official and approved. That might have been too much weight brought to bear upon another person. Other people got bits and pieces of me; Lucy got the whole damn thing. Isn't that what she wanted? No, she just wanted the good parts. Yet if I couldn't be wholly myself with her, I could hardly lay claim to having a self worth the keeping. All I knew was that I would rather hear her railing at me – "loving, rapid, merciless – / break[ing] like the Atlantic Ocean on my head," to quote Robert Lowell – than listen to a consultant drone on about time management surveys or some such crap.

Maybe some of that alienation was self-created – too many Antonioni movies, perhaps. So far from being alienated from her labor, Lucy liked to show me the wondrous floor plans she drew up at work. Most of my library friends and colleagues went about their jobs without any of my customary handwringing. My friend Al Avant turned the reference desk in the Language and Literature Department into something like a personal fiefdom. Al loved trash fiction as much as modernist poetry – definitely the right man for the job. He was a good example of what I might call the undivided self, and a good role model for my divided one. If on any particular day he was suffering from the effects of alcohol withdrawal, wooziness from antidepressants, and lingering anxiety from the fear of AIDS (of which he eventually died), he said so. I myself was merely trying to overcome my longstanding shyness. Having new, worldly, and sophisticated friends like Al over for dinner was a good place to start. He liked Lucy and Lucy liked him, although the presence of an adorable, rambunctious, and manifestly heterosexual little boy clearly discomfited him. Al just didn't give a damn, really. He was who he was. Lucy, in some ways, represented a more normative version of the same undividedness. Whatever demons tormented her (or us) at two in the morning, she could roll with just about anyone in just about any social situation. At a party with some artist friends of hers, a garrulous World War II veteran – the father of the hostess – discovered that she was from Manila, where he had been stationed during and after the war. Many inappropriate jests followed, the brunt of which was that Lucy might have been his daughter. Did she glower? Did she glare? Did she smile tightly and ask for the canapés? Actually, the old guy was pretty funny, and Lucy laughed heartily, but she would have treated him with the same deference even if his jokes had fallen flat. And when she had to deal with someone she disliked, she wasted no time in recrimination – unlike Al, who had an enemies list a mile long and was never funnier than when expiating upon it.

I especially liked the way she interacted with three of her coworkers, who sometimes played up their philistinism for comic effect but were really quite steady and competent. They came over a few times to help us paint the apartment, and we met once or twice at a garden party in Queens. Two were African-American, one was Polish-American, and all were utterly unlike her in background, interests, and inclinations. That's what made seeing them together so much fun. The three amigos played the lottery, shopped at Kmart, kept an eye on the Mets and Yankees, checked out women on the street – well, one of them did, and he was so openly a dog that Lucy couldn't help but laugh. She let them be their funny, streetwise, unaffected selves, and they let her be the architect that everyone deferred to without any egotism or grandstanding. One of them, I always suspected, was half in love with her. The other two were merely in awe. Her dealings with other architects, contractors, construction workers, electricians, and carpenters – all male and many gruffly macho – were another point of wonder with me, especially in later years, when she hired a crew to do some major work for us. All these terse, heavy-smoking, Eastern European guys with their impenetrable accents intimidated the hell out of me – I, for whom seventh and eighth grade shop class was unmitigated trauma. But here was Lucy confidently giving orders and conferring with the blunt, laconic foreman about where and when to "rock it" – meaning, not as I originally thought, celebrating a job well done, but installing a wall of sheet rock. All freely gave her the respect that I couldn't have won from them if I lived to be a thousand.

Lucy did some freelance commissions with one of the three amigos (she took care of the designs, he the business stuff) after she returned to work from her six months of maternity leave. Our childcare arrangements were so complicated that I couldn't possibly reconstruct them. Suffice it to say that after she had gone back to work and my sister (Jonathan's babysitter) back to Florida, we shuffled schedules to the extent possible and placed Jonathan in a local and massively expensive daycare center. Life suddenly got much, much harder, not least for a two-year old boy who deserved better than being hustled off to daycare five days a week. After about a year of this craziness and endless discussion regarding possible alternatives, Lucy decided to avail herself of additional maternity leave, which the city allowed its employees for up to five years. She would stay home with Jonathan three days a week and take him to daycare the other two, during which time she would work on her quilts and Jonathan would mix it up with the other kids at the daycare center, where they were well provided for and where, upon pick-up, the parents were solemnly informed in a report of the day's momentous events. ("Jonathan made pies out of play-dough with Barret, while Sarah . . . ") The only catch was money. We would be living on one exiguous salary rather than two, but the solution to that was simple enough – when we ran out of money (which happened, as I recall, in about a year), Lucy would go back to work.

Life did in fact get slightly easier with this arrangement, excepting for continuing "discussions" at two AM about my former crush Maria and other complications arising from my fecklessness – but also, I think, from the sheer difficulty of being alive. Neither of us was capable of taking things lightly. Maybe some of Lucy's frustrations derived not solely from my inadequacies but also from the ultimately tragic extinction of all our deepest hopes and dreams, which she indirectly laid at my door. Don't blame me, it's the world's fault. Oh, there was plenty of blame still to come, all of it richly deserved. Read on.

If the idea was for Lucy to create art two days a week, the stuff she did with Jonathan on the other three days (as well as weekends) was hardly less amazing. I've already mentioned the play-dough menagerie, but there were also costumes, watercolors, origami, flip books, panel paintings, and a series of mini graphic novels about "Tipple," Jonathan's imaginary mouse friend. He apprenticed with the best, and it shows. Certainly he didn't get any of his talent from me. My job was to bounce him on the bed and recount over and over again the plot from *Abbott and Costello Meet Frankenstein*, skills more within my wheelhouse. That movie, though he never saw it, made quite an impression. "Mommy," he would say excitedly, "draw me a picture of Wolfman fighting Dracula and Dracula turns into a bat and they crash out the window of the castle and Frankenstein crashes too." And she would.

I kept a record, with much photographic evidence, of all the Halloween costumes she made for him: a cheetah, a brontosaurus, Hercules, Sherlock Holmes, Spiderman, Superboy. His friends so coveted the last that we passed it on to others, and for a few years it could be seen on smaller boys and younger brothers in the Park Slope Halloween parade on Seventh Avenue. It may be moldering in someone's attic even as I write. Once we took him to the Greenwich Village Halloween parade – not a very kid-friendly experience, as we should have known, but he turned out to be one of the unwitting stars of the show. In photo albums possibly gathering dust in attics across the New York Metropolitan Area and beyond, there may well be found dozens of snapshots of little Jonathan perched on my shoulders as the world's most adorable cheetah.

The cheetah costume eventually got recycled into one of Lucy's quilts. With more time for her to experiment, her quilts were starting to approximate the abstract paintings she would soon take up. Although she never quite broke over in that market, now and then she would sell one for four hundred or five hundred dollars – a lot of money for us in those days. I used to jokingly suggest titles that would boost their market value: "Homage to Neil Young," "Breakfast of Champions," "In What Sense Can a Dog 'Know' Its Parents?" Sometimes, too, her work was shown in quilting exhibitions around the country – usually too far away for us to attend. One exception was a solo show in the office of David Dinkins, the Manhattan borough president, soon to be the mayor of New York. At the opening we nibbled cheese and crackers, and everyone marveled at the quilts, which had a grandeur when seen together, like a suite of Mark Rothko paintings without the despair. What I chiefly remember about that night, however, was the arrival of Dinkins himself, who made a few jokes and then hugged Lucy a bit too

– well, *intimately.* He passed that off as a joke too, and everyone laughed. They might not laugh today. But really, it was a very mild faux pas, and Lucy, being a *femme du monde,* took no great offense. Dinkins turned out to be a pretty decent mayor. Could he help it if the artist selected by his staff turned out to be such a dish?

David Dinkins was an elegant and classy gentleman. A rather less gentlemanly person once propositioned Lucy in a dismal waiting room in Penn Station, where we sat for a few minutes before boarding a train to New Jersey. I was reading to Jonathan from a few seats away when out of the corner of my eye I saw a rather shabby guy approach her and exchange a few words before hurriedly moving away. What was that all about? I asked her when we got on the train.

"He asked if he could sleep with me," she said.

"Wow. What did you say?"

"I said, 'Sure, just let me check with my husband, who's sitting over there.'"

So there we were, *nel mezzo del cammin di nostra vita*, with an enviable (if complicated) domestic life, a good place to live, decent jobs, no crushing financial burdens, and still very much in love. Wish I had appreciated it a little bit more. Don't it always seem to go, asked Joni Mitchell, that you don't know what you've got till it's gone? Yes it do. I remember a cool, clear, sunny day in early October at the Bronx Botanic Garden with the tupelos and dogwoods just starting to turn and Jonathan scarfing down French fries at the restored millhouse on the river that served as a cafeteria in those days. Wouldn't an outing like this be even nicer, I kept thinking, somewhere in the lower Hudson valley? New York City, as previously noted, was slowly emerging from its decline, but it still had a long way to go – the interminable, rackety, rerouted trip we had taken on the D train from Brooklyn to this garden proved that readily enough. So I started thinking about library jobs outside of the city.

I'd like to take this opportunity to apologize to all of those library directors and department heads whose valuable time I wasted in the late eighties and early nineties. I *thought* I was serious about my job prospects, but deep down I really didn't want to leave New York. Neither did Lucy. When I finally abandoned the pretense, New York was off life support and Jonathan a thoroughly formed city kid. The whole idea had been to provide him with a healthier environment, but were the suburbs really a healthier place for a child than Brooklyn, where his friends represented every ethnicity in the world and no one thought it odd that his parents didn't own a car or a washing machine? We stayed.

Nevertheless, a friend of ours, now living in Amherst, Massachusetts, made the case that "stepping over homeless people," as she put it, was not a life skill that she wanted to impart to her son, a much-missed former playmate of Jonathan's. With their example in mind, I applied for a job as a high school librarian in the nearby town of Ware and bombed at the interview. Oh well, that was one decision I wouldn't have to make. Yet the trip to Massachusetts in a rented car furnished the means for a happy little domestic adventure, as did one or two of my other ill-fated job interviews. In Massachusetts we visited our transplanted friends, hiked for a spell in the Quabbin Reservoir, failed to find Emily Dickinson's house, and back in our crummy hotel watched a television interview with Mario Vargas Llosa, then running for the presidency of Peru. (He lost, by the way.) I had botched the interview, but I didn't care. There was a lot of love in that hotel room.

Another job-related adventure transpired in my hometown. Since I had extremely mixed feelings about Westport,

Connecticut, I probably had no business applying for a job in the public library there, but I wanted Lucy and Jonathan to see the place where, to quote Philip Larkin, "my childhood was unspent." We took the train from Grand Central and Lucy and Jonathan puttered around downtown while I, perhaps deliberately, botched another interview. The head of reference was appealingly straightforward. Neither I nor anyone on the staff, she told me, could afford to live in Westport on their librarians' salaries; most had a spouse who made the real money. That was a wall I kept running into – the frank acknowledgement of the barely subsistence wages I could expect from a well-heeled town like Westport or an elite college like Sarah Lawrence. That institution, after a grueling round of interviews that I did not, for a change, screw up, peremptorily dismissed my candidacy upon being informed, as required, of my "salary requirements." I was asking for twenty thousand dollars.

No hard feelings. I was more remiss than any of the libraries to which I half-heartedly applied. Even when offered the job, as occasionally happened, I found pretexts to decline: insufficient vacation time or too many bureaucratic hurdles to leap. I especially regret having trifled with the staff of the State University of New York library at New Paltz, who took me out for a posh lunch and all of whom seemed as artsy and unstuffy as I could have wished. And maybe I should have taken more seriously the offer from the Hingham, Massachusetts Public Library. The director was in town to see an opera and pick up some books at the Strand. We met at the fountain at Lincoln Center, where, he pointed out, Nicholas Cage and Cher had their rendezvous in *Moonstruck*. Personally, I told him, I preferred the cinematic rendezvous of Jack Nicholson with a fellow mobster on the Brooklyn Heights promenade in *Prizzi's Honor*. Our interview took place in a coffee shop on Broadway. He didn't ask me for my "philosophy" of cataloging, and I didn't have to pretend to have one.

To the extent that I succumbed to the fantasy that Life Is Elsewhere, these pointless job interviews perpetuated an unhealthy strain of magical thinking. Fortunately, the sheer impossibility of relocating – of finding, with next to no savings, decent jobs for two people, an affordable home, a car, a new daycare center, and so on – grounded me in necessary realities. And yet the temptation to what the French philosopher and literary critic René Girard called "metaphysical desire" was always there. (Metaphysical desire: the belief that someone else always has what you want, until you get it, and then you don't want it anymore.) One of the assignments I was then working on for my *World Authors* reference books was that of the novelist Louise Erdrich. I was supposed to compose an objective overview of her work to that date and the critical reception of it rather than impose upon the reader the question I kept asking myself: Gee, wouldn't it be nice to have a life like that? Barely in her mid-thirties, she was the author of three acclaimed works of fiction, the inheritor of a rich and storied Native American ancestry, as beautiful as a fashion model, and so much in love with her husband that she wrote dedications like, "For Michael: complice in every deed, essential as air." It was only with some difficulty that I could imagine her taking out the garbage or arguing with the clerks at the Motor Vehicle Department – very foolish of me, as I knew, but such was the insidious contagion of metaphysical desire. According to Girard in *Deceit, Desire, and the Novel,* everybody in the modern world was infected. Everybody, to one degree or another, envied someone else who envied someone else who envied someone else. But here the theory broke down. Lucy never envied anyone.

Louise Erdrich was the least of it. There was also the Paul Auster Problem. The subject of yet another reference article of mine (this one my critique of his work commissioned for a book called *Contemporary Novelists),* Auster lived a block away from us – I knew exactly where because, once I began escorting Jonathan to and from the local elementary school, I used to pass him almost every day, as he escorted his son to the local prep school. Sometimes we sat at adjacent tables at Pino's Pizzeria, treating our boys to an afterschool snack. The scenario was almost too much like a Paul Auster novel to be believed: the unknown writer for reference books continually crossing paths with the famous, broodingly handsome novelist, who never notices him and remains entirely unaware that the first writer has composed a fawningly adulatory analysis of his oeuvre for an obscure reference book. What saved me from metaphysical despair was the dawning realization that maybe he wasn't quite the genius I had first taken him for. It shouldn't have mattered one way or another. It did.

My younger sister, who used to see him around the neighborhood, thought Paul Auster was to die for. Lucy never got around to reading him. Her favorite contemporary novelist, incredibly, was Philip Roth. Yes, she understood that Roth had a little trouble depicting fully rounded female characters. Feminist polemics would simply have to yield to Roth's wit, energy, inventiveness, and brio. I used to hope that her fascination with Roth's wayward male protagonists might translate into a somewhat more sympathetic attitude toward her husband's own errancy, but that would be to mistake literature for life. Lucy made her share of mistakes. That, unfortunately, wasn't one of them.

René Girard implied that the cure for metaphysical desire was belief in God. He also decried the tendency of moderns to make Gods of their fellow mortals. Although I wouldn't profess belief in God if you put a gun to my head, neither did I deify Lucy. Boy, was she human: loving, impatient, empathic, unforgiving, steadfast, loyal, angry, generous, guilt-ridden, and with a tendency (which always turned me on) to perspire slightly in warmish weather. When we first fell in love I wanted to show her off, and I even considered attending my wretched high school reunion with her as arm candy, but that would have been to succumb to the promptings of metaphysical desire. The cure for that disease wasn't God, it was love. I don't know if I'll ever be wholly cured, and I wouldn't even say that Lucy – as opposed to another wise, loving and endearingly imperfect woman – was uniquely equipped to heal me. But all those years of loving her made me a better person: kinder, happier, more accepting. Less metaphysical.

12

[T]hough the vast majority of the world's inhabitants may organize themselves into permanent and semi-permanent arrangements of two, even the most cursory cross-cultural glance reveals that the particulars of these arrangements vary greatly. In our own day and part of the globe, they take the form of what historians of private life have labeled the "companionate couple," voluntary associations based (at least in principle) on intimacy, mutuality, and equality; falling in love as the prerequisite to a lifelong commitment that unfolds in conditions of shared domesticity, the expectation of mutual sexual fulfillment. And by the way, you will have sex with this person and this person alone for the rest of eternity.

If the above paragraph, from Laura Kipnis's bracingly unillusioned polemic *Against Love,* reads, for present purposes, like a pre-emptive rationalization of my faithlessness, that's because it is. I'll spare the details, out of mercy for the reader no less than for myself; my cluelessness and self-absorption can be imagined readily enough. Perhaps I can sum up the mess I made by rephrasing Edith Piaf's famously self-assertive motto as a more realistic appraisal of the little defeats we manage to inflict on ourselves and others: *Je regrette tout.*

At various times in my life I've tried to make myself believe in Friedrich Nietzsche's concept of *amor fati* – "that one wants nothing to be different, not forward, not backward, not in all eternity. Not merely bear what is necessary, still less conceal it . . . but *love* it." All my mistakes, missteps, delusions, and gaucheries have brought me to this moment, have made me who and what I am no less than their opposites. It's such a beautiful idea. Too bad I had to trample over Lucy's feelings to get here.

A guy screws around, his wife finds out, what more is there to say? Quite a lot. Fortunately, I'm not going to say it. With or without my slippages – not many and never concealed or equivocated – Lucy would have fallen out of love with me. She was worldly enough to know that a man (or woman) might succumb to temptation. We might have lasted a few more years without the additional damage caused by my infidelity, but probably not. There are many other ways to screw up. I seem to have discovered most of them.

Unlike Laura Kipnis, I'm wildly in favor of love, but she certainly put her finger on a real problem. Fidelity is *hard*. It exacts a cost. The alternative, admittedly, exacts an even greater cost, as my case proves, but as with every problem, the first step toward a solution is acknowledging its existence. That may be why I find the solution proposed by Saint Paul – "it is better to marry than to burn" – so profoundly unsatisfactory. You can't "contain," said Paul, so you get married and find, contra the good saint, that you *still* can't contain. The problem of other bodies and wayward desires remains exactly where it was. One common understanding of the problem is to say that the erring partner (let's call him Stephen) is "acting out" rather than bravely confronting the character flaws that compel such behavior in the first place, or seeking extrinsic satisfactions for the lack of intrinsic ones. But "Stephen," in this case, never bought into those pious explanations. His motives were, at once, more squalid and less so.

So what hidden wells of self-loathing and marital discontent led me down the primrose path of dalliance? None. Or none that I can see. Sometimes a cigar is just a cigar and sometimes sex is (mostly or partly or at any rate not delusionally) just sex. Ascribing an unconscious psychological motivation to our every desire hardly does justice to the anarchic force of human sexuality. Why should I stray? I lacked for nothing in that department. In fact, my handful of encounters with other women were much like my encounters with Lucy – very exciting but without the tenderness. Truly, it was better at home, except (this being the whole point) that it *wasn't* at home. I thought Lucy would be O.K. with my having a few meaningless clasps under my belt. Initially, she tried to understand, then gave way to her fury. Of course, I stopped when I saw the harm I was causing. What a guy.

Once, a few years earlier, we had met a bunch of Lucy's International House friends at Carnegie Hall for a recital by the pianist Rudolf Serkin. Walking to a café after the performance, I ended up talking with a very attractive married friend of Lucy's named Carmen. An evening of Beethoven sonatas in that august temple (even if we sat in the last row of the balcony) was not something a lowlife like me could take for granted, and maybe a faint hint of Carmen's delicate perfume turned my head slightly. Anyway, we got separated from the crowd, so that when we realized our mistake and later found our friends and spouses settled around a big table in the café, there was some ribald jesting (what have *you* two been up to har har har) at our expense. All in good fun, and Carmen and I had discussed nothing more alarming than the development of Beethoven's piano music, about which I knew virtually nothing. And yet a man, a woman, and a swirl of perfume . . . Something was calling to me beyond the jesting voices in the café and certainly beyond the entirely innocent conversation of Carmen, an accomplished musician who, for all I know, considered our rambling tête-á-tête the most tedious five minutes of her life.

It's never a good sign when you start hearing voices in your head. One voice, emanating from somewhere deep within my psyche, urged me on to more life, more feeling, more experience, more – to be blunt – sex. A second voice, not so deep but a lot clearer, told the first voice to shut the hell up. I listened to the first voice. And there was a third voice that I heard every time I switched on a television or opened a magazine or passed by a department store window display. This was the voice of American consumer culture, emanating from the great ozone but vibrating to tuning forks implanted in my head. I remember seeing a movie poster in the subway stations around that time showing a beautiful, half-dressed couple half copulating on the beach. Lucy and I were an attractive young couple but we didn't look like *that*, and if we made love outdoors it didn't happen on a tropical beach. Sex sells – no news there. But consumerism works in part by selling you images of your own inadequacy, and although Lucy and I paid little or no attention to the blockbuster movies and TV shows that enthralled most of America, the same images and noises bombarded us as everyone else. As usual, she dealt with the ramifications better than I did, shutting out the worst ugliness but enjoying a bawdy B-52's song as much as the next person. At any rate, she didn't need to fornicate with a third party to obtain the blessing of more life, or the illusion thereof. Having been exposed, unlike her, to mass culture from earliest childhood, I was easier prey. To give Laura Kipnis and other disbelievers in monogamy their due, I did enjoy my few indulgences in extracurricular "activities." It couldn't have been all inadequacy and bad faith – just enough to haunt me forever.

This mess went on for a few years, I'm sorry to say. For a while, I thought I could have it both ways, so I tried negotiating. When you agree to no secrets, there's a lot to negotiate. In fact, what infuriated Lucy far more than my very few infidelities was my continuing hankering, as she saw it, for my adolescent crush Maria. The former merely betrayed her bodily, the latter betrayed her spiritually. To the end of our days I could never persuade her that I harbored no such hankering. Sacrificing that friendship – indeed, making a lifelong enemy of someone I once held dear – made no practical difference. For months – years! – that name would come up and round about midnight we would revert to our attack/defense mode for the next two or three or four hours. After the tears and the avowals and the make-up sex, we were back pretty much where we started. It's small consolation to say that, in regard to any conscious designs on Maria that Lucy imputed to me, she was wrong and I was right. You can be wrong by being right. I was the master of it.

Part of the problem was language. They're just words, Lucy used to tell me after some of my more ardent professions of love and atonement. You talk and talk and talk but nothing changes. Well, yes, they were just words – on the one hand, a pathetically inadequate toolkit for the hopeless tasks of representing complex, extra-linguistic realities, and, more specifically, of appeasing Lucy's wrath. On the other hand, I thought and still think (maybe because I'm a writer) that words are the most important and beautiful things we have. Funny how this debate, the one about words versus things, language versus reality – the one that thinkers have been wrestling with from Plato to Wallace Stevens (Lucy's favorite poet) – played out in our relationship. I could say that our arguments reified certain key issues in the philosophy of language. Or I could say that Lucy sometimes felt like ripping my head off.

If I hadn't been the cause of it, Lucy's fury might have been almost funny. I will refrain from quoting some of her more colorful execrations, which wouldn't have been out of place in a few of the Philip Roth novels she was then reading. I myself had no cause to execrate Lucy, but what if she had followed my grievous example? What if, to relieve the pressure or satisfy her curiosity or from whatever other motives, she had chosen to have a meaningless fling or two? I was guilty of everything else; I wasn't guilty of hypocrisy. If she wanted or needed the female equivalent of getting her rocks off, she was welcome to it, and I said so. It might even have been sort of . . . *interesting*. It might also have wounded my soul exactly as I had wounded hers. I never had to find out. In the midst of all this wreckage, our desire for each other never flickered.

All of this, I'm aware, makes our life sound like an Ingmar Bergman movie, with the lovers offering up their souls one moment and flaying each other alive the next. And there were indeed some bad nights, when the make-up sex didn't happen and I woke up after three hours of restless sleep on the living room sofa. Once Lucy called me up at work to take the blame for the previous night's debacle. I nearly dropped the phone. She almost never apologized – admittedly, I had a lot more to apologize for. Normally, she showed her love in less dramatic fashion, principally by remaining so supportive and demonstrative and affectionate. Even with all the Ingmar Bergman stuff in the background, the foreground was still our little empire of nuzzling and private jokes and raccoon love. Ordinary life, blessedly, went on.

I was of two minds about ordinary life: one, it got a little boring sometimes, and two, the mere fact of being alive, of sipping orange juice in the morning, of hearing Lucy's calm, familiar voice, of watching our child sleep, of breathing in the fragrance of the blossoming linden trees in city parks in June, of feeling the slight lift of an uphill sidewalk under my sneakers – all that was so miraculous that any dream of "transcendence" instantly became otiose. I now incline wholeheartedly to the second view, but all the same it was a healthy thing to exchange our daily routine once or twice a year for vacations in Vermont and Florida. Furthermore, although we loved/hated New York in just about the right proportion, 365 days of it were altogether too much. Hearing the crickets and seeing the night sky became even more important once Jonathan was able to walk, but even before then Lucy and I had used our visits to my father and mother as occasions to reconnect with the earth and with each other. Less grandly, those visits also furnished the occasion to take advantage of some freely offered babysitting.

A photo never taken: we were climbing Mount Hunger in the Green Mountains one September in the 1980s. As we hauled ourselves up over the rocks on the approach to the summit, I looked down a few yards at Lucy in her jeans and work shirt just as she was looking up, a smile on her face, the mountain winds whipping her hair, the whole Champlain Valley spread out below her. Christ! To be blown off the mountain would have been a fair trade-off for the ecstasy I felt in that moment. I suppose there's more to be known of human happiness than was given to me then and there, but I don't particularly want to know it. Just wish I had remembered to pack the damn camera.

I did remember to pack the camera on another hike, this one on a rare trip to Vermont in winter. In the deep snow drifts of January, I led Lucy to a high bank on an oxbow curve of the Winooski River where I used to tumble as a child and where my friend Sean gleefully destroyed the nests of a colony of bank swallows after slaughtering tadpoles by the dozens with his BB gun. (I once killed a barn swallow with that BB gun. I think it's the worst thing I've ever done. Readers of this book might beg to differ.) Before crossing the river by foot, we stopped for a photo opportunity, with me standing on the river just off the bank and Lucy snapping the picture from a few feet above. And there it is, in one of the twelve or thirteen photo albums I keep in a cedar chest: Stephen grinning into the camera and standing next to the inscription he had carved into the snow with a stick: "STEVE HATES LUCY." For readers convinced of my adamantine puerility, this anecdote will serve as a sufficient indictment of the subconscious motivations I have never understood or as an apt premonition of our tragic undoing. Actually, Lucy thought it was pretty funny. I could have drawn a heart with an arrow through it but, I don't know, "STEVE HATES LUCY" just seemed more romantic.

Our hikes through northern forests and southern bottomlands were often pretty tough, but not tougher than Lucy. She had no sense of direction (I navigated – someone had to), but cheerfully accepted a certain amount of mud, sweat, and discomfort in exchange for the exhilarating sense of expansion she felt in those sacred spaces no less than I did. Whenever possible we got off our feet and into a canoe – she powered from the bow, I pulled and steered from the stern. I can't imagine many people remaining as calm as she did on one of our paddling trips on the Myakka River in Florida, which took us way beyond the parkland visited by most tourists. Huge beds of invasive water hyacinth forced us to navigate through narrow channels that gave us very little room to maneuver away from the alligators sunning themselves on the banks. During one especially tight stretch, four or five sizeable gators slipped successively off the bank and under the water just in front of the prow, where Lucy sat negotiating the current. "Uh, Lucy," I suggested, "maybe it wouldn't be a good idea to look down just now." Slightly disconcerted but unwavering, she sailed steadily through.

The alligators took some getting used to. Not so the Florida scrub jays, which we sought out on the arid prairies of Oscar Scherer State Park, one of the last refuges of that highly endangered species. No luck – until, unexpectedly, just as we were about to return to the car, there they were, half a dozen or more, hopping about inquisitively with their long blue tails and raspy chatter. They seemed especially curious about Lucy. What a treat. Here was one of the rarest songbird species in North America, and they were virtually perching on her shoulders. Yes! Even the scrub jays were in love with Lucy.

Because I was much closer to my mother than my father, we extended our visits to Sarasota and enjoyed ourselves most when just lolling around. Lucy taught my mother to do needlepoint and bravely consumed the boiled vegetables and flavorless potatoes that constituted Peg's home cooking. One night my sister and I were comparing stretching exercises on the plush living room carpet when three-year-old Jonathan interceded with his version of toddler aerobics. Much laughter and hugging ensued. As I lay there on the floor, sweating slightly and surrounded by the four people in the world I most loved, I tried to think of a philosophical formulation that might account for this blissful feeling of egoless serenity, but all I could come up with was what my mother would have said: It was very nice.

Not so nice was a return trip from the Ding Darling Wildlife Refuge on Sanibel Island, a two-hour ride in a rented car on Highway 75. Lucy, who had never learned to drive, read the *New York Times* to me on the way down. On the way back, after a long day of canoeing and hiking, she slept soundly in the passenger seat. Thus she was unaware that a crazed redneck in a pickup truck, who apparently didn't like seeing an Asian woman with a white man, was following us neck and neck at high speed for sixty miles, leering at her from his open window and addressing obscenities to me that I took care not to acknowledge. Failing to get a rise, he eventually gave up and peeled off to threaten someone else. I told her the whole story when we got back, but I don't think it completely registered. She had slept through the only incident of overt racial harassment we ever experienced. On a subsequent trip to Corkscrew Swamp Sanctuary, when we ended up on what seemed to be a road to nowhere distinguished only by the extraordinary number of vultures roosting in bare trees, I thought it advisable to leave Lucy in the car when I pulled into a roadhouse to ask for directions. It was not yet eleven AM and the locals were already getting tanked up. Yep, Corkscrew Swamp was thataway. Or maybe it was the other way. Or maybe it wasn't nowhere at all and I was in the wrong state. What do you say, Frankie? Frankie, or someone else, eventually did me the kindness of directing me properly. Perhaps the only prejudice here was mine. Even so, I was relieved that the barflies hadn't seen the young Chinese woman waiting in the car.

Should I have got into a bar fight with Frankie and his friends? Not my style, obviously, and nothing repelled Lucy more than displays of assertive masculinity. Although our sexual orientation was wholly binary, living with Lucy challenged any lingering notions I might have of conventional gender roles. Fortunately, I didn't have many of those. My generally soft-spoken, reflective demeanor resonated with her; indeed, she loved me for it. The one traditional masculine trait she might have liked to see more of was confidence – not, alas, one of my strong suits. In my post-Lucy years, I've discovered I can go toe to toe with raging macho assholes. Not long ago I cleared a subway car by getting into a shouting match with one such guy;

maybe he thought the raging macho asshole was me. Which reminds me of one of Lucy's finest moments. A relative of mine was lecturing his young son on the prerogatives and obligations of masculinity.

"Now, what do you do," he asked, "if a boy hits you?"

"You hit him back harder," came the trained reply.

"That's right," he continued. "And what do you do if a girl hits you?"

"You never hit a girl!"

"How about you never hit anyone?" said Lucy quietly.

I hope it wasn't masculine overcompensation that lead me, in my fifth or sixth year with Lucy, to the rediscovery of my adolescent passion, basketball. But no, playing that glorious game – a Bach cantata with bodies moving in intricate patterns around an airborne object – entailed no motivation more complex than the sheer exhilaration of running up and down the court, even when getting outgunned, more often than not, by players, bigger, stronger, faster, and a hundred times more athletic than I. In one of the leagues I joined, the girlfriends of some of the younger players came along to cheer on their menfolk from the sideline. Golly – I liked to imagine them thinking – weren't these grunting, sweating, half-naked guys with their three-day stubble just *hunks?* Lucy never saw me play. Her frank indifference to my athletic endeavors charmed me more than any cheerleading could have. Fine, I'm glad you like the game, she said (in so many words), just don't expect me to pretend to any interest in it, and no, I don't think men look as irresistible in their basketball shorts as they think they do. On the other hand, she understood that if I couldn't play the game like a maniac, there was no point in playing at all. She brought the same intensity to everything she did, but she went about it so quietly that many people never noticed.

That's how she learned to ride a bicycle: with quiet intensity. I taught Jonathan; I could have taught her. Characteristically, she chose to do it her way, which meant enrolling in a class for adult learners taught by a young Chinese man in Riverside Park. During her sheltered upbringing in the family compound in Manila she had never acquired that skill. Lucy was not one to go easy on herself, and learning to ride a bicycle as an adult is not easy at all. Even after a summer of lessons with Michael Chang, she always wobbled a bit going uphill, and getting started was even harder. Once, a bunch of schoolkids saw her struggling up the steep hill approaching Grand Army Plaza in Prospect Park and made a few passing comments. It was useless to tell her that kids will be kids. She was furious, and barked at me instead of them. Did Lucy push herself too hard, was there something self-punishing in her tireless exertions? I knew a couple of people who thought so. Here I believe I can assert a counter proposition with confidence: they were wrong. They didn't see the simple pleasure she took in her art and other endeavors, they couldn't understand the existential imperative of all that making and doing. If she was too hard on anyone, it wasn't herself; it was me. Without saying so, she expected me to be as focused, as disciplined, as driven as she. I wasn't, and never could be. She did, nonetheless, make me demand more of myself. I hate to think what a slacker I might have been without her. Anyway, learning to ride a bicycle in her thirties wasn't merely (or only) a trial undertaken subconsciously to propitiate her ferocious mother; it was *fun*. We took many a turn around Prospect Park, Jonathan and I accompanying her on our rollerblades, sometimes skating backwards to stay even with her. That too was driven, hyper-motivated Lucy: a little leery of her balance but riding her newly acquired bicycle with the innocent pleasure of a child and having at least as much fun as the two show-offs zooming around her.

It would have been lovely to bicycle in Florida, but somehow all I remember is canoeing over alligators and conversing with scrub jays. Those vacations were so relaxing that coming back to New York always felt like a bit of a shock. Everything was so much harder here, and the taxi ride from Newark or LaGuardia Airport so astoundingly dismal. Within a day or two I would get my rhythm back, and although I continued to explore employment possibilities elsewhere, my heart wasn't in it. All three of us, whether we realized it or not, were confirmed New Yorkers. Once Jonathan reached the second or third grade, we were anchored.

Jonathan got a pretty decent and very touchy-feely education at P.S. 321 in Park Slope, and Lucy and I got something even better: friends. We had been friendly with some of the parents in Jonathan's daycare centers, but this was different. I had to spend a lot of time waiting for him outside the schoolyard each day and in the process I met some like-minded parents whose friendship I had time to cultivate. And I had the time because of a detail I omitted to mention: in August 1989, I quit my job at the Brooklyn Public Library. My ostensible motive was to care for Jonathan outside of his half-day kindergarten class and to make some money from my freelance reference writing, but a deeper motive was simply to give myself a sabbatical, since no one else was going to. Nice while it lasted, but of course we ran out of money and I went back to the Cataloging Department a few months later as a part-timer while continuing my reference writing. By then I had made the friends that would constitute the nucleus of the little neighborhood social circle that in those years made Park Slope seem like a Norman Rockwell village with subway stations and lesbian bars. I couldn't step out to pick up a quart of milk without running into someone I knew. Not that Lucy and I idealized the place excessively; it was starting to become very, very expensive. And our neighbors still hated us.

Such literary dreams as I had came mostly to naught in my five months of reprieve from regular employment, except for one article in *The New Republic* ("McLibraries," 26 February 1990) that caused something of a stir. I mention this only because the episode presented me with a question I would have preferred to avoid, to wit, Did I want to become a "name," even if a small one? It wouldn't have been that hard. Every subculture has its niches to be filled. With my *New Republic* article critiquing the radical dumbing down of public library acquisition policies, followed by an op-ed piece on the same subject that I wrote for the *Washington Post,* I had suddenly become something of a hot property in the small of world of public libraries. Would I agree to debate the director of the Baltimore County Public Library System on National Public Radio? Yes. Would I accept the invitation to speak at the annual conference of the Washington State Library Association? No. If I had written a few more articles, attended a few more conferences, networked with a few other dissidents, I could have been the go-to guy, Mr. Stephen "McLibraries" Akey, on the not-so burning issue of the cultural and educational responsibilities of public libraries. But it all seemed so dreary. Although I believed enough in the mission of public libraries to write several articles (and later a book) about it, I couldn't see myself as a respectable spokesperson for anything or anyone. No doubt my abnegation looks like a classic fear of success, with which I was almost wholly unacquainted. After all, Philip Larkin, whose magnificently discomfiting poetry I had recently discovered, managed to have it both ways, being, as he was, one of the leading figures of British librarianship on the one hand and a fearless explorer of the inner life on the other. Yet even if the conflict was all in my head, I reasoned that I would do better to err on the side of love and domesticity, especially given my recent and spectacular failures in that arena.

Around the time that Charles Robinson, the Baltimore County library director, and I were bloviating like a pair of windbags with Diane Rehm on her National Public Radio program, I had a colloquy with Jonathan from the perspective of two pterodactyls, he the old hand, I the new kid on the block. I have transcripts of both conversations, the one with Charles Robinson about the commercialization of public libraries, the one with Jonathan about neighborhood prospects for friendly dinosaurs. It's no contest.

STEPHEN: Hey, I'm new around here. Are there any dangerous dinosaurs around?

JONATHAN: No. Yes. The worst is tyrannosaurus. The next baddest is dienonychus. The next baddest is allosaurus. The next baddest is I don't know how to say their names.

STEPHEN: Are there any friendly ones?

JONATHAN *(casually)*: Oh, yes. Brontosaurus and diplodocus. The one with three horns is good too, triceratops. He fights tyrannosaurus with his horns. Dad, don't ask me any more questions about other dinosaurs.

STEPHEN: Are there any exploding volcanos nearby?

JONATHAN *(reflectively)*: Well, some. No, they're not . . . the volcanos . . . some volcanos, well . . . They're sixteen hundred miles away!

STEPHEN: Wow, that's far away! Did you ever get any lava on you?

JONATHAN: Me? Oh, no, I just flew up past it.

STEPHEN: Hey, what do you eat around here?

JONATHAN: Me? Oh, I just dive down for fish. Pretend the quilt is the ocean, Dad.

STEPHEN *(swimming)*: Didn't a tylosaurus ever get you?

JONATHAN: I'm not afraid. I just hit it with my wings.

13

Being a librarian, I had for some time deeply involved myself with reference books – cataloging them, annotating them, explicating them, writing for them, even occasionally reading them. It's one of the things that most dates me; *Wikipedia* will always seem to me an impoverished, colorless, and less than trustworthy substitute for the exhaustive, ingenious, eccentric, and now mostly forgotten reference works of yore: Kane's *Famous First Facts, The Encyclopedia of Associations, The Baseball Almanac, The Statesman's Yearbook, Brewer's Dictionary of Phrase and Fable, The Statistical Abstract of the United States.* For three years I had ransacked these and hundreds of other indispensable volumes for our demanding and sometimes rather trying patrons in the Telephone Reference Division of the Brooklyn Public Library. One of those indispensable volumes was *Who's Who of American Women* (Marquis Who's Who, 1988), where, in the sixteenth edition, a long and detailed entry may be found for "KUNG, LUCY HA, quilt artist; designer." I'd love to transcribe it, but I'll limit myself to what I consider the key datum: "m. Stephen Michael Akey, Jan. 9, 1981." We didn't buy a copy; Lucy was self-conscious about owning one, and it wasn't cheap. However, perusing the copy held at my former place of employment, the New York Public Library at Forty-second Street, I'm reminded that Lucy was the architecture editor of her college magazine; that she was the assistant to the senior partner ("asst. to sr. ptnr.") at her architectural firm in the Philippines; that she had exhibited her prints at a group show in the Brooklyn Museum and her quilts at the New England Quilt Museum; and that she made me look like a chump.

It's no accident that the people at Marquis Who's Who solicited Lucy, not me. But if they had, I would have been ready:

AKEY, STEPHEN MICHAEL, librarian; guitarist; b. Norwalk, CT, Sept. 22, 1955; m. Lucy Ha Kung, Jan. 9, 1981; 1 child, Jonathan; B.A., U Connecticut, 1978; M.L.S., Columbia U., 1979; postgrad Columbia U., 1982-1984; librarian, Brooklyn and New York Public Libraries, 1979- ; promoted, 1982; demoted, 1984; public school teacher, Brooklyn, N.Y., Sept. 1984-Sept. 1984; graduate, Mel Bay Home Study Guitar Method, 1985 (presentation piece: "Powderfinger" by N. Young); small forward/ shooting guard, Never Too Late Basketball League, 1989- ; Democrat. Membership: Bronx Zoological Society (family/student discount). Home/studio: Brooklyn, N.Y. 11215. Quotation: "Ask a hog what is happening. Go on. Ask him" – J. Ashbery.

In the next few years Lucy could have bulked up her *Who's Who* entry substantially, with accumulating distinctions as an architect and artist, but she never bothered again. As for me, the only way I was ever going to be listed in reference books was to write for them, which I had been doing as a freelancer for a number of years. In fact, I was starting to get slightly sick of reference writing, so that when the editor of a multi-volume project to be called *World Authors 1900-1950* asked for my participation, I thought about it, then politely declined. A few days later I got another call: if I wasn't interested in freelancing, would I consider a full-time staff position? Indeed I would. After passing a fairly grueling trial period, which required absenting myself from Lucy and Jonathan for much of the next month, I resigned once again from the Brooklyn Public Library. I couldn't have planned it better, and I hadn't planned a thing.

I got unsick of reference writing fast – a good thing, given that I was to spend the next five years at it. Contracted to compose readable and reliable articles on major, minor, or barely reputable writers of that period, I became expert at writing within a formula while concealing the formula. Some people, I suppose, would call it hack work; I think it was better training than any M.F.A. program, and I'm no less proud of my articles on Fyodor Gladkov (didactic Soviet novelist) and Royal Cortissoz (reactionary art critic) than of my articles on Dawn Powell and Wallace Stevens. Who ever (if anyone) read these articles was not my concern; I was being paid the equivalent of my librarian's salary (no benefits or pension) to be able to say casually, "Oh, I write," when asked what I did for a living. Since then I've written a few books and a fair number of essays, but I've never been able to make the same claim.

Whatever my staff position with the H. W. Wilson Publishing Company did for my confidence, it did more for my skills in household management. I met my editor a few times a month at the Forty-second Street Library, but mostly I worked from home. The timing, which corresponded with Jonathan's elementary school years, couldn't have been better. With Lucy still commuting to her office in lower Manhattan, I no longer had any excuses. The shopping, the cooking, the cleaning, the laundry, and most importantly the shepherding of a young boy to and from his school, with all the additional after-school, sick, and vacation time, were now largely my responsibility. Yes, I *would* like an award, except that early on Lucy had done far more than her share of all of that stuff. I was just making up for lost time – hers.

The cooking worried me a bit. Grilled cheese sandwiches and scrambled eggs would get us only so far. Basically, I learned by imitating Lucy. My staple was a variant of her stir-fried vegetables over rice or noodles. She used a wok, I a frying pan, the difference being that her meals tasted like authentic Chinese cuisine, mine like the stuff you get from an inferior take-out, without the additives. Still, most nights I provided a reasonably nutritious, substantial dinner, with the table set and the mess cleaned up before Lucy walked through the door. For serious occasions – birthdays, special guests, and so on – she took over. Although I never liked cooking and got through it only by playing very loud rock and roll music, I enjoyed being the house husband, chiefly for the pleasure of confounding expectations. When my mother arrived for her annual visit from Florida, I cooked her exactly the sort of soggy chicken casserole that she loved.

"Lucy, that was such a delicious meal," she said. "You're such a good cook."

"Mom, Lucy didn't cook it, I did," I said.

"Honestly, Lucy, I don't know how you do it. You work so hard all day and then you come home and cook us such a nice meal."

"Hey Mom, I cooked the friggin' meal, OK? What do I have to do to prove it – chop off my finger for you?"

My mother's culinary primitivism only endeared her all the more to Lucy and to me. She liked dining out, but since she didn't eat ethnic food and since virtually all the restaurants in Park Slope were ethnic, we struggled to find a suitable bill of fare. Lucy discovered the solution at a cozy Italian/Cajun' restaurant on Second Street that offered a promising honey glazed spiced chicken. We'll have that, she told the waitress, but could they hold the honey? And the glazes? And the spices? The waitress obligingly brought out a heap of plain boiled poultry for my mother, while Lucy and Jonathan and I had our usual jambalaya and catfish. Peg was thrilled, and I got to play Link Wray and the Ronettes on the house jukebox.

I don't claim that Lucy required any mothering from Peg. Lucy had a mother, whom she loved in a very complicated way. Nevertheless, it couldn't have hurt, being so far from her own family, to have a mother-in-law so rapturously admiring of her. It was easy for Lucy to make the little accommodations for Peg's comfort that she would have made for (almost) any other guest, but she made more of them for Peg. One of my responsibilities during those visits was to accompany my mother to mass on Sunday, which I relished for the chance to take in the architecture of Park Slope's exquisite (and severely under-attended) Catholic churches. (I once jokingly offered to receive communion; she wasn't amused.) Lucy had a harder job; she had to find a beauty salon able to accommodate the stylistic preferences of a silver-haired grandmother from Florida. That would have seemed an even less likely possibility than finding bland American food in a Park Slope restaurant, but she came through. Tucked inside a limestone rowhouse on Sixth Avenue and Third Street was a little Russian salon where they spoke the same stylistic language as my mother: 1950's suburban Moscow! Lucy waited in a chair reading a magazine while Peg luxuriated under the blow dryer.

My mother died and Lucy divorced me. I love life; I just wish it weren't quite so overwhelmingly, unrelentingly, inhumanly hard. When life was at its hardest – the last unhappy years of our marriage, with my mother now in a nursing home – I had no consolation but this, though it was a major one: that Lucy bore my filial grief with unstinting compassion. She bore very little else; all my other worries, she made it clear, were my concern, not hers. Furthermore, if I felt wounded by her apparent coldness, she briskly dispelled any illusions I might have about the cause of all this sorrow. I, and I alone – don't delude yourself, Stephen – was responsible. Also, the coldness wasn't apparent; it was real. Lucy owned up to moments of irritability that she wasn't proud of. That was really the only concession she allowed me. She had, she said, grown harder, more impatient over the years. Maybe that would have happened anyway, but I speeded up the process.

Nevertheless, when I came back guilty and heartsick every Saturday from that long train ride to the nursing home in New Jersey, I knew I could unburden myself to the person in the world I most needed in those moments. Lucy just listened, which was all I wanted, or let me cry, which I sometimes did. That lovely old woman, slowly losing her mind and dying by inches in a nursing home! Lucy grieved with me, or through me. But when, too many years later, my mother's death finally came as the blessing it was, I grieved alone.

I always thought my family was very good to Lucy, and she to them. I myself hadn't had to pass the son- or brother-in-law test. That changed in 1990. Twelve years after saying goodbye to her parents and seven siblings, Lucy finally said hello to one of them – the youngest, Tommy, the manager of a McDonalds in Manila, who was stopping off in New York on his way home from mandatory training at Hamburger University in Illinois. She did more than say hello; she cried when she met him at Kennedy Airport and cried again when she saw him off. Their reunion was all the more touching in that they scarcely knew each other. Lucy had been a rising young architect, Tommy an innocent junior high school student, when she stepped on that airplane in Manila. He was still pretty innocent. During his week-long visit, he placidly reminisced with his sister, played with Jonathan, watched our rarely used TV, and followed us wherever we led him around the city. We never had an easier guest.

Watching Lucy with Tommy, and in the years to come with three of her other siblings, I had two leading thoughts: one, she was just like them; and, two, she wasn't anything like them. Although thought number two prevailed, there was something clannish about the Kungs. In the first place, all the children had to deal with their larger-than-life mother, about whom she and Tommy spoke at great length. I think Lucy found it comforting to learn, as an adult, that each of her brothers and sisters had a greater or lesser *agon* with Brave Orchid; hers differed only in degree, not kind. Also, since they had been raised in what they called a "compound," with servants and cooks and drivers (luxuries long since surrendered in the wake of financial insolvency), the children had created something like a secret society, one with its own language, a pidgin of Fukienese, Mandarin, and Tagalog. Not much of the family pidgin remained, but I loved the private names the siblings used for their eldest sister, "Tsetsi" and "Hong-a," meaning, in fact, "eldest sister." And yet, hearing them speak those names with such affection, I thought a better translation might be something like, "You Are My Eldest Sister And I Too Am Slightly In Awe Of You."

Tommy was much given to Jackie Chan movies, a subject entirely unknown to his eldest sister but one that his American brother-in-law could and did discuss with avidity. (We bonded over Jackie Chan; whatever else Tommy thought of me, he knew I couldn't have been a complete stiff.) That lacuna pretty well typified Lucy's relationship with her family – none of them had any interest in her interests, she had none in theirs. Practical, business-minded, and apolitical, the Kungs tended scrupulously to their own gardens. How this one person in a family of nine (plus a live-in grandmother and great grandmother) came to have a passion for modern art, feminism, and Western discourse must have mystified them, though only her parents pushed back. As the tears of joy occasioned by Tommy's visit clearly showed, she loved them all. But they would have to come to her, not she to them.

My last service for Tommy was to accompany him to our local supermarket, where I helped him to select a mountain of oversized candy bars (Crunch, Cadbury, and Kit-Kat, plus quantities of Hershey's Kisses, Butterfingers, and M & M's) to distribute as gifts back in Manila. This came as an order from his wife – a nutritionist! – whose displeasure he feared to incur. She had also mandated that he take up smoking to project an image of "manliness." Boyishly chubby, Tommy didn't look especially manly, either with or without a cigarette in his mouth. Lucy gently reproved him for his smoking and urged him to adopt a healthier diet. I don't remember whether his wife was Chinese or Filipino, but it was a striking fact that he identified easily and unselfconsciously with Filipino culture. He spoke Tagalog proficiently; Lucy's was (by then) too rusty to be of much use.

Some of the siblings had married or were to marry native Filipinos; that shook up the parents a bit, but they made their peace. The one who never made her peace with Filipino culture was Lucy. It's not that she had a V. S. Naipaul complex, though she read him with interest. Rather, like Naipaul (reared in Trinidad, resident of England), she felt that she had simply been born in the wrong place. Sometimes that happens, and when it does, it takes integrity and strength of character, not ill will and bad faith, to get out. In fact, I resented almost as much as she the occasionally encountered implication that she had somehow "betrayed" her group identity or had succumbed to the values of her imperialist overlords. That accusation didn't merit a response, but if it had, no better justification could have been found than in the chorus of the Animals' magnificent and incendiary single from 1965, "It's My Life":

It's my life and I'll do what I want!

It's my mind and I'll think what I want!

Admittedly, Lucy knew almost nothing about rock and roll and had never heard of the Animals. Nevertheless, she ended up hearing that song quite a lot, for reasons more coincidental than inspirational: I could play the bass line. I'm afraid my singing and guitar playing offered very little inspiration, but she knew I was on her side. We were decadent bourgeois individualists together.

The fact remained that Lucy had lived more than half her life in the Philippines. If she felt more Chinese than Filipino, she also felt more American than Chinese. And she felt more a woman than an American. It was her life and she did and thought what she wanted. What she didn't want to think about was the past. Outside of bits and pieces of family lore, I could rarely gather much about her childhood. Soon after we fell in love, she sang for me, like the schoolgirl she once was, a children's song in Tagalog about a peasant dwelling in a little hut. And thereupon my heart was driven wild: / She stood before me as a living child! (William Butler Yeats.) But that was the rare instance. With enough prodding, I could get her to mention schoolfriends or various Filipino customs, but she did so somewhat grudgingly. By contrast, I had an endless supply of vignettes from my Tom Sawyer-like boyhood in the suburbs: of playing insanely dangerous games with cherry bombs and other explosives; of aiming for the face with our pellet guns; of operating, unsupervised, my uncle's speed boat at the age of thirteen; of guessing which of my high school English teachers obtained their marijuana from my classmate David; and so on. Different world back then.

Lucy had once been an adorable toddler, dressed up in flounces and bows by her doting parents. I know just how adorable, because I have her baby pictures. (No, she didn't want them either.) What a princess! Being the eldest, she was pampered as were none of the others, except for the eldest boy, a spoiled ne'er-do-well. (Resistance to The Patriarchy, in her case, began early.) In my favorite, she sits on the floor, a satin dress billowing out to the edges of the frame, laces encasing her tiny shoulders, some sort of head-dress atop her carefully brushed hair. There are Chinese scroll decorations on the wall behind her, and she's looking shyly into the camera. We could have been playmates! I would have taught her to throw cherry bombs at people. She would have taught me trigonometry. As she laughingly admitted, she had been such a goody-goody that her idea of unsupervised play was to corral her siblings into a game of "schoolroom," with her as the teacher.

What was the story behind the taking of that photograph? I never found out. The ratio of my stories to hers was about ten to one. Was I not listening? Was I a monster of self-involvement? When Lucy got angry enough, she would have answered yes to both of those questions, but really I was trying to draw out her childhood memories without making her feel uncomfortable. I never succeeded, and in the process of sharing my own memories, I probably did come across as self-involved. That's because I *was* self-involved. But so was she. Our tendency to brood and keep morbidly introspective diaries had drawn us together in the first place; I saw no reason to stop now. All the most interesting people were tortured introverts! If I had a propensity to obsess unhealthily about the past, she had a counter propensity to deny it altogether. Which hurt us more? Probably a draw. When we split up, her propensity served her better. She moved on. I got stuck.

Well, there's no time like the past. I mean the present. I mean the past. Anyway, whatever our difficulties living in time, we appreciated, for the most part, being where and who we were: a young(ish) married couple in New York City with a wonderful child, a few good friends, decent jobs, and more interests than we could keep up with. Lucy tended to be more focused than I, and in 1990 she got very focused indeed. That year she applied for and won a fellowship at a printmaking workshop on West Nineteenth Street. Bob Blackburn, the master craftsman who ran the operation with benevolent authority, had produced print editions for Romare Bearden, Jacob Lawrence, and other luminaries, so getting this nine-month fellowship was quite a coup. The inductees were honored in a ceremony at the Studio Museum in Harlem, where I used my "I'm her muse" line more than once. Truly, I loved being eclipsed by Lucy. Even allowing for her shyness, which she had gradually overcome in the course of years, she could have been with just about anyone. She chose me.

Lucy threw herself into the techniques and methods of printmaking with her customary zeal, which meant that she spent most weekends at the workshop, while leaving me sufficient solo time for my creative endeavors – chiefly, going to the movies. From time to time she brought home the tools of the trade; copper plates, burins, etching needles, lithographic stones, which I beheld with fascinated incomprehension. Lucy loved the technical stuff of art; I could never quite grasp it, but then again, I can't grasp anything technical. Through me she became friendly with the art director of the Brooklyn Public Library, a talented figurative painter whose passion for fixatives and alkyd gels possibly surpassed her own. Hearing the two of them together was like eavesdropping on a pair of prizefighters: Yeah, this trick will get you through the ninth round, and try this when your knees begin to wobble. I can vouch for the maxim sometimes attributed to Picasso: When critics get together, they talk about style, form, meaning. When artists get together, they talk about where to get the best turpentine.

On one of those lithographic stones Lucy drew a loose, impressionistic study of Mount Denali segmented into vertical bands that she printed in a small edition and gave to a few friends and relatives. One copy hangs on the wall of my brother's living room in New Jersey, where I see it once or twice a year. I ended up with something even better: two of Lucy's largest, most sumptuous paintings, one of a kingfisher hitting the water, the other a landscape of the Long Meadow in Prospect Park, each collaged with strips of fabric separating one gorgeous swirling surface area from another. After we split up they hung in my one-bedroom apartment in Clinton Hill for a couple of years. My apartment never looked better. But they were killing me. They had to come down, and they did.

That year the workshop fellows produced a lavish portfolio featuring one print for each artist. Lucy contributed a rather austere etched cross-hatching – not her best work, but it hardly mattered. She had found a community of artists that would henceforth support and encourage her, or, to put it more plainly, she made some good friends. I did too. These people – Margo, an abstract expressionist, Cindy, a junk sculptor, Selda, a pop artist, Jacqueline, a conceptual artist, Burton, a graphic designer, and (usually) their partners – knit themselves into the fabric of our lives: group shows, studio visits, birthday parties, picnics in Prospect Park, New Year's celebrations, babysitting and all the rest. What did it matter that none of them were quite so talented, so intelligent, or indeed so attractive as Lucy? They were thoughtful, creative people who weren't going to bore me with talk about automobiles or investment opportunities or the Super Bowl. (Did I bore them with talk about the NBA play-offs? That's different!) When Cindy one night showed off her new dishwasher, she laughed at the absurdity of it. Yes, we were typical American consumers but we were *ironic* about consumption. Years later, when push came to shove, they all chose Lucy over me, not that I asked or expected anyone to choose. I could say much about the hurt and anger they caused when they abandoned me, or about the impossible situation they suddenly found themselves in, but I'll leave it at this: I miss them. I know I didn't make it easy for them. Anyway, Lucy ended up with all the friends. I felt like Vladimir Nabokov's hapless refugee Timofey Pnin, who at a similar point in his life exclaims, "I haf nofing left, nofing, nofing!"

All these friends had two things that Lucy didn't: MFA's and studios. The first might have been supererogatory, but an artist needs a studio. Yet another regret: I carped, I caviled, I kvetched. René Magritte had painted in his dining room; why couldn't Lucy? How could we possibly afford the rent for a studio when we were incapable of saving a dime? So Lucy did the only proper thing: she went out and got a studio anyway. I never found out how much the rent cost us, which was just as well. Lucy's various studios couldn't have been cheap, but we always managed. Once again, I had been a very great fool.

To make amends, I professed nothing but delight when I first visited the studio that she shared with three other artists in the basement of a nondescript building on White Street in Tribeca. And in truth it was exactly the sort of work space – a dingy chaos of brushes, rags, spilled paint, and heaped canvases – that non-artists like me tend to find so mysterious. It cheered me to see Lucy so much in her element. I thought a celebration was in order.

"Let's fuck," I said.

There was in fact a ratty old sofa that would serve well for the purpose, but Lucy objected that someone might come in. That's why it'll be so much fun, I said. And it was.

With her studio as refuge and clubhouse, Lucy began producing a stream of semi-abstract drawings and paintings of ever greater richness and authority. (The quilts definitively ceased production. Oh well, you can't have everything.) I always thought that Lucy was slightly self-conscious about her own facility. Without any training, she had a sureness of touch that, in my opinion, none of her friends attained to. In particular, her brush stroke – luminous, feathery, seemingly effortless – recalled that of Renoir at his absolute best, a comparison she did not at all appreciate. She held to the modernist credo that art must disturb, not comfort. Fortunately, she just couldn't help herself. However brooding they might be, her paintings were consistently beautiful. Not that she disdained the simple pleasures of picture-making. Just for fun, she rummaged through our snapshots and, using oil sticks, added fanciful details and highlights in bright colors to scenes of the three of us messing around on the beach in Florida or pulling a sled through an icy Prospect Park. I've seen it done since; I've never seen it done better. I hate to think they ended up on Lucy's promised bonfire of unsold artworks, but they probably did.

Making art was one thing, selling it something else. Lucy approached the latter with the same even-handedness as she did the former. While she busied herself with artistic creation and the means of getting it out into the world, I backed into an unexpected realization of my own: Jesus, maybe I can create something too.

14

Glassboro State College is not listed in *Peterson's Selected Colleges*, let alone in *The Insider's Guide to Colleges* compiled by the staff of the *Yale Daily News*. It can, however, be found in somewhat less discriminating directories such as Cass and Birnbaum's *U.S. Colleges*, where the number of students (4,000 M, 3,500 F [FT], 2,100 M, 1,500 F [PT]), tuition ($3,000/annual + expenses), and average SAT scores of entering freshmen (500 M, 440 V) are duly noted.

That's the opening paragraph, subsequently dropped, of my first book, a serio-comic memoir of collegiate misery and class consciousness at Glassboro State College and the University of Connecticut. I was forced to write a new opening when the industrialist Henry Rowan made front page news in 1992 by donating a hundred million dollars to that unassuming teachers' college in southwestern New Jersey, instantly transforming Glassboro State College into Rowan University. I'm grateful to Mr. Rowan for necessitating an improved opening to my book, but my deepest gratitude for the genesis of *College* goes to Paul Auster – yes, *that* Paul Auster, my doppelgänger, the famous novelist whom I was now encountering weekly on Seventh Avenue as we walked our children to their respective schools.

In the course of my readings by and about Auster for my critique of his work in *Contemporary Novelists,* I was much taken with *Moon Palace,* an extravagant bildungsroman about a brilliant Columbia University student who crashes sensationally into poverty and homelessness but nevertheless dazzles everyone he meets (including his gorgeous girlfriend) with his intellectual and verbal gifts and to whom the most extraordinary things continually happen. Pretty interesting, I thought, but how about a story concerning a lonely and hapless student at not one but two mediocre colleges who never once says a clever thing, who doesn't come close to getting the girl, who never even talks to the girl, and to whom nothing at all ever happens? And what if the story were told not as fiction but as fact, thus refusing the consolations of symmetry and symbol? And what if the autobiographical experience could be projected outward so that the story – *my* story, as it happens – might encompass intractable social realities overlooked by fabulously successful postmodern novelists? So far, so good. Now all I had to do was write the thing. Not coincidentally, I chose this moment to abandon, as a necessary means of saving time, my journal-keeping. From this point on, the chronology of this story might get a bit slippery.

There would have been no book without Lucy. I wouldn't have had the confidence to contemplate it, let alone complete it. And I had the confidence to write about my gaucheries and insecurities because I knew I was no longer the complete fuck-up I had been in college. And the proof of that was the presence of the intelligent, desirable woman sitting up in bed with me, listening to me read, sentence by sentence and paragraph by paragraph, the book I was now writing. The path was littered with mistakes, but I had got one thing irrefutably right: this person, sharing my bed, my life, and, at the moment, my prose.

Not that I had exhausted all of my gaucheries and insecurities. No, there was still plenty of that stuff to go around and there always would be, but I had the sense of writing about weakness from a position of strength. That sense has sustained me ever since. My psychic life – messy, disordered, but mine, if you please – isn't so different from everyone else's. I just write about it a little more openly.

Also, I needed a reader or, strictly speaking, a listener. Lucy would be that listener/reader. What I didn't need, at that point, was an editor. Later, I acquired one. His role was to say, Well, maybe we could use a little more of this and a little less of that. Lucy's role was to say yes. She seemed happy to do so. We both had the sense, if I'm not mistaken, that I had hit on something significant, that just possibly I might be more than a help-mate to a real artist – her "muse," as I self-consciously joked. After living for years with someone who breathed creativity, I was shocked to discover that I had a little talent too.

Lucy knew when and how to say yes. Did I? Apart from that foolishness over my resistance to her studio, I believe I did. There was, in the first place, the sheer wonder I had always felt in the presence of her endless creativity. As time went on, more and more occasions arose for her to share the results of that creativity in group shows, small galleries, and alternative spaces. (At a café in the East Village hung for the occasion with a dozen of Lucy's best paintings, the profligately tattooed waitress took my order with perfect insouciance: "What'll it be, sailor?") Normally awkward at parties, I relished the openings of Lucy's group shows, where I could banter easily with our artist friends, whose work invariably paled beside her own. Lucy knew that perfectly well. More importantly, she didn't care. So what if the others were a bit derivative or still groping for a signature style? They were all in this together, they inspired, stimulated, and supported each other. Worrying about whose dick was bigger – well, that was something Stephen might do, if he had been an artist.

I never felt remotely competitive with Lucy, and I think she would have said the same about me. It helped that we were both so conspicuously unsuccessful, at least relative to the art stars and literary celebrities of the moment. That was a standard of success that didn't obtain in our world. Yes, everyone would have liked a few more sales or a review in *Art News*. But Lucy and her friends knew what the egregious Jeff Koons and Julian Schnabel didn't: that commercial success was a secondary goal, often a dangerous and delusive one, and that the primary goal – namely, the joy of making art and sharing it with an appreciative audience, however small – had already been achieved and would always be achieved so long as one remained open and honest and willing to grow. Maybe that sounds like the rationalization of the chronically disappointed. On the other hand, can anyone truly believe that the race is to the swiftest? Artistic communities, in New York or Paris or Saskatoon, Saskatchewan, are sustained, not by rare genius, but by cadres of skilled, imaginative, and hardworking people – people like Lucy and her friends, all of whom had day jobs, none of whom knew anybody who knew Andy Warhol. Why worry about stuff outside your control? Lucy took reasonable measures to get her art exposed and when she failed to become the next Jeff Koons, cheerfully returned to her studio and the fellowship of her equally unstarry companions in art.

I was a writer, not a painter. Would Lucy and I have been so blissfully uncompetitive had our creative fields aligned rather than diverged? I would have trusted Lucy; I'm not so sure about myself. Inclined to writerly envy (René Girard's "metaphysical desire"), I desperately needed the lesson that her example provided: Do your thing, don't worry about the rest. That I even had a "thing" still came as something of a surprise. Reference writing, dilettantish humor pieces, yes, but a full-length literary memoir? Maybe publication was a fantasy, but there was no reason to give up on this memoir, the composition of which was starting to make me feel almost like – well, Lucy. No wonder she was more grounded that I was. All the time I had been brooding on the traumas of my adolescence and early adulthood, she was losing herself in quiltmaking and printmaking and painting. Like anyone else, she will carry a certain amount of baggage to her grave, but all that artistic activity lightened her load. The key, I was beginning to see, wasn't to "work though" unresolvable problems but to find productive ways of evading them.

That's not what my therapist told me. Everyone else in Park Slope, including Lucy, seemed to be seeing a shrink. Why not give it a whirl? Not to have at least some personal experience of therapy, in our milieu, was like not reading *The New Yorker;* it just wasn't done. And unquestionably, I had some very disturbing stuff to get therapized about, stuff that was, all too obviously, still hanging me up: the agony and humiliation of my college years, the parental alcoholism that had blighted my childhood, and (by far the worst) the systematic bullying I had endured in early adolescence. Furthermore, I realized that if these things were dragging me down, they might also drag down Lucy and Jonathan. So long as I ruminated over the public humiliations seared into my consciousness as a thirteen-year-old, I couldn't fully become the cheerful, loving, and responsive husband and father I had the duty to be. So in my middle thirties, for about six months (which was all I could afford), I got myself into therapy with a bearded, tweedy, and austerely old school shrink. It helped. I'm grateful. But then I started writing my book and I found that all the therapy in the world couldn't do for me what the writing did. To be specific, the nightmares that had visited me since college about social disgrace and academic failure dissipated over the course of the writing. By the time I finished the book, I was almost nightmare-free. Years later the nightmares came back, more harrowing than ever. This time they were about Lucy.

Another nail in the coffin, I suppose. Lucy never forgave me for resorting to a therapist on what she considered insufficient grounds. She thought it another instance of my incorrigible self-involvement or, worse, an excuse to grumble about her to someone else. Wrong on both counts, but I had given her enough cause to raise those doubts. Lucy's therapy was her business, not mine, and I was careful not to pry. I knew perfectly well that she used her therapy primarily to work out her *agon* with her mother. In our last years I knew equally well that an even larger psychic problem had displaced Brave Orchid as Topic Number One in Lucy's ongoing therapy: her husband.

Well, weren't we an artsy-fartsy, duly therapized, politically progressive New York couple? No one wants to think that his or her identity can be reduced to a social type. Although Lucy and I hit some of the marks of the yuppie identikit, we didn't have enough money or professional prestige to fully qualify. Wherever the Hamptons were (I wasn't a hundred percent sure), we had no desire to go there. I remember reading a review somewhere of Woody Allen's *Hannah and Her Sisters* in which, apropos of one of the characters, the critic said something like, "We've all met people like this at certain parties – smart people who take too much cocaine and blurt out their insecurities." Well, no, actually, we never met anyone like that, and we certainly didn't go to parties where people took cocaine. It's what I loved about living in Park Slope – that despite its odd mix of lesbians and investment bankers (or lesbian investment bankers), we and our friends could live our utterly middle-American lives as if we were good citizens of Wabash, Indiana, except that we went to art galleries and voted for Democrats. The Greenwich Village Halloween parade was famous for its outrageously creative defiance of social norms. The Park Slope Halloween parade was just a bunch of parents trudging along with their kids. I preferred the Park Slope parade.

Now, however, we were about to enter a slightly more glittering world. It happened like this: Seeking greater exposure for her paintings, Lucy hired as an agent a gay, middle-aged connoisseur of contemporary art who claimed to have connections with certain galleries and collectors. Stanley really did have an eye, and he really did appreciate Lucy's work, but his connections proved to be dubious. What he was really good at was throwing parties. He went all out for one in his apartment in the East Village, which he hung, for the occasion, with Lucy's glowing semi-abstractions, many, by that point, executed on small wooden boxes, like mysterious Joseph Cornell constructions with flat surfaces. The guest of honor was Quentin Crisp, the frail and elderly icon of queer identity. Known for never turning down a free meal, he was unlikely to forgo this invitation, however much his fashionable tardiness unsettled the desperately expectant Stanley. That was just the problem. When Quentin finally arrived, Stanley spent more time fussing over him than Lucy – not a good omen, I thought, for her salaried promoter. Lucy and I would have fussed if we knew how, but we were at a loss when, for a few ghastly minutes, we somehow found ourselves alone with the Naked Civil Servant himself, he enthroned on a winged armchair, mascara lightly coloring his eyelids, a foulard wrapped gently around his throat. He looked at us. We looked at him. Nothing. I was tempted to say, "Well, Quentin, think the Yankees will win the Series this year?" when several guests burst in from the kitchen, doing him the obeisance that we couldn't.

Was Stanley conning us? Probably not. He just wasn't a very effective promoter. Characteristically, Lucy wasted no time berating herself when she let him go after a couple of years. What's the use of an experiment if it might not fail? And it hadn't failed entirely. She used the occasion of Stanley's social gatherings not to suck up to strangers, as she probably should have, but to have fun in mixed settings with her new and old friends. (Stanley once put her in touch with a grande dame in a Fifth Avenue apartment overlooking Central Park. Stephen, she said when she got home, you think rich people are different? You don't have *any* idea.) Furthermore, she enjoyed, as did I, his hardboiled style. In particular, he had a way of dangling a cigarette from his lip that held me in acute suspense. When would the butt, bobbing up and down in rhythm with his wised-up patter, finally succumb to the law of gravity and drop from his mouth? Never! He had the manner of a street intellectual from the 1940s, rather like Clement Greenberg, the philosopher-king of abstract expressionism, whose bald-headed, bulldog appearance resembled his own. Clement Greenberg, however, did not develop crushes on handsome, young (and straight) male painters, as Stanley did with another of his protégés. Lucy could see that Stanley's infatuation had clouded his judgment. The young man in question (British, with a calculated flair for combining high and low) was a better hustler than artist, and Lucy watched the elaborate dance between the two men unfold as if in an updated Henry James novel. Yet Henry James novels were better read than lived. Time to end this particular experiment.

Stanley had no part in a commission that came closer from home. The client was me. I had sent off a chunk of my memoir to the *New England Review,* where it ran in 1995. That modest success emboldened me to submit the manuscript to a handful of small presses, one of which, Orchises, in Alexandria, Virginia, accepted and published it the following year. No marketing, no advertising, no bookstore readings, and not a whole lot of sales: such are the parameters of small press publishing. On the other hand, I worked with an editor and publisher who regarded me as a writer, not as a "brand," and who brought out the best in all of his poets and essayists and memoirists. Apart from the quality of the writing he published, Roger Lathbury's other chief concern was elegance of design. I can't speak for the text, but *College* (Stephen Akey, Orchises Press, 1996), is one of the most beautiful trade paperbacks I've ever seen.

I had asked Lucy for a cover design that would show a bicycle – my bicycle being something of a leitmotif in the book – against a background of my college transcripts. (If you look closely you can see the six credits I earned for "HLTH C PHYS ED COED," my two required gym classes at Glassboro.) Although I joked that I deserved a credit for "cover concept," as was sometimes seen on the back of rock and roll LPs, the mystery and lyricism of the artwork were all Lucy's. She and Roger chatted like old friends on the telephone, exchanging ideas about margins and color resolutions. He told me that she had the most delightful laugh he had ever heard.

For the dedication I briefly considered something lofty and literary ("complice in every deed, essential as air") but settled on the unadorned "For Lucy," which, I think, said it all. Lucy appreciated it but rightly expected no less. As she joked to a friend, "He had *better* dedicate it to me, if he knows what's good for him." And she said something else. "You'll like it," she mentioned to another (female) friend. "It's honest and funny. But it's really a book that men will appreciate much more than women."

No it's not. Just as many female as male readers have told me that *College* speaks feelingly to their experience, or, alternately, underwhelms them profoundly. I wanted to catch people between laughter and tears. With some readers I succeeded, with some I failed, but their gender, as far as I could tell, had little or nothing to do with their response. It's true that Lucy had never read the book; she had heard it in so many iterations that she didn't need to. Still, that comment stung slightly. Esthetic disagreements were allowed. But what if this disagreement didn't really concern esthetics at all?

I thought the literary/publishing world, where, essentially, you couldn't get established unless you were already established, was sufficiently venal, but it seemed like a bastion of rectitude compared to what I saw of the art world. Lucy knocked on the doors at all the galleries in SoHo and Chelsea and rarely got a first let alone a second glance. In the art world, unlike the literary world, you could get away with complete unadulterated bullshit. With her rigorous painterly values, Lucy would never be the flavor of the month. Nonetheless, she invested much time and energy getting her slides prepared, for a while turning our dining room into a mini-photography studio. As was only to be expected, she mastered that art as readily as everything else she put her hand to. We got some good family photos out of it.

Rejection seemed hardly to touch her. First of all, her paintings just kept getting better. She could choose to be quietly satisfied or clamorously frustrated. She chose the former. Secondly, she appreciated more than ever the fellowship of her peers, which is to say, she liked hanging out with her girlfriends. (There's a famous photograph of Joan Mitchell, Helen Frankenthaler, and Grace Hartigan laughing arm in arm at a gallery show in 1957; that could have been Lucy and Cindy and Selda.) She now shared studio space closer to home with two of those friends in an old industrial building on the Gowanus Canal and Union Street. Possibly the most toxic waterway in America, the Gowanus Canal glowed with an eerie, purplish iridescence by night. Just before reaching the studio you passed a coffin factory, with the caskets sometimes piled high on the sidewalk as a bracing memento mori. Ah, the old industrial Brooklyn! Lucy feared that gentrification would drive the artists out of their studios, but it never happened; the stench from the canal kept realtors and developers away. Anyway, it was great riding the rickety storage elevator up to her studio on the third floor to see her beavering away on her latest projects and maybe catch up with Selda and Cindy. I couldn't help envying the lot of them; compared to writing, making art looked like so much fun! Of course, they encountered difficulties and obstacles, but seeing Lucy at work in her studio in the midst of her peers was a life lesson even more valuable to me than those coffins on the sidewalk: Find what you love and do it.

Since this story doesn't end well, I suppose I should be looking for premonitions of disaster. They're not hard to find, even in a setting as apparently innocuous as Lucy's Gowanus studio. What began as a practical necessity – affordable studio space at a convenient location – became, as the years went on, something very different: a refuge. From me. And that camaraderie with her artist girlfriends also evolved into something darker. Lucy's genius for friendship never ebbed, but its expansion in one direction entailed a contraction in another: more room for the friends, less room for me. Maybe it's a good thing I had abandoned my diary. The diminishment that marked our last years would have been too painful to chronicle.

Well, the end was hardly in sight, or even imagined. We lived, we loved, we ordered sensible clothing from the L.L. Bean catalog. I might have been living in a fool's paradise. Perhaps the pleasure of ordering less sensible articles of clothing with and for Lucy from the Victoria's Secret catalog blinded me to the fact of her anger; it was always there, ready to kindle at an insensitive comment or failed joke. And although I watched myself very, very carefully, my caution availed nothing. Either I would slip and let loose the wrong words, or Lucy would imagine I slipped. It came to the same thing.

Once, while vacationing in the Adirondacks, I made a passing comment about a pair of tight, dayglow slacks that she was wearing. Fury. Rage. Despair. She got over it in a day or two, but I wonder: Did my foolish remark about her dayglow slacks end our marriage? She might have said that this small instance epitomized all my worst qualities: my stupidity, my thoughtlessness, my censoriousness. And she might have been right. She couldn't have been blamed for not noticing what I had so signally failed to express – that she looked pretty sexy in those tight pants.

For eight successive summers we stayed for a week or two in rented cabins or lodges in the Adirondacks. Rage and despair over Stephen's inane comments about Lucy's wardrobe constituted only a part of our summer vacations. The Adirondacks was our Special Place, where we rediscovered the world and ourselves away from the bustle of the city and our daily routines. For me it will always be consecrated ground, and it never seemed more sacred than one afternoon on the shore of Blue Mountain Lake, where Jonathan and I met Lucy after the two of us had spent the day at a water park in Old Forge. However sublime those mountains and rivers, a nine-year-old boy wants his fun. So, for that matter, does a thirty-seven-year-old man, one more inclined to such amusements than, say, wine tasting or chamber music. Anyway, we arrived back in Blue Mountain Lake to find Lucy, in the golden light of the afternoon, sketching in a secluded spot on the shore, happy to put down her pencils and listen to Jonathan's excited babble about our eventful day. And it *was* an eventful day. How often do you get the thrill of plunging down water slides only to live it all over again in recounting the tale to a gentle, nurturing, and loving mother? Or how often does that same mother hold out her hands so that an eastern newt, which we discovered on the trail to Sawyer Mountain, might skitter over them, like a magical wind-up toy invented by an artificer from the Arabian Nights? Eastern newts, by the way, are poisonous. Sometimes ignorance is bliss.

She climbed the mountains, she portaged the canoe, she foraged for blueberries, she did not, as I did, find it necessary to impress anyone by diving from an eighteen-feet rock in the middle of Blue Mountain Lake. Most of all she kept Jonathan happy and distracted in the midst of all our rambles and on the days when we got rained out. In spite of my inapposite comments, I believe she treasured these Adirondack trips as much as I did. If there was a more beautiful wilderness in the world, we hadn't seen it. Then again, we hadn't seen much. In 1995 we got a chance to see a little more of the world, for a change. We were going to Paris.

A colleague of Lucy's owned an apartment share in the Marais; we could have it for a week in February for eight or nine hundred dollars. For a ten-year-old boy, the City of Light could hardly compete with a water park in Old Forge, New York. Apart from the promise of authentic Tin-Tin memorabilia in various tourist traps, we offered as an additional incentive a special guest: Grandma Peg was coming with us. Well, Paris is Paris, and I don't need to describe its painterly light, which we didn't see (the cold gray skies never lifted), nor its sumptuous cuisine, which we didn't taste (unthinkable – with my mother to feed, we shopped for cold cuts and vegetables at local markets).

Jonathan and Peg entertained each other like the best friends they were, and on occasion Lucy and I were able to slip out by ourselves while they rested. I have photographs of Lucy in the twilight on Île Saint-Louis looking as glamorous as a spy in a film noir.

There was, however, a problem, which I mention only to adduce Lucy's unending resourcefulness and thoughtfulness. Like Anne Elliot in Jane Austen's *Persuasion,* she never panicked, she dealt calmly and efficiently with whatever difficulties presented themselves. And I was like Captain Wentworth in the same novel: completely outclassed. The problem, as we should have foreseen, was that our spacious "fifth floor" apartment was, of course, on the sixth floor, and that the stately winding staircase was far too steep for my mother to manage. On the morning of our arrival she had to stop at every landing and by the third was bent over and panting.

"I'm fine," she said.

Lucy wasted no time. She had noticed a small hotel on the same block and, while Jonathan and my mother were sleeping off their jet lag, arranged at the reception desk for the soonest possible transfer of Peg's person. Although Peg apologized profusely for the "trouble" she was causing us, Lucy wouldn't hear of it. For the rest of the week, Peg rode up to and down from her tiny room in an elevator. We congregated around her bed in the evenings, reviewing that day's outing and eating select pastries, the one French food my mother would countenance. Yes, Peg hobbled us a little and necessitated the standard tourist itinerary, but as Lucy reminded me, "We'll come back here, she won't. Let her enjoy herself, Stephen."

We never did come back – not together. But even this unromantic, hurried family vacation afforded me a few treasured moments with Lucy: exploring Île Saint-Louis, resting our weary feet in Place des Vosges, or –what we would have dismissed as a cliché if we hadn't seen it the very first time we left the apartment together– observing a *jeune fille en fleur* with a baguette under her arm, peddling her three-speed bicycle down the street through a light rain.

Although I firmly resisted the notion that intimacy required "work" – no, intimacy was a *reprieve* from work – I had to admit that our regular trips to the Adirondacks and Florida or Boston or Washington or (now) Paris served a larger purpose. The day-to-dayness of our lives back in Brooklyn sometimes alienated us from our deeper selves. Little by little, without even realizing it, we got disconnected. We too were sometimes numbed by all the commuting and the cooking and the cleaning, we too required special occasions to be loving and demonstrative and silly. The Fra Angelicos at the Louvre or an eastern newt on a mountain trail were wonders, but what really mattered was collapsing on a rented bed after a long day of sightseeing or hiking, too tired to do more than snuggle sleepily. Thus it was that one warm and sunny August day, while Jonathan poked a stick in the mud a few feet away, I lazily nuzzled Lucy's neck from the stern of our beached canoe in the shadow of Blue Mountain. She nuzzled me back. Thou hast ravished my heart, my sister, my spouse; / thou hast ravished my heart with one of thine eyes!

There would be fewer of those transcendent moments until, of course, there were none. In our last few years, Lucy decreed that there would be no more vacations; we couldn't afford them anymore. A fatal mistake. We should have taken out loans or borrowed from friends or robbed a bank – *anything* to preserve that time-stands-still feeling of being in love and lost to the world that our vacations afforded us. A more terrible possibility exists. We could have scraped together the funds. Lucy just didn't want to be with me.

15

One of Lucy's many, many grievances was that there was an imbalance of power in our relationship. It pained me to hear her talk that way. Love, I needed to believe, was the place where power had no voice. I didn't plan the details of our vacations because I was a control freak; I did so because Lucy had no discernable relish for it, had never driven a car, and (initially) didn't know the Adirondacks from the Catskills from the Berkshires from the Poconos. On this subject, as on so many others, I might have been deluded. What the hell did I know? As Lucy pointedly reminded me, I was a *man*. I had the luxury not to think about power because I could take it for granted. So when she started asserting her authority more deliberately, I wasn't in a position to object. Sometime around 1995 she laid down the law on a matter of some import: we were going to move.

That was fine with me. Although we had a good financial deal with the ongoing rent strike, her chief arguments – that our neighbors were hateful and that it was about time we owned something – were unassailable. So we began hunting for an affordable co-op apartment in Park Slope. Getting driven around the neighborhood by friendly real estate agents for private apartment tours turned out to be a diverting little adventure. Who knew there we so many funky and eccentric interiors in Park Slope? Also, the real estate bubble had recently burst; it was, fortunately for us, a buyer's market. We had finally saved some money from the rent strike, and Lucy borrowed considerably more from her sister Connie in Australia to pad our accounts. I used to think it was our charm that won over the co-op board at our new home, a yellow-brick walk-up on Second Street and Sixth Avenue; in fact, it was the money that we didn't, technically, have.

I loved that apartment. It was the last place where we were happy. After the poisonous atmosphere of our previous building, the easy, matter-of-fact pleasantness of our new neighbors disarmed us. Nobody was going to pound the ceiling if Jonathan dropped something on the floor. We lived on the fourth and top floor, with a view to the street. On occasion I have business that takes me to that stretch on Sixth Avenue. Should I look up at the window where I used to stand, sometimes with Lucy, watching a streaky sunset over New York Harbor? I can never quite decide. Someday, I hope, I'll be able to look up at that window with equanimity.

The view of the harbor from our living room was lovely but compromised. One floor up, on the roof deck, it was unobstructed. We read, dined, entertained our friends, and watched the nighthawks diving for insects up there. "On the roof, it's peaceful as can be / And there the world below can't bother me." That lilting New York City nocturne by the Drifters could have been our theme song. The neighbors, who sometimes joined us, had reason to be glad we spent so much time aloft. Little by little, Lucy was turning the roof deck into a botanic garden in the sky.

Gardening was yet another arena of her omnicompetence; she could make virtually anything grow. Before Jonathan's birth, she had turned our one-bedroom apartment into a little greenhouse. Now she had the chance to garden on a larger scale. A few planters with geraniums and marigolds would hardly suffice. She trained climbers over the pagoda and trellises, she balanced colors and textures, she experimented with difficult-to-grow mosses and herbs. Why do it the easy way if you can do it the hard way? She allowed me to water and haul dirt up the stairs; that was the extent of her trust in my botanical abilities. Watching her garden was like watching her paint or draft: the absorption, the purposefulness, the confidence, the sense of losing herself in the task at hand. I had my basketball, my birdwatching, and (lately) my tin whistle playing, all of which afforded me intimations of the sort of existential engagement that seemed to come so naturally to her. There was this difference, however, between her favored activities and mine: She excelled at everything she attempted. I kinda sucked.

I wrote a good portion of my second book on that roof deck, under the shelter of Lucy's floral pagoda. (Moonflower – or was it star jasmine?) Writing was the one activity in which I escaped mediocrity. It afforded some consolation, and I needed it. After five years as a staff writer, I turned in my last article for the now completed *World Authors 1900-1950* and was out of a job. When signing my first contract, I had been promised a lifetime of writerly employment, but the vice-president who made that promise was also out of a job. I'll never know what office shake-up sealed my fate. I did know I had to find another job, and fast – for the first time in our lives we had a mortgage to meet. Fortunately, there was always the Brooklyn Public Library, chronically in need of qualified librarians. Although I wasn't welcomed back with open arms, I qualified. As punishment for my disloyalty, management exiled me to Siberia – the severely underfunded, dilapidated, and "high security" (as it was euphemistically called) Red Hook Branch. I felt like Raskolnikov in penal servitude at the end of *Crime and Punishment*. And like Raskolnikov, I learned – in my case, from my wonderfully down-to-earth co-workers and a few of the regulars from the housing projects – to roll with it a little better. Here was another lesson, of which we can never have enough, in the virtue and necessity of humility. I used that experience to form part of the book (*Library*) that I would soon begin writing on the roof deck.

Transitioning from writing literary reference articles, at home and at my own pace, to beseeching the children at the Red Hook Branch to stop shrieking, was about as unenviable as it sounds. Did I detect a little less than wholehearted sympathy from Lucy? She expected me, rightly, to do my job with a minimum of fuss and complaint. Nevertheless, I remembered how she had reacted years before, when I had come home from my first day on the job at the New York Public Library numbed with despair. Somehow she had found the perfect balance of indulgence and firmness. This time there was a lot of firmness but not much indulgence. Fortunately, I knew that Red Hook wasn't forever. After serving my sentence for a little more than a year, management deemed me sufficiently re-educated and allowed me to return to the Central Library.

If you came to the Language and Literature Division of the Brooklyn Public Library from 1997 to 2000 and found me or my estimable colleague Amy, a bustling and energetic Midwesterner of a certain age, on the reference desk, you were, if I may say so, in luck. We knew that collection inside out and took pride in furnishing reference materials, suggesting avenues of research, citing Dewey Decimal numbers off the top of our heads, and placing in the hands of expectant readers the bodice rippers, vampire mysteries, and (sometimes) works of challenging literary fiction that they coveted. Nothing lasts. Within a few years the advent of the Internet turned my department into an outpost of the Port Authority bus station, with glassy-eyed pornography addicts squabbling over access to computer terminals. That situation would eventually stabilize, but I had had enough. When an opening arose in the Cataloging Department, where some of my old friends still worked, I jumped at it.

And nothing lasts, or stays the same, at home. I did perceive, to quote from *King Lear,* "a most faint neglect of late" – faint enough to be ignored, for the time being. Coming home every day to Lucy remained a presumptive joy. And the time being was pretty nice too: a lovely new apartment, friendly neighbors, a few close friends, a good middle school for Jonathan (not so easy to find in New York City), even an affectionate little pug to keep us company. (Her paws smelled like chrysanthemums.) If the writing was on the wall, I couldn't read it.

Certainly it was hard to imagine, on the September night in 1997, when Lucy had the opening of her first and only solo show in SoHo, that we would ever be apart. It's not as if she required the sanction of an approved gallery in the art capital of the world to validate her identity, but SoHo was assuredly the big time. Why not enjoy the moment? And she did. She was at her gracious, self-effacing best as friends and family came by to offer congratulations and marvel at the swirling surfaces and mysterious spatial configurations of her latest abstractions. The gallery assistants were sleek and beautiful young women. It was like a scene from a movie – *The Lucy Show,* starring Lucy and Stephen as an ordinary couple from Brooklyn impersonating for one night the kind of sophisticates who might turn up in the pages of a magazine. Then we returned in our pumpkin coach (the F train) to our workaday lives in Brooklyn and brushed off the fairy dust.

Lucy sold but not enough; there would be no more solo shows in SoHo. And so she returned, as focused as ever, to her creative outpost on the Gowanus Canal. But even Lucy might have had some doubts. All this knocking on doors and preparing of slides and rewriting of artists' statements – was it really worth it? Maybe the game was rigged, maybe it wasn't. Maybe she didn't need to play this game at all. Hunkering down with a few artist friends and giving her pictures away seemed a happier alternative to persistently banging her head against the wall.

It's a firm conviction of mine that talent will *not* out; undiscovered Emily Dickinsons, I believe, go to their graves all the time. In Lucy's case, there was the added temptation of her gardening, which afforded the same sort of creative fulfillment as her painting but required no walls to be breached or curators to be mollified. She could no more stop creating than she could have stopped breathing, and she had by no means given up on the art world, where she continued to have sporadic success in group shows, alternative spaces, and competitions. But little by little, her gardening was pulling her in another direction – away, as I did not see at the time, from me.

Gardening was one of the innumerable activities for which I had no aptitude, but I would have helped more if Lucy had let me. She didn't seem to want me to, even doing most of the grunt work herself. So I read or wrote as she puttered away, involving myself less as she involved herself more. By the time she started assembling a comprehensive botanical library and memorizing the Latin names for her plants, I had been excluded from a domain where we should have lived and loved and worked together.

At a party on that rooftop garden one night in 1996 or thereabouts, we met Danny Kalb, former lead guitarist for the Blues Project and, as he ruefully admitted, a rock star for a few minutes in the sixties. I've written elsewhere about my fraught relationship with Danny; what mattered for the present was

Lucy: she couldn't stand him. His assertive masculinity and burgeoning neo-conservatism rubbed her in all the wrong ways. Also, a friendship with the perennially impecunious Danny entailed some slight financial sacrifice, which she objected to on principle. Danny's entry into our lives was in some ways ill-omened. Until then (with the exception of Anne-Sophie proving the rule), her friends had been mine, and vice versa. That began to change, first with Danny, then with others. In our last couple of years, Lucy's best friend was a woman who repelled me precisely as Danny Kalb repelled Lucy. Dining with us in a restaurant a few days after September 11, 2001, her new friend placidly rationalized the murder of three thousand innocent people and delivered with preening self-satisfaction a screed about American "arrogance." Lucy shot me the briefest of glances, which said, unmistakably, Don't, don't you *dare* say a word. I found myself getting almost nostalgic for Anne-Sophie.

We were in our early forties now. Complications were to be expected. I wished Lucy hadn't seemed quite so angry quite so often, but I could put off thinking of that for the present – or at least until I noticed, sometime thereafter, that her subway reading included a book called *The Dance of Anger*. Just what I needed – an author telling Lucy she *should* be angry. Yet hers was still the voice I longed to hear, even if it had lost most of the Chinese accentuation that had once enchanted me. One night, a couple of years after we had moved into our new apartment, I came home from my evening shift at the library to news that Lucy was bursting to deliver: my mother had called to say that she had unexpectedly come into an inheritance from a recently deceased relative in Ireland. Peg's financial worries were over! Well, not quite. It took years for the money to materialize, and lawyers pocketed more of it than my mother ever got. But Lucy's joy was my joy. That night we strolled around the neighborhood, excitedly speculating about my mother's prospects and sharing the simple, unguarded pleasure of being in each other's company. I remember that night less for the news about my mother than for the news about us; it was the last time we were ever completely, unselfconsciously happy together.

Lucy had some family news as well. Her second youngest sister, Annie, was coming to stay with us for a few months. I would have liked to tell Annie what I sincerely believed: that she was the gentlest, sweetest person I had ever met. I couldn't. She would have died of embarrassment. Her shyness was so extreme that she once tried to approach me at the reference desk in the library but scurried away when another patron intervened. The most touching thing about her was the way she clung to "Tsetsi" or "Hong-a" as the worldly, accomplished older sister who had all the confidence that Annie so signally lacked. Eventually she moved to Vancouver and, I'm happy to say, got married. Forsaking my deepest principles and firmest convictions, I offer this atheist's prayer: May the Lord and Savior, in whom she so devoutly believed, forever bless and guide her.

I have a snapshot taken in the Brooklyn Botanic Garden of Annie, who looked like a slightly plainer version of Lucy, standing stiffly in an arbor and clutching her big sister's arm. What were her impressions of New York? Of me? Of Jonathan? What did she confide to Lucy? I never found out. Apart from their obvious affection for each other, Lucy didn't tell me much about Annie. In fact, she wasn't telling me much about anything. That "most faint neglect of late"? It wasn't so faint anymore. When I began writing *Library* a year or two later, I would read out, as usual, the day's passages to Lucy in bed. I stopped reading when, after a few months, she stopped listening. At first, she would doze off now and then until it became something like a concerted policy. Really, she couldn't have been *that* tired or the book *that* boring. One night I put the manuscript aside, and she never asked about it again. It was a bit like that montage in *Citizen Kane,* when the young Kane and his bride lovingly share the morning's newspaper only to end up reading, in passive-aggressive silence, rival publications. Lucy never did read *Library* and to this day is unaware of the little tribute to her that I planted on page 120.

That hurt. A lot. I was a writer, and the reader I most wanted to reach had abandoned any pretense of interest in my writing. Inch by agonizing inch, the distances were growing. I have no intention of tallying up those inches, but for the sake of verisimilitude, I'll note a few of the more obvious signs, the ones I couldn't ignore no matter how I tried:

One. Eye contact. I still loved looking into Lucy's limpid brown eyes. She, apparently, took no such pleasure in gazing into my muddy greenish ones. Like everything else, these manifestations of disenchantment grew so slowly as to be almost imperceptible, until, like a river carving itself into rock, a canyon had appeared. It was only at the very end that Lucy avoided my eyes as if I were a basilisk. In the interim, I merely noted that she no longer held my gaze for more than a few seconds. I remembered how, in our hot youth, we used to lock eyes and nuzzle nose to nose. Maybe that was the first of all my losses. The love had gone out of her eyes.

Two. Foot speed. If you live long enough in New York, you learn, as a survival skill, to walk very fast. My habitual pace approximates that of a middle-of-the-pack marathon runner, but I slowed my step for Lucy until, to my cost, she started outpacing me. Once again, this ominous road sign ("DANGER: HOPELESSNESS AND DESPAIR AROUND CURVE") came into focus only when it was too late to turn back. It struck me, at some point, that Lucy was lagging half a step behind me;

maybe age was catching up with us. So I slowed down; now I was lagging half a step behind her. In our last few years, during our increasingly infrequent walks, we ceased pacing shoulder to shoulder. There was our relationship, once a harmonious reciprocity of interests and inclinations, in a nutshell: When I slowed down she sped up, when I sped up she slowed down.

Three. Movies. Pauline Kael once said that a friendship can't survive too many disagreements about movies. Neither can a marriage. Although we tended more and more to operate in separate spheres, one day I prevailed on Lucy to accompany me to a local showing of a new film by Alexander Payne called *Election.* One of the plot points concerns a high school teacher who has an affair with a student. By way of justification for the catastrophe that ensues, he exclaims to his best friend and colleague, "Her pussy was so wet!" Lucy was much taken with the film and in particular with that line. That's how men really talk, she said, that's how they think about women, that's what they'd all do if they could. I protested that *I* didn't talk like that and that I knew hardly any men who did. In fact, I considered the line frankly unbelievable – which might say more about my limited experience than the verisimilitude of Alexander Payne's *Election.* But we weren't really arguing about the movie. We were arguing about us.

Four. Laughter. It's bad enough when you can't get your spouse to laugh; I couldn't even get Lucy to smile. Maybe, in my growing sorrow and anxiety, I wasn't so damned funny anymore, but no, we still got together with our friends and they seemed to think I was sufficiently amusing. Hence a scene that played out more and more often – the two of us sharing a dinner with Cindy and Nathan or Burton and Maude, and everyone but Lucy laughing at what remained of my sense of humor. Once, to the considerable amusement of Cindy, I compared her toddler son's wobbly posture to the contrapposto struttings of Mick Jagger. Uh-oh. Not only did Lucy not join in the laughter, but I had a sudden premonition of being attacked later that night for my stupid and belittling jokes at the expense of her close friend. No such attack followed. We were both losing all sense of proportion.

And then I broke my ankle playing basketball. Not so bad, really – I had Lucy to look after me, and I used the sick time to work on my book. Feeling antsy one sunny Saturday in May, I asked her to accompany me to the Brooklyn Academy of Music to see a new French movie called *The Dream Life of Angels*. We couldn't get a car service, so I hobbled all the way there and back on my crutches. I worked up quite a sweat. No matter how furiously I propelled myself, Lucy remained two steps ahead. Nor did she have much to say about the movie afterwards, not even about the gross exploitation of male over female that the story depicts with such grim realism. Instead of the breathless debates we used to have after seeing a good movie, I had to listen to my own boring monologue. The dream life of angels was nearing its expiration.

That night I asked: Lucy, what am I doing wrong? I'm trying very hard, but you're clearly unhappy about something. So she told me. She wasn't sure if she loved me anymore. She wasn't sure if she wanted to be with me. Anyone else would have seen it coming. I was floored. I sobbed, I begged, I pleaded. In the years since, I've sometimes wondered, Well, what if I hadn't pleaded? What if I had made a few demands myself – for instance, that Lucy forthwith begin treating me with the respect that all of us owe to every human being, whether we have fallen out of love with that person or not? Idle speculation – damaging, delusive, and probably unfair to both parties. Looking back, I've had and continue to have occasional flashes of anger, always tempered, however, but this thought: Lucy surely has them too, but more, and worse. Anyway, I'd rather live in sorrow than in anger; sorrow seems more, I don't know, poetic. Besides, as she surely would have pointed out, I was in no position to insist on anything. We did make some progress, however. At the end of that long and sleepless night, we resolved that (1) we still loved each other, (2) we would make a new start, and (3) we would move again.

Of the three resolutions, only the last obtained. Number two was entirely false and number one only half true: I still loved Lucy. It was all over that night; it just took us a few years to realize it. What happened during those years? I'm not going to say. Neither of us, to put it mildly, was at our best and I have no desire to make us look any worse than we already do. So I'll just skip ahead to the worst day of my life: May 1, 2003, the day I moved out.

Three years earlier, in accordance with Lucy's wishes, we had sold our Park Slope apartment and bought a brownstone on the other side of Flatbush Avenue in the slightly less expensive neighborhood of Prospect Heights. (Another bad sign: at the closing, the person she tearfully embraced was our realtor, not me.) The idea was to live on the ground floor and rent out the other floors, thus covering our mortgage through the rent rolls. I hated being a landlord, but Lucy can't say I didn't give it my best shot. I interviewed prospective tenants, I vacuumed the hallways, I shoveled snow off the stoop, I helped move in (on the hottest day of the year) a gay couple on the top floor when one of the two men claimed to be incapacitated by a migraine. It was a classic New York City brownstone. How the middling have fallen! I live in a perfectly serviceable and thoroughly nondescript one-bedroom apartment in Clinton Hill. My Prospect Heights apartment with Lucy had three marble fireplaces, stained-glass windows, parquet floors, and oak columns intricately carved by anonymous nineteenth-century craftsmen. (A community group asked us, shortly before the bitter end, if we would participate in the annual open house tour. We declined.) This marriage-saving expedient had failed. Lucy was no happier with me in our opulent brownstone than she had been in our more modest co-op apartment.

So, that day. Jonathan was away at college, Lucy got up and out early, and I awaited the arrival of the movers. When they showed up, I had to shut Puggles in the bedroom, where she barked furiously. (Leaving behind a dog you love is not the least of all sorrows attendant upon a domestic breakup.) The movers were two burly Rastafarians, who did their best not to notice my tears. They were moving me only a few miles away, to a tiny ground-floor studio apartment on a tree-lined block in Brooklyn Heights. They seemed so tough with their dreadlocks and biceps that I felt ashamed to be whimpering as I looked out the window of their van on the slow drive along Atlantic Avenue. Surely, they had seen this before; I couldn't have been the first brokenhearted spouse or partner they had moved under the tragic circumstances of divorce and disunion. Throughout that long morning they comported themselves with a tactfulness and even a gentleness that helped shore up my wavering self-control. If I hadn't been so depressed, I might have taken more to heart the lesson they were so clearly imparting: There were good people in the world.

By agreement Lucy called to check on me when she got home from work. At the sound of her voice I burst into violent, uncontrollable weeping. Between my sobs, I heard much the same on the other end; Lucy too was crying, nearly, from what I could tell, as abjectly as I was. That sense of fellow feeling gave me just enough strength to be able to stammer, "I'm here – can't talk – call later."

Around ten o'clock that night I said what I had to say in a
rush, before, as in fact happened, a flood of tears could stop my
words. What I said was something like this: "Be together again
– need time – stronger, better – admire you – love you – grew up
together – always in awe – mistakes – sorry – learn – not kids
anymore – smarter – real life – love – forever."

"We'll see, Stephen, we'll see," she said. It was the last time
she ever spoke lovingly and gently to me. "But all this *projecting*
all the time won't do any good. You'll live your life, O.K.? And
I'll live mine. We'll just have to see where that takes us. You'll be
all right, Stephen. We're always going to care about each other."

In other words: No. Which I took to mean yes. That
mistake set me back another two years. I never believed anything
so firmly as that we would be together again, so that when she
definitively disabused me, it felt as if I had been divorced all
over again. One spring day, at my request, we met on the Long
Meadow in Prospect Park. Lucy, I said, there's been enough time.
This separation has been needful and healthy, you were right to
make it happen, but now we can be together again, we can love
and be strong, we can be who we were. No, Stephen, no, she said,
looking at the ground and struggling to remain collected and
dispassionate. It's over. I must understand that. It's really over.

It had been over even before the end. Sometimes after the
enervating battles of our last few years, Lucy would say, "You
don't want to live like this, Stephen, you don't want all this
grief and conflict in your life." Yes I did. It was better than the
alternative, which was a frictionless and annihilating loneliness.
Unlike me, Lucy had an alternative, namely, her friends. Always
the most steadfast friend a person could possibly have, she now
devoted herself to them with an exclusivity that utterly sidelined
me. I used to beg her – such was my desperation – to give
me half the consideration she gave them and I would never

complain again. That was hardly the strongest argument to be made for a trusting and reciprocal relationship, but when you're losing love, you tend not to think too clearly. For that matter, Lucy acted no more rationally than I did. On that terrible night when all was revealed, she pledged to make a new start with me and thereupon did everything in her power to undermine that pledge. Why not just say, It's over, Stephen, I don't love you anymore? She had the right. Maybe she was trying to let me down gently, maybe she didn't want to be seen as an "angry bitch" (as she once said), maybe she honestly believed she was making a good faith effort while she rehearsed every known grievance in twenty-three years of cohabitation or rolled her eyes in silent contempt. Sounds terrible, doesn't it? Not as bad as it really was.

It took over twenty years, but Lucy had finally caught up with me: she could be just as reckless and hurtful as I was. She had a motive, however, whether she realized it or not; she wanted to end the marriage, whereas I was just clueless by nature. She barely noticed, it seemed to me, that I had long since ceased making the mistakes that had so infuriated her: no more gawking at other women, no more dogmatic opinions, no more jokes that might offend her. Indeed, I took such excruciating care not to aggravate her that I couldn't have been much fun. Nothing I did or didn't do mattered anyway; she said no to everything. No to Florida, no to the Adirondacks, no to museums, movies, galleries, concerts, plays, no to the network of splendid hiking trails I had belatedly discovered in the Hudson Valley. This last continues to be a source of inspiration for me. Maybe one day Lucy will read, if not this book (highly unlikely), the magnum opus I am destined to write: *The Public Transportation-Dependent Day Hiker's Guide to the New York Metropolitan Region.* She would have loved seeing the wintering bald eagles I visit annually at Croton Point Park on the Hudson.

There was no going back, she told me; even with the best of faith, which we didn't have, there was too much hurt and anger to be unremembered. But I was like our Puggles; with a little affection, I would have been wagging my tail more or less contentedly. I knew that Lucy was more complicated than I was, but I thought there was a way back for her too, so in the midst of the fruitless arguments and hostile silences that we were then bringing to the conjugal bed, I proposed a corrective. We'll take off our clothes, we'll hold each other, we'll speak, if we speak at all, only words of love. The result? Bliss. Deliverance. Salvation. Overnight, it seemed to me, we erased all the rancor and resentment in a rapture of tenderness and nonpenetrative sex. Of course, I couldn't sleep for my raging hard-on, but what did that matter? We had saved our love through the primal realities of nakedness and exposure and vulnerability, we had found our way past ego and possessiveness and jealousy. But nothing is ever that simple. Although Lucy seemed to respond in kind, I should have noticed that I was the one murmuring all the endearments. After three or four nights of this ecstasy, she put her night clothes back on. No, she said, I was dictating things on my terms alone, as always. She would not be coerced into loving me.

So why endure the rejection, the disdain, the grotesque disparity between the way she treated her friends and the way she treated me? Because Lucy was still Lucy. Her intelligence, her strength, her thoughtfulness, her sensitivity – all those things were still there, albeit bestowed more often on others than on me. Yet even then I benefited from her presence. All this time my mother had been going from bad to worse in the New Jersey nursing home where I visited her weekly with my brothers. Coming home from those desolate trips, I felt restored by Lucy's patience and concern. How was Peg? Did you get her to laugh? Would she eat anything? There was nothing special about any of those questions – until I had no one in my life to ask them anymore.

Anyway, there was still love amid the ruins. A few years of growing resentment couldn't entirely extirpate two decades of rooted affection. Furthermore, we had a son to guide through a typically thorny adolescence. Naturally, we made every effort to shield him from our domestic turmoil, and naturally we failed, yet I still marveled at Lucy's maternal wisdom, her easy way of nurturing Jonathan while respecting his independence, her refusal to get hysterical over this or that infraction. "They fuck you up, your mum and dad," wrote Philip Larkin. While this truism remains applicable across the board, I can only say that one of the things I loved about Lucy, even (or especially) at the end, was watching her be a mother and – to the extent that any normal, that is to say, "fucked-up" parent ever does – getting it right. She broke the news to him. I tried but I couldn't get the words out.

When did we break the news to each other? Like a mother approaching her second pregnancy, I've blessedly forgotten many of the more excruciating details. One day, I seem to recall, I said something like, O.K., you win, I don't want to live like this either, I'll move out. It was sheer anti-climax, borne of numbness and despair, but I had enough clarity to foresee one eventuality. Lucy, I said, if the day ever comes when we pass each other on the street and we nod to each other stiffly as we go on our separate ways, I will fall to my knees and beg the earth to swallow me up. Did that day ever come? It did, and no earthquake or avalanche or conflagration could have harrowed me more thoroughly than the desolation I felt in that moment.

A second prediction has yet to be realized. I know what will happen, I prophesied from the depths of my despair, when we're old and about to die: nothing. I'll die, you'll die, there will be no reconciliation, no final words of good will or atonement or blessing. You won't want to hear from me and I'll know not to try. Lucy calmly and wisely advised me to stop tormenting myself about unrealities that couldn't be foreseen. She had often deplored my tendency to fixate on the past. Now I was fixating on the future. Could I not for once live comfortably in the present? Given that the present consisted primarily of agony and vastation, no, I couldn't live comfortably in the present. And yet if I were to make of the living moment something tolerable, even desirable, I must determine to do so myself. She couldn't do that for me. Neither could my friends.

My friends. I had helped some of them through their own time of crisis, but now that my turn had come, I didn't know what to say to them. So I didn't say anything. Lucy made it known that I didn't want to hear from any of them. She might have overemphasized my Garboesque wish to be alone; I never intended it to be forever. In time, a couple of them made somewhat equivocal gestures of support, then gave up on me entirely. They didn't ask to be put in this ghastly situation. Then I got angry at them, which was like getting angry at cancer – it didn't help. Also, this: what Lucy loved about her friends was what she used to love about me. They were intelligent, talented, creative, caring, sensitive, pretentious. I was, I liked to think, all of those things, and more. Lucy wouldn't or couldn't see those qualities in me anymore, a situation unlikely to dispose me favorably to those friends.

Maybe because there weren't so many of them, I remember the better moments Lucy and I shared in the midst of our decline. The time we surreptitiously planted saplings in the city-owned lot adjacent to our side yard. (Guerrilla gardening, I called it.) The time we laid out tile samples in an ante-room in our basement, creating a mosaic on the floor that looked like one of Lucy's quilts in marble and granite and onyx. The many times we speculated on the impending marital dissolution of our mismatched friends Cindy and Nathan. (They survived; we failed.) And all the times – admittedly fewer – that we fell asleep in each other's arms, as if in memory of the raccoon love that had once enfolded us.

Those were the good moments. The bad moments are, even now, too searing and humiliating to recount. This book by no means tells the whole story of our lives together. I can almost hear people from my past objecting, "Wait a minute – Stephen was a much bigger asshole than that." They wouldn't be wrong. I've left out some of the good stuff too, stuff that – hard to believe – might make me look a little better. On balance, I think I've shown Lucy and me as the ordinary, fumbling human beings that we were, but even ordinary, fumbling human beings get a shot at sublimity. We had ours. It ended. It was still sublime.

So here's a last look at Lucy and Stephen in their profoundest unsublimity a few months before the end. Lucy had been accepted, with a few of her friends, at a group show to be held in the main library of Long Island University in downtown Brooklyn. For the first time in our lives, she had created a work of art that I actively disliked – no, I hated it. A handball court adjacent to our property furnished an endless supply of blue rubber balls that sailed over a chain-link fence into the large back yard that Lucy was transforming into a magnificent garden. Taking a dozen or so of those balls, she placed them in a huge plexiglass box filled with soil and seeds, there to form part of a growing, organic, shaggy work of conceptual art. All her friends loved it, but all her friends knew about the handball court and the garden and the rubber balls that turned up in her hydrangea. A self-referential bit of conceptual bullshit for a coterie or a fun and playful experiment in democratic process art? Although I now embrace the latter view, I didn't have to worry about expressing my former opinion; Lucy didn't ask, and wouldn't have cared. She did, however, have to transport the thing to Long Island University and accordingly hired a mover for the job. He was stumped. The plexiglass box was so heavy with soil that the three of us could barely lift it off the floor. With her usual patience and good humor, Lucy shrugged it off as a minor stroke of bad luck and prepared to set off for the opening to cheer on her artist friends, who merely had a few canvases and figurines to transport. What followed was an unprecedented example of mechanical ingenuity on my part. I reasoned that by unscrewing the door to the basement bedroom, where the monster resided, we could use it as a plank and lever the box out the window into the back of the waiting truck, which was just what we did. How we got the box into the library I can't recall. I do remember that Lucy had a great time at the opening. And spoke not a word to me.

So what does this exemplum illustrate exactly – that love dies but life continues? That Lucy had already checked out while I was still hanging around? That plexiglass boxes full of dirt and debris are heavier than they look? I'm afraid it doesn't illustrate anything very clearly. It's all a muddle, rather like human existence in general. So that's how it ended – in a muddle of hope and despair, incommensurate needs and unresolved conflicts. One thing, however, strikes me as abundantly clear: We loved. It was real. It was true. Ordinary, fumbling Stephen and Lucy, like most lovers everywhere, were touched, to quote Ford Madox Ford, by "the true sunshine; the true music; the true plash of the fountains from the mouth of stone dolphins."

16

As self and beloved alike become, with greater
or lesser velocity, the final dwarfs of themselves,
and as social awareness diminishes dreams of self-
transcendence, the poet sees dream, hope, love, and
trust – those activities of the most august imagination
– crippled, contradicted, dissolved, called into
question, embittered. This history is the history of
every intelligent and receptive human creature, as
the illimitable claims on existence made by each one
of us are checked, baffled, frustrated, and reproved –
whether by our own subsequent perceptions of their
impossible grandiosity, or by the accidents of fate and
chance, or by our betrayal of others, or by old age and
its failures of capacity.

Crippled, contradicted, dissolved, embittered, checked,
baffled, frustrated, and reproved: thus Helen Vendler in *Wallace
Stevens: Words Chosen out of Desire.* Is this truly the "history of
every intelligent and receptive human creature"? I find it oddly
comforting to think so. This belief absolves me of at least some
of my guilt; with or without my mistakes, Lucy and I would
have become "the final dwarfs of ourselves." On the other hand,

it's easy to imagine a sort of autumnal splendor for us, gardening together, birdwatching, reading, waiting to die. Which leaves me approximately where I started: it's all a muddle.

We're not friends. After a few years of fraught and fitful conversation, Lucy decreed that there would be no communication with me – ever. That, I suppose, is my greatest sorrow; I'd just like to call her up sometime to talk about her gardening. Or our son. All of which must make me sound like an emotional zombie, stuck in the past, obsessing about the ex-wife who rejected me, unreconciled to any meaningful future. And indeed, I was that person for a while, though I prefer to think of myself in the years immediately following our breakup as a perfectly polite and only vaguely suicidal middle-class depressive. How I rejoined the human race and made a future for myself I will briefly tell, but not before clarifying a few essential points.

The first point is that whatever murky psychological motives exacerbated the severe and prolonged depression I went through after our breakup, psychoanalysis can't explain everything. A year after moving out, I began seeing a therapist who spent much time exploring the hidden blockages, many rooted in childhood and adolescence, that imprisoned me in a hopeless cycle of longing and regret. Personally, I considered myself no more damaged than the next person ("We are all ill," as Freud said), but my therapist seemed unwilling to consider an alternative explanation. That explanation can be found in every pop song, every tearjerker, every soap opera you've ever heard or seen, namely, that losing the love of your life, whoever you are and whatever your psychological background, feels like and *should* feel like the end of the world. Maybe it's true, as Freud claimed, that romantic love requires the "overvaluation" of the loved object. But maybe there are deeper truths in Hank Williams and Etta James and Paul McCartney. "Changing my life with a wave of her hand," Paul sings in "Here, There and Everywhere." That's what Lucy did for me – or, more importantly, that's what it felt like she did. With my therapist I dutifully explored the root causes of my despair, merely glancing at the most obvious one: that my baby didn't love me no more.

And what of the "overvaluation" of my loved object? Hence my second point. When I was twenty-four I met a beautiful, kind, talented, and intelligent woman with whom I shared many interests and avocations. I got lucky. Was she the only one? Did fate appoint her as my unique soulmate from among the two billion two hundred nineteen million other women in the world who wouldn't have quite measured up? To believe that would be to succumb to the narcissism that, I like to think, my shared life with Lucy refuted. We weren't Tristan and Isolde or any other archetype of all-consuming passion. Tristan and Isolde, as Denis De Rougement points out in *Love in the Western World,* were so busy declaiming their grand passion that they barely noticed each other. Lucy and I spent twenty-three years noticing each other – our bodies, our minds, our souls, our endearing and not so endearing tics and habits. And yet if circumstances had been different, I might easily have spent twenty-three years noticing another. So might she.

In fact, I have since noticed others in the very same way. I'm aware that this book might seem hurtful to several of those others. They too have their stories, no less rich, complex, and worthy of the telling than Lucy's. It's thanks to them that I've gone on to live and love and make ever more mistakes, sometimes new ones, sometimes the old ones; the difference, as Lucy said, is that the two of us grew up together. By the time I started meeting other women, I had, for better or worse, already grown up.

So it's the first spring-like Saturday in March 2003, and I'm walking in the sunshine, with my baseball cap pulled low and my eyes on the pavement, along Lafayette Avenue in Fort Greene, with all the other young couples, the yuppie families, the Black bohemians, the skateboard kids. But rather than reveling, like my neighbors, in this blissful premonition of spring, I'm walking very fast from one Brooklyn neighborhood to another in search of an apartment in which to live, when, as Lucy ardently desires, I move out in the next few weeks. Also, I'm crying. Generally speaking, I got pretty good at hiding my tears, at compartmentalizing my life into the endless, agonizing, sleepless nights and the merely depressing but more or less tolerable days. Every now and then, however, as on this day, my guard slips. I once had an amusing conversation with a female friend at the library about the stalls in the staff bathroom where she resorted for the occasional cry over ongoing romantic troubles. Hey, me too! On this day I stifle my sobs sufficiently to persuade the landlord of a rowhouse on State Street in Brooklyn Heights that I'm a good-enough risk for his tiny ground-floor studio apartment. Once I move in, I can cry all I want.

I cried while eating my dinner. I cried while playing the tin whistle. I cried while hiking in the Hudson Valley. I cried – sometimes – while talking to Lucy. In the first two or three years of our separation we talked fairly often. Trying and failing to work out a meaningful friendship, which she claimed to want as much as I did, we kept in touch and got together for family occasions. On the phone, however, my emotions sometimes overwhelmed me and my throat would catch. That infuriated her. It might have looked like emotional blackmail. It wasn't. Almost anything could set me off. I often went to the Metropolitan Museum on Friday nights after work, where I invariably waited in a long line to check my knapsack before buying my ticket and proceeding into the galleries. One night in the confusion and hurly burly (the Met really needs to do a better job with its coat check system), a woman accused me –wrongfully – of cutting in front of her. She might as well have spat in my face and arraigned me for war crimes. I stood there, speechless, as the tears started from my eyes. Whatever resilience I once had was gone. It would have been another night lost to depression and despair if not for an encounter minutes later in the museum lobby with an unexpected visitor: John Updike! (I could see his nose from halfway across the lobby; just as on the jacket flaps of his books, he wore a suit to go to a museum.) Breaking my fixed rule about never gawking at a celebrity (you see a lot of them if you live in New York long enough), I politely asked him if he were there to review an exhibition for *The New Republic*. No, just looking, he said, in a joking reference to his book of that title. He allowed me to gush for a few minutes about the Rabbit novels, all of which I had just read. Although his courtliness and modesty helped me to regain my composure, they couldn't prevent me from thinking the thought I knew I shouldn't be thinking: I wish I could tell Lucy about this.

My fixed belief in the first year that all would be well after our excruciating but temporary separation didn't lessen the tears, the insomnia, the loss of appetite, and every other classic sign of depression. A part of me must not have believed what I thought I believed. Lucy, of course, never had the slightest intention of reconciling, as I should have known all along. I certainly should have known it when, about half way through that first year, I came over to see the brownstone she had bought on Tenth Street in Park Slope after selling off our previous brownstone in Prospect Heights. (After our split, she moved up in the world; I moved down.) A postcard was lying on the coffee table and I couldn't resist. There on the back I read a thank you note from an unknown friend gushing about the *fabulous* party Lucy had thrown in her *fabulous* new home to celebrate her *fabulous* new life. No more than what I deserved. Still, although I kept quiet about the postcard, it did strike me that Lucy had got rather the better of this deal. Where genuine grief ended and self-pity began seemed to me a moot point. Lucy firmly believed that my problem was the latter, not the former. If, as she said in moments of wrath, I was such a fucking asshole who felt so fucking sorry for himself, then I could fucking well spare her the fucking misery. On the contrary, I maintained and still maintain that whether the world regards your depression as socially acceptable grief or reprehensible self-pity, it feels like death either way. There is nothing either good nor bad, but thinking makes it so, said Hamlet, a notable depressive himself. And that's the whole point, really – when you're depressed you can't prevent your thoughts from making life feel unlivable. You become something of a solipsist.

Fortunately, I had obligations to others that kept what my therapist called my "suicidal ideations" safely at bay. In that regard, I probably had more to learn from Oprah Winfrey than I did from him. The pop psychology adage that you "fake it until you make it" proved, in my case, to be worth any number of solemn psychoanalytic interrogations about my father's alcoholic neglect. I had to be strong for my mother and son. Maybe they knew my "strength" was a fiction as much as I did, but the will to believe goes far. Moreover, despite my constant depression (or willful self-pity, for the less charitably inclined), not to mention the sickening discomfort of unceasing insomnia, I never at any point lost my zeal for art and literature and music and birds and basketball and all the other passions I had spent my adult life pursuing. I had never imagined, for example, that my love for Japanese cinema could ever have any practical effect in my life, but Film Forum was showing a Yasujiro Ozu retrospective and I had to be there.

Lucy and I, with Jonathan, still celebrated birthdays and holidays together. I assumed we always would. Wrong again. It was, I believe, on my third post-breakup birthday that the phone failed to ring. Not long after that, in response to a desperately needy email of mine, Lucy informed me that all communication would henceforth cease. That was her right, of course; I just wish she hadn't sounded quite so much like a lawyer. For more than two years we had tried, and failed, to arrive at a sustaining mutuality that would preserve our affection and concern while respecting our freedom and independence. Mostly we ended up squabbling over what she considered my manipulative and cringing self-pity. I can't help thinking that she picked fights with me precisely to avoid having a sustaining mutuality. I didn't want a sustaining mutuality anyway. I wanted her to love me again.

This process of disintegration was too painful and rancorous to recount, but it traumatized me pretty thoroughly. After more than a year of record-breaking insomnia and appalling nutrition, I betook myself to the therapist I should have been seeing from the start. Why had I delayed so long? Well, as I saw it, my wife had dumped me; I had lost all of my best friends virtually from one day to the next; I couldn't sleep; I could barely even eat. What was a therapist going to tell me – Get happy? Not very rational, but there you have it. What looked like self-pity to Lucy looked like bedrock reality to me. And yet, confused as my thinking was, I knew I couldn't go on this way. If nothing else, I figured, therapy might help me with the insomnia.

Do therapists have a protocol regarding sessions when the patient does almost nothing but sit there and cry? My guy – the same austerely old school Freudian whom I had seen briefly seventeen years earlier – summoned a look of professional concern and pushed a box of Kleenex in my direction but remained otherwise impassive. It felt like God the Father was looking down on me with stern benevolence. At last, even if I had to pay for it, I had someone on my side. And I paid a lot. Earlier I had attempted to avail myself of the limited but free mental health services available to municipal employees and welfare recipients. Once past the brutal and bullying desk clerk in the dingy clinic in downtown Brooklyn, I found myself in the presence of a psychiatric social worker who couldn't process the thought that I was neither the perpetrator nor the victim of physical abuse. Then what was I doing there? Good question. Unlike the other broken people sitting uncomplainingly in that cramped waiting room, I had options. I could pay for qualified assistance; they couldn't. If only for their sake, I should have slapped the desk clerk on the way out.

After sobbing through the first of our weekly sessions, I soon began making progress with my therapist. I wasn't, we agreed, a *complete* fucking asshole, as Lucy – in the only way she knew how to extricate herself from a situation in which she felt trapped – had so tirelessly insisted during our last year few years. "If I am not for myself, who will be for me?" Once I got a little clarity, I took Rabbi Hillel's question much to heart. I had some serious ego-rebuilding to do, in the process of which I was paying my therapist most of my remaining discretionary income. It was well worth the cost. The only problem was that he wanted me to hate Lucy.

No, she shouldn't have treated me with such contempt. That was a fault, one that had fairly ruinous consequences for my mental health. But if, as my therapist urged, I was to weigh her faults against mine, I knew only too well how badly I would come out in the balance. Besides, all the while Doctor Feelgood was telling me to blame everything on her, Lucy's therapist, whom she had been seeing for a number of years, was surely telling her to blame everything on me. Eventually my therapist and I hit a wall, yet I stuck with him for several more years. Once you get in, as many a Borscht Belt joke has it, it's not so easy to get out. Although I greatly benefited from the support and insight my therapist gave me, he beat back every attempted discussion of "termination" as patent evasion on my part. Finally, I hit upon a fail-proof expedient: lying. I've really made extraordinary progress, I told him. I hardly ever think about Lucy anymore.

My secret goal – and my therapist considered it important to set goals – was to think about Lucy once a day rather than every twenty minutes. Anger, regret, guilt, jealousy, shame, humiliation – that was a lot of emotion for a repressed ex-altar boy to handle. More than anything else, I struggled with disbelief. Of all the couples in the world least likely to split up, I would have put ourselves at the top of the list. Maybe the Gods or a malevolent Cosmos or the Furies or were punishing me for my hubris. In some ways, nothing had changed. All the picnics and the parties and the holiday celebrations were still going on with Lucy and our best friends; it's just that I wasn't there. I had occasionally heard about men who, through a combination of bad luck and their own fecklessness had lost seemingly everything in one fell swoop. Welcome to the club. How had I suddenly ended up as the punch line in a bad joke? This stuff was supposed to happen to other people, not me. But no, there was from time to time that special feeling of crawling out of my own skin to remind me that this was indeed happening to me and that my sense of unreality was the only illusion. Everything else – the loneliness, the loss, the shame – was fact. Around that time, I had a nightmare that put things in their proper perspective. (My dreams, when I managed to fall asleep, were almost exclusively nightmares.) I dreamed that Lucy and I had split up and that I was living alone in agony and despair, while she prospered ostentatiously and disdained me. Then I woke up with unspeakable relief to find her sleeping snugly in the hollow of my arm. And then I *really* woke up.

If disbelief was problem number one, shame was probably problem number two. I'm ashamed to admit I felt so ashamed. Millions of people get divorced and face the consequences bravely. Not I. At the doctor's office, filling out the forms, I quailed at the box for Single, Married, Divorced or Separated. How was I going to handle this question, not just at the doctor's office, but, more painfully, everywhere else? Well, I could lie, which I sometimes did, but generally I preferred the route of elaborate evasion. When that failed, I was left tongue-tied and stammering, as on the day after I moved into my studio apartment on State Street. Having dozens of errands to take care of, I chanced to run into my former boss in Telephone Reference, recently retired and a longtime resident of Brooklyn Heights. Funny meeting you here on Remsen Street in the middle of the weekday, Milo said.

"Well, I just ... I just ... " I just what? Couldn't bear to tell him the simple truth? After a long and agonizing pause, I finally came out with it, or the nearest I could come to it:

"My circumstances have changed."

Milo, who had been a fiercely demanding supervisor at work, looked at me with the great compassion of which he was equally capable.

"Oh Stephen," he said. "Oh Stephen. Oh Stephen."

Not the least of the many things I couldn't handle was the legal reality of separation and divorce. To this day, I don't know when we were legally divorced. One day – I've deliberately forgotten the date – I met Lucy in a pharmacy to have our signatures notarized. Those were our divorce papers. I averted my eyes from everything but the blank line for my signature. For all I know, the divorce agreement accuses me of ritual Satanic abuse. I didn't, and don't, care. Nor am I any less ignorant of the financial details of our settlement. Lucy, who kept the books, gave me half the proceeds from the sale of our Prospect Heights brownstone, and that was that. Later, I met people who thought I was crazy to trust everything to her. I may be a fool, but I would never knowingly cheat or dishonor anyone. Neither would she.

In what I thought was a happy premonition of our "sustaining mutuality," Lucy helped me to remodel the one-bedroom co-op apartment in Clinton Hill that I bought in year two of my new and unwanted life. Although her manner was brisk and businesslike, price shopping with her for bathroom fixtures in Home Depot cheered me perhaps more than it should have. This was still lovely, generous, omnicompetent Lucy, and for a few minutes she was at my side. The major design feature in my new apartment was her artwork; she covered my walls with some of her biggest and best paintings, for which – as always with her completed works – she had little or no use. Bad idea. A couple of years later, as my therapist accurately predicted, those pictures would come to haunt me. Lucy wouldn't talk to me, and her paintings were staring me down from the walls. They had to go. Remembering how she had decorated the hallway of our first apartment so many years ago, I replaced them with a mini-gallery of classy reproductions – Fra Angelico, Albrecht Durer, Howard Hodgkin, David Hockney. All very nice, but my apartment has never looked as good since.

My therapist also considered it ill-advised for me to attend, as I forewarned him, the sessions of a depression support group sponsored by Beth Israel Hospital in the East Village. Maybe I should have listened to him. One of the things I was to discover in my new life was just how much more suffering there was in the world than I had ever imagined. He reasoned that surrounding myself with mentally unstable people might only destabilize *me*. And so it was that I entered a world where people had been trying to kill themselves from the age of nine. Who had been kicked out of advanced mental health clinics for being past care. Whose parents hated them. Who had never had a friend until joining this support group in late middle-age. The problem wasn't that the extremity of their suffering further depressed me. On the contrary, I considered them the most courageous and heroic people I had ever met, and tried to tell them so. The problem was, contrary to the reassurances of the "intake" person who had interviewed me, that there was no one remotely like me in the group. I was just an ordinary, unmedicated guy with no history of mental illness, one whose situational depression must have seemed insultingly lightweight to everyone else sitting on those plastic chairs in a broad circle in that over-lit room. Furthermore, I didn't have the pharmacological vocabulary to comprehend half of what was being said. I had briefly and disastrously tried the sleeping medication Ambien, which only bought me a few hours of bad sleep and gave me worse nightmares than I already had. When they started talking about Klonopin, Temazepam, and Lithium, as they invariably did, I was utterly out of my depth.

All my life I had avoided groups, clubs, affiliations, and associations of any sort, so it was with considerable trepidation that I found my way to another support group after bailing out of the charmed circle at Beth Israel Hospital. (For the record, I briefly tried a second, more informal depression support group, from which I derived some of the above anecdotes.) This was the New York Meetup Divorce Support Group, which convened weekly around a long table in a café opposite Carnegie Hall for some serious talk and also convened less regularly at various bars around town for some serious drinking. I skipped many of the more overtly "social" sessions, which tended to be for a smaller group of insiders. No matter how sincere and well-intentioned its core members, group dynamics inevitably made themselves felt. Indeed, I was to discover in a year or two – when, incredibly, I began running the group myself – just how difficult it was to banish the middle-school proclivities that most of us carry into adulthood.

When first glimpsing the fifteen or twenty people gathered around that table, I had to fight the instinct to flee – a common experience, I was to find. Even asking a waitress at the door about the presence of a divorce group felt shameful, and now I was to reveal my most intimate sorrows to a group of strangers. The strangers, however, proved to be warm, welcoming, and understanding, and if I could do so without violating their privacy, I would gratefully name the four or five regulars who most propped me up and helped me to gain some perspective on my Lucygrief. Also, some of the women – not the least of the attractions of the New York Meetup Divorce Support Group was the pool of possibilities it provided for both sexes – were really hot.

They might have been hot, but, at least initially, I couldn't have imagined being with any of them. Nor, given the way I droned on about my Lucygrief, would any of them have wanted to be with me. One attractive woman in the group told me so quite plainly. She needed help driving out to Pennsylvania to retrieve some of her belongings from the house she had shared with her husband. When we arrived, she pointed out the hole he had punched in the wall during one of their customary arguments, and she casually informed me (not that this bothered her especially) that he was an anti-Semitic biker nut who refused to accept the idea of their separation. Where was he now? I anxiously asked. Oh, he was out around town somewhere. Maybe we should hurry to get these things in the car, Stephen. It probably wouldn't be a great idea to run into him just then.

We managed to get out of there without encountering the furious redneck, and as a reward Wendy treated me to dinner in a coffee shop near her subsidized high-rise on the Lower East Side. Thanks so much for helping me out, she said. I always like talking to you at the meetings. The way you listen to people is really nice and when you talk about Lucy you sound like such a pathetic loser, it kinda shows me what I need to do not to be like you, ya know what I mean?

These were largely unchartered waters for me. Outside of work, in my twenty-three years with Lucy I had associated with people much like us – liberal, culturally curious *New Yorker* subscribers, essentially. Now I had thrown in my lot with people from every conceivable social and ethnic background, many or most of whom had no use for the *New Yorker* and the other accoutrements of my circumscribed, middle-class life. Oh my God, people got drunk, watched stupid TV shows, listened to crap music, and wasted their money in shopping malls. Yes, and these very same people had a firmer grasp on reality than I did and graciously pointed the way to a firmer acceptance of my own reality. But first I had to learn how to comport myself in a bar.

Many years earlier my cousin had dragged me to a few bars to get me not drunk but high. (He got drunk *and* high.) O.K., that was moderately interesting, but I saw no reason to repeat the experiment and I hadn't darkened the door of any such establishment in more than twenty years. So here I was, in my second outing with the divorce support group, nursing a ginger ale in an East Side bar with eight or nine hard-drinking strangers, all laughing very hard at the inane patter of a standup comedian. And I laughed too, or tried to. A few years earlier, Lucy and I had been laughing easily and conversing amiably in the homes of our closest and most interesting friends, and now – *this?* Yes, this. Don't be such a prig, Stephen. Maybe these people know some things that you don't. Maybe you've got something to learn here.

Well, I learned to order tomato juice, which might be mistaken for a Bloody Mary and thus forestall any hostile interrogations about my abstinence, as once or twice happened. More importantly, I learned that my new friends were in some ways just as interesting and a lot more supportive than my old ones. One of them had an object lesson for me in the value of adaptability. All his life, he told me, he had done exactly as expected of him: attended synagogue, graduated cum laude, married a proper Jewish girl, became a successful accountant. Divorce was not part of the plan. And yet here he was, after being knocked to his knees, dating (thanks to the auspices of match.com) a working-class Dominican woman from Queens, learning a few words of Spanish, trying out a few Salsa steps, and living, as far as he was concerned, *la vida loca*.

Many more of the stories I heard had to do with *la vida trágica* or, more properly, la *vida chingada*. Lawyers, money, court hearings, custody disputes, police intervention, and unyielding hatred: I blanched from hearing about such things, and yet if I were to return the support that had been offered to me, I must condole with the embittered litigants no less than with the sorrowing romantics. And maybe there was a little more of the embittered litigant in me than I cared to recognize.

We had a little questionnaire that we sometimes used to generate discussions with newer members of the group. Are you divorced or separated? Who initiated the proceedings? How long were you together? Are there children? And so on. The real question, however, always boiled down to one word: Why? Most people had a fairly ready answer. He was cheating on me. She was married to her career. He beat me. She was psychotic. We never loved each other. I myself never had a good answer to that question and I dreaded being asked. Of course, my fecklessness and faithlessness went far towards providing an answer, but Lucy would have been the first to admit they weren't the whole story. She fell out of love with me before I fell out of love with her, but that's not the whole story either. So what is the whole story? After many years of brooding on this question, I think I can offer this ringing affirmation: I don't know. Love is complicated. I'm tempted to suggest that I might have been slightly better at intimacy than Lucy, at allowing for frailties and failures, at seeing the best rather than the worst in her, at making more reasonable demands of life in general. "There can be no end to our sense of emptiness and incompleteness," wrote Alain de Botton. "But none of this is unusual or grounds for divorce. Choosing whom to commit ourselves to is merely a case of identifying which particular variety of suffering we would most like to sacrifice ourselves for." Lucy felt lonely, and said so. I protested that loneliness was part of the human condition, even in a happy marriage. Fine, she said, what do you call loneliness in an unhappy marriage?

Any claims I might make for a superior understanding of intimacy will probably sound, to the ears of my outraged readers, like the worst sort of special pleading, so I hasten to add that to the inherent difficulties of sustaining romance over the long haul, I contributed more than my share of impediments. Lucy used to say there was no going back, that in the end there was too much damage to undo. I disagreed. She was a more driven, complex person. I was just a raccoon. In matters of the heart, however, a veto determines the outcome.

I heard a great many more stories when, the following year, I became the official "organizer" of the divorce group. The original organizer and founder, a lovely man who had partnered up with someone in the group, was eager to move on. That was just the problem. Almost all, after a few months or a year or so, were eager to put the group behind them. The transient nature of the membership made it difficult to sustain friendships, and in fact I never succeeded in doing so. As invaluable as it was to me, the divorce support group was no substitute for the close friendships that Lucy and I had cultivated over many years. There was also, as previously mentioned, the middle-school aspect that became part of my purview. When pressed into service as organizer, I had to settle disputes between a few overly zealous members and monitor the message board for "inappropriate" content. The latter activity turned out to be kinda fun. Some guy was making heavily misogynistic comments online and I was asked to rein him in. As expected, he called me a limp dick and a pantywaist and I had the pleasure of returning the compliments and banishing him from the group.

For all their experience of sorrow and loss, some people nonetheless felt the need to apologize for their grief. Can there be anything more soul-crushing than the cult of American optimism? So I instituted a new rule: If you feel like shit, say so. I also proposed that if people were having a bad night, they could call me up; I had nothing better to do anyway. One or two took me up on the offer, and I found, through listening to them and through my other ministrations with the group, that the old bromide about serving ourselves in serving others was quite true. Nor was this obvious conclusion to be avoided: You think you've got it bad, Stephen? Listen to *this*.

So I listened. Of the scores of stories I heard, I'll briefly recount two as illustrative of – what, exactly? I don't know – maybe that divorce crosses a threshold that some human beings will never be able to bear. Anyway, once upon a midnight dreary, while I pondered, weak and weary, the phone rang. The voice on the other end belonged to a young and extremely handsome African American man who had attended two of the previous sessions. He could have had any number of willing and attractive women in the group if he had noticed them, which he didn't. He didn't notice anything. Here was a guy who seemed to have it all: youth, movie-star looks, Ivy League education, family connections, money. What he didn't have was his sexy Italian ex-wife, who had tortured him with her infidelity when they were together and now tortured him with her silence when they were apart – an unremarkable, even a banal story, except for the depth of his despair. Nothing I said, as we spoke over the next few nights, made the least difference. He soon gave up on me, gave up on the group, and, from what I could tell, gave up on himself. Who was I to say he should appreciate the advantages he had when to him those advantages weighed in the balance as absolutely null? I believe there are two lessons here: one, that respectful and civilized as divorce can and should be, sometimes it's a death sentence; and two, that if you're overcome with suicidal despair, you need to be talking to trained mental health professionals, not to the hapless "organizer" of a local support group.

Case number two, the Argentine psychiatrist. I know it sounds like a cliché, but she really was from Argentina and she really was a psychiatrist. If anyone should understand the importance of shielding children from the wreckage of divorce, it ought to be a psychiatrist. And in fact, Luisa, as she tearfully told me, knew just how wrong it was to compel her thirteen-year-old daughter to share her bed every night in the absence of the husband who had abandoned them for a much younger woman. (This also sounds like a cliché, but the story I heard more often than any other was that of husbands ditching wives for younger women.) All of Luisa's psychiatric training and motherly wisdom availed nothing. Her life had suddenly become a tragic tango ballad about *amor perdido* and the only way she could cope was by clinging to her daughter in bed and crying herself to sleep.

If I had had the perspicacity, I might have told Luisa something my therapist told me. All those hours of quasi-Freudian speculation were as nothing compared to one exasperated outburst provoked by my implacable and self-defeating Lucygrief: "Life isn't a fairy tale, Stephen!" he almost shouted. "No one is guaranteed a happy ending. You need to make a new life for yourself. Yeah, it's hard – that's why you're here. You got an alternative?"

No, I didn't have an alternative, and I've been working on that new life ever since. A few years later, further help arrived from an unexpected quarter: Lucy. It wasn't much, but somehow it felt like everything. Despite her ban on communication, family occasions had, once or twice, brought us together. In the course of the abortive email conversation that ensued, I mentioned an insinuating third-person report regarding her emphatic indifference to anything having to do with me. She had something to say about that. "Please know that I care," she wrote. "I have always cared, even when I said I didn't. How could I not?" What kind of person, I ask myself after all these years, would say something like that? But I've always known: A kind person. A beautiful person. A raccoon for love.

Admittedly, Lucy's words weren't quite so healing as the psilocybin I later ingested in a therapeutic and highly illegal experiment in self-understanding, and certainly not so healing as the love that I've been lucky enough to give and receive in recent years. But a little kindness from the person you loved for twenty-three years always helps. Did we utterly fail? Are we merely a cautionary tale? Some will think so; for all I know, they may be right. Yet I firmly believe that being in love with another person and having that love reciprocated, however badly it may end, however briefly it may last, is the biggest, greatest, grandest thing that will ever happen to any of us. It was certainly the biggest thing that ever happened to me. Life is a serious business, and spooning over your wife or girlfriend, in the long run, makes up a fairly small part of it. I've tried to live a responsible and honorable life, to be a good citizen, father, son, brother, friend, and all the rest, but I know very well what I'll be thinking of on my deathbed: when I was young and spooning over my wife and girlfriend.

About the Author

Author Photo: Bob Rock

Stephen Akey is the author of two previous memoirs, *College and Library*, and of a collection of essays, *Culture Fever*. His writings have appeared in The New Republic, The Smart Set, The Millions, and other publications. He lives in Brooklyn, New York.